BOUND TO LOVE –
Romantic BDSM Erotica

Edited by Maria Isabel Pita

BOUND TO LOVE – Romantic BDSM Erotica
Copyright ©2006 by Magic Carpet Books, Inc.
All Rights Reserved

No part of this book may be reproduced,
stored in a retrieval system, or transmitted in any form,
by any means, including mechanical, electronic,
photocopying, recording or otherwise, without
prior written permission from the publisher and author.

First Magic Carpet Books, Inc. edition September 2006

Published in 2006

Manufactured in the United States of America
Published by Magic Carpet Books, Inc.

Magic Carpet Books, Inc.
PO Box 473
New Milford, CT 06776

Library of Congress Cataloging in Publication Date

BOUND TO LOVE – Romantic BDSM Erotica
Edited By Maria Isabel Pita

ISBN: 0-9766510-4-1
Book Design: P. Ruggieri

TABLE of CONTENTS

Summerhouse – 5
Jonathan Marchant

Staying Present – 35
Ariel Graham

What it Means – 69
Brooke Stern

Necessary To Her Good – 105
Marilyn Jaye Lewis

Comfy – 139
William Gaius

Pony Penning Days – 173
L.A. Mistral

Janice and Kyle – 199
Reena Anne Hovermale

A Night Without A Moon – 233
N.T. Morley

Natural Bondage – 269
Maria Isabel Pita

Summerhouse

by
Jonathan Marchant

Joan Roth had heard of neighbors calling a weekend resident about damage to a house after a storm. She knew contractors often kept an eye on things even when they were booked, but when was the last time an *architect* had called? Maybe it happened, but this was the first time it had ever happened to her. Then again, it was exactly the kind of thing a man like David Riggs Mason would do.

Joan stood motionless in the corridor of the courthouse as she gazed at David's number on the tiny screen of her cellular. Just seeing it lodged among the others gave her a thrill. She knew she ought to call some of those other numbers first. The first call was from her secretary at the law office, the second was from an opposing counsel, and the third was the District Attorney. They were going to have to wait; when she pressed the button to dial David, she wanted her mind clear.

"Joan?" The rise in his baritone showed he had recognized her number.

"Hi, David, I got your message." She walked down the hall away from the courtroom as she spoke. "How bad is it?"

"Nothing too bad. You lost a patch of shingles on the western side. I didn't see any damage to the underlying roof, but I'd like to get one of my contractors over for a closer look. Will you be around this weekend?"

"Tomorrow's what... Friday?" she blurted even though she had consulted the judicial calendar three times that day. Normally a fast-thinking lawyer, she rolled her eyes at the way talking to him on the phone suddenly turned her into a ditz. "I'd love to quit early, but I have a deposition in the afternoon which will probably run until five, so I think Saturday morning is better."

"That's good. It'll give us the chance to see the house in full daylight."

They set the time at ten o'clock. She had planned on a working weekend, so clearing her desk in such short order was going to be a major juggling act. She would have to delay discovery on the Brownwirth case, assign extra research to one of the interns anxious to climb the legal totem pole, and then scramble to recover on Monday.

She made her business calls from a private room with a window at the end of the hall. Outside it was sunny and calm. Scattered branches torn from trees and some residual wet spots were the only trace of the front that had moved through the day before – a midsummer hailstorm that pounded the building, dimmed the lights and made the hanging traffic signals swing like insanely blinking cathedral bells. She wondered what the storm had been like upstate, where her summerhouse was. Worse, probably, *much* worse, but that was history. Her mind settled on the weekend and the slim but existing possibility that David had called not so much about the roof but as a way of renewing their acquaintance. His having seen the house was no coincidence, she thought with a smile. Considering the fact that it was half-a-mile off the public road down a shaded, private drive meant he had trespassed to get there. And no, she thought as she folded her phone closed and left the room, she didn't mind. She didn't mind at all.

The only problem was that David was married, or at least he had been when she built the house two years ago as a gift to herself for making Partner. She had not only seen his ring; she had confirmed his unavailability when she did diligence on his reputation as a builder. That was sterling, she discovered. A Riggs-Mason Signature Home was money in the bank. But if houses stood, people changed, and two years was a long time.

Almost as long as it's been since I've gotten laid, she mused. It wasn't true, but when she was horny it certainly felt that way. She re-entered the courtroom vowing to herself that if David was married she would have the roof fixed and leave it at that. *No Married Men* was a rule chiseled in stone. But if he wasn't married, well then…

"The court will now come to order." Judge Gavin's announcement – amplified by a microphone into a resounding command – jolted her back to reality. She had daydreamed through his entry; stood up and sat down again by rote. She cleared her mind for the summations. It was a moderately difficult case; she bore down and made notes. Judge Gavin was not one to brook any shenanigans in his courtroom, including attorneys who weren't paying attention.

For the next day-and-a-half, Joan worked extra hard to ease her conscience over skipping out for the weekend, sipping decaf coffee as thoughts of David wove through her mind. She didn't even watch the clock. It was amazing the way time flew when you were busy, hopeful and curious.

On Friday afternoon she thought of Pete Petras, the investigator she had used on and off for years. *Do it*, she thought. It was a bit soon to have David checked out, but she had been lied to before, and when it came to relationships, she had learned by getting burnt.

"What you got?" Pete's no-nonsense response reassured her. She had used conventional means to check into David's business in the past, but this time she was going straight to a pro. She instructed Pete to check David's marital status, past divorces, driving record, drug or alcohol troubles, priors and arrests, if there were any, which she seriously doubted.

"How about financials?" Pete asked.

"Check those, too."

"When you need this by?"

"Next week, if you can."

"That's walking on water, you know."

"You always have in the past," she shot back.

He laughed, and his tone softened. "Who is this guy, Joan?" He was a friend who would look out for her if he had to.

"I might be dating him, if you must know."

"I'll do my best. Be careful, and take care."

Saturday morning promised a stellar weekend. It was bright, sunny and clear, without the humidity that had plagued New York in recent weeks. Joan chose a pair of light-beige summer pants, a madras blouse, and sturdy flats for the trip. She applied the least amount of makeup possible, then brushed out her shoulder-length brown hair. She didn't need the sporty four-wheel drive on such a bluebird-clear day, but driving it for two-hours put her in a country frame of mind. She stopped for takeout coffee on the last leg of the journey, at the same place she always did – a crossroads carriage house with real red barn-siding turned into a deli that served hot, no-nonsense coffee that tasted great.

Should I get him one? She wondered. She even remembered how he took it – cream, no sugar – from the days they spent poring over blueprints, plans, and brochures. Two years later, and she still remembered. As she fastened on the lid, she felt the heat of the cup in her palm together with a corresponding warmth between her legs.

No coffee for David, she thought as she paid. Once the roof issue was out of the way, the offer of a drink at the house was the right way to invite him in.

As she neared the end of her driveway, she saw his sedan parked next to a roofer's truck. Both vehicles were considerably out of the way. On the far side of the house, the base of an aluminum ladder protruded out onto the lawn. David was standing on the elevated front deck leaning against the railing, the sleeves of a white cotton shirt rolled back up his forearms. He looked just the way she'd been picturing him, with tousled sandy hair and khaki chinos, clean running shoes and a wide brown leather belt. The house – an alpine-style cedar home with large sliding glass doors across the front – was built into the side of a hill so he was twelve feet off the ground. When he heard her car pull up, he turned and waved.

"Hello, Joan," he said as she walked up the steps. He extended his hand for a firm handshake.

"How've you been, David?" As his fingers slid from hers, his nod told her he'd been fine. There was no trace of the wedding ring he'd worn before, and no telltale band of pale to advertise it's recent removal. "How bad is it up there?" She indicated the roof with her eyes.

He shrugged dismissively. "It's a pretty big patch. Jim has some heavy plastic, so he can cover it until he gets back here on Monday to finish it up. He's booked, but he owes me one. If you approve, that is."

"Sure. And *thanks*." It was a relief to have the problem taken care of so easily. There would be no question of competence, no guesswork and no issues later.

"I'll take care of the cost," he added. "We stand behind what we do. The damage is minor, and the house is still new, so don't worry about it."

"Are you sure?"

"You can forget all about it," he insisted mildly but firmly. "Unless you want Jim up there sending you a bill for work on a Saturday." He smiled.

"Okay!" She raised her arms in mock surrender.

He gave a thumbs-up to Jim high above, who went to work with the temporary sheeting he already had in hand.

As the roofer finished up, they took a professional walk around the corners of the house he had designed. David checked the basement, the foundation, and even laid a level on the deck. Joan looked him over as he moved. In two years it seemed he hadn't aged a day. When he went down on his haunches to inspect some joinery, he hung there with the springing resiliency of an athlete. He had worked in carpentry for years before getting his architectural degree. He had managed to keep the fitness the trade had given him and his walk exuded confidence. His toned forearms were light with hair, and he was still narrow at the waist and broad across the shoulders.

When Jim came down, there was a brief conversation about shingles before he hoisted the ladder on his shoulder and hustled off to enjoy the rest of his Saturday. Tires crunched on gravel as the truck disappeared down the drive.

David and Joan were left alone on the porch.

"Care to come in?" she asked casually. "It's warm out. I'm sure you could use a drink."

"Sure." He followed her in as she unlocked the door.

"So, how have you been these last two years?" She stepped into the cathedral-ceiling living room. She opened the sliding doors for some welcome air, and then drew the semi-opaque sun curtains in front of the screens. The varnished hardwood floors, large throw rugs, and the fieldstone fireplace in the corner all seemed to welcome her home.

"Working hard, as usual. Business is booming. Other than that, just fine."

She concealed her taut nerves in the moment of truth. "And how's the family?"

"Kate and I divorced last year."

"I'm sorry." In a way she was, but she was much more thrilled by possibilities made real.

"That's okay. It was amicable enough. Sometimes things just aren't working and it's time to call it quits."

She gave a small nod of agreement. It wasn't difficult to see he didn't want to go into details, at least not yet.

"I thought of you," he added.

"Really?" She ached with desire as she asked him to sit down, the warmth between her legs swiftly transforming into a deep wetness. She wanted him, she decided. She wanted him! "And exactly what did you think?" she asked with a sly smile.

"Just thoughts," he replied as he sat down on a brown leather couch. The center of the room held one other couch and a chair that all formed a three-sided rectangle arranged with the open side toward the high glass doors that offered a view of green fields through curtains waving languorously in the breeze.

She looked at him quizzically. Most other men would have jumped at the opening she had given him, but he sat back as calmly as if he was attending some architectural conference. "What can I get you, David? Tea? Coffee? Mineral water? Maybe an Irish coffee to start the day?"

"I'd like a glass of cold water."

"That's all? Anything in it?

He smiled. "Just a glass of water, very cold, with no ice, and served, by you, in the nude."

Joan was so surprised her mouth fell open. She stared at him as she took an involuntary step back. She made a sound as if to speak, but then didn't know what to say. *How dare you?* She thought reflexively, the same way she would have indignantly brushed away an impertinent, out-of-order move in court. But she didn't say it. Her brown eyes narrowed. She shook her head to show she simply could not believe what he had just said. "*Excuse* me?" Her emphasis on the first word indicated she was willing to believe she had misunderstood him.

"I would like a glass of cold water, with no ice, served by you, completely in the nude," he repeated, "and placed right here on the table. And don't forget the coaster." His gaze held hers like an inescapable illuminating ray.

She stood transfixed like a deer in headlights as she looked this way and that for escape. No man had ever spoken to her in quite that tone. No one had ordered her around like a servant or, more accurately, a serving-girl. Not her father, not her ex, a professor of law, or even a judge. What she was loath to admit was that it excited her far more than the simple sexual craving she had been experiencing up until that moment. It was as though an accelerator had been applied that raised her desire to a point she had never known was possible. As her pussy juiced, her mouth went dry and she actually went weak in the knees. The problem was, she had never allowed herself to admit the truth. The expectations of her peers, law school, and the stab and parry of the courtroom had caused her to raise a shield. And she had done more than that, she suddenly realized. Over the years, she had gone to work to conscientiously chisel this submissive thrill out of every corner of her being. But now here it was, back in full force, and then some.

She had two options. She could ask him to leave and end it right there and then, which is what she would have done if it had been anyone else. But he was a good man and she wasn't afraid of him; she could play along and see where it went. And wasn't the idea of weekend trysts one of the unspoken reasons she had commissioned such a private house in the first place?

Years of unfulfilled desires welled up inside her as she bent before his will and let go. "Okay," she said. Her voice was almost a whisper. She looked straight at him as she raised her voice to make sure he heard her. "Yes, David." As the words came out, she felt a burning in her cheeks. She quickly turned away and walked down the hall to the kitchen.

She stopped in front of the refrigerator. Her hand dropped from the handle. *Nude*, he had said. All right, so be it. She took off her shoes and socks. Then she slid her pants down, stepped out of them and, always neat, folded them and put them on a chair. She took off her blouse, removed her panties, and unhooked her bra. When she was fully exposed, the coolness of the air against her skin brought her unexpected pleasure as it swirled around her breasts. The knowledge that David was waiting to look at her made her tremble. She felt mysteriously more exposed than normal because she was nude under orders.

She let the tap run until the well water ran ice-cold. She filled the glass, and wiped the moisture from the outside. The wooden coaster was handy, near the wine rack. Then she saw the circular silver serving tray. *Why not*, she thought. It would make a nice touch. She put the glass in the center with the coaster nearby. Before starting down the hall, she touched up her hair in the black reflective glass of the microwave with her free hand.

She had never waited tables, so she was careful with the tray as she padded down the hall. When she entered the living room she saw that, while she was away, David had moved the coffee table out of the central space of the seating area. She came around in front of him and set the coaster on the end table, then placed the glass precisely in the center. "Here you are."

"Thank you, Joan," he said very quietly, as if he realized what she had just accomplished.

"You're welcome," she said almost breathlessly. She put the tray aside as she stepped back to where the coffee table had been. She stood for long minutes with her hands at her sides while he looked her up and down slowly, her nipples hardening from his appraisal alone.

"You are truly beautiful, Joan."

She smiled, then she turned all the way around to show him her back and her firm round ass.

He took a long drink, then put the glass down.

"Would you like anything else?" she asked as she faced him again. There was a distinct bulge in the front of his pants.

"Just your company."

"May I sit down?" Her voice was playful as she tried to make light of the situation.

"Yes, but not there," he said as she moved towards the chair. "On the floor."

"The floor?" Abruptly, she realized that was why he had moved the table. The varnished hardwood was covered with a large woven rug. "Yes, David," she said for the second time that day. Just saying it that way made her heart pound as she sank to her knees, and then stretched herself out on her side. She lay with her right hand holding her head up and her legs, slightly bent, resting one on top of the other. She flexed her toes, then kept them curled slightly inward. Her right elbow was planted on the floor, giving her the look of a movie star positioned languorously on an ornate bed. "It's not fair, you being dressed while I'm naked," she said coolly.

"It wasn't meant to be fair, but you seem to be enjoying yourself, so I think I'll keep you that way for a while."

Instead of answering, she rested in silence as she luxuriated in her enforced nudity and in a desire so strong she was beginning to perspire. She ran a hand over her hip and down her leg, yet still he sat impassively. She wanted him so much she was ready to leap up and take him right then and there, but she didn't dare make the attempt. Letting him take complete control made her feel confused and anxious, yet for some reason it excited her even more.

"So, judging by your actions, I assume you're going to do as you're told today, Joan?"

"I am."

"Good. Very good. Do you think you can manage to control yourself until I decide if I'm going to let you come over here or not?"

"David, please..."

"Just stay there."

"Okay," she agreed, even though she wanted him to strip, get on top of her, and make love to her right there on the floor. Instead she listened attentively as he talked to her about his life and his business, about how things had gone into a big upturn and it was becoming more and more difficult to put the kind of quality into his houses he had vowed to from the beginning. As he spoke, she began to squirm.

"All right then." He stood up abruptly. "Come on over."

She met him halfway to the couch. She stopped in front of him, and he used two gentle fingers to raise her face to his. He kissed her full on the mouth, his lips pressing hard against hers. She wrapped her arms around his neck to bring him close, and when their lips finally parted, she felt his hand flat on the top of her head. The firm, gentle pressure only meant one thing. Slowly, she sank to her knees before him, and found herself staring at his promisingly tented slacks.

"Go ahead," he said, his voice both understanding and encouraging.

Using her thumb and forefinger, she lowered his zipper one shiny connector at a time. She unbuckled his belt, and he didn't resist as she lowered his pants, and then his fine-print boxer shorts. His cock leapt straight out, pointing at her. It was long and thick, with a classic circumcised head. His erection wasn't enormous, but its proportion and form were in perfect balance with his quiet authority.

"You've earned a taste, Joan."

She looked up at him quizzically. "Is that all I get, just a taste?"

"For now, yes."

She took his cock in one hand and stroked it, her other fingers toying gently with his balls. She pressed her lips against the side of his shaft and ran her tongue along its firm length from just beneath his head and back again. Then she looked up at him again. "I've never let a man come in my mouth before," she told him.

"And if I asked you to?"

"Then I would let you." She leaned forward, ready to begin sucking him down until he ejaculated between her lips.

"Not today, Joan, but I want you to suck me for five minutes, no more, no less."

"Yes, David," she said as she faced his cock straight on. She wanted to pause to savor the idea of being made to wait, but he was the one waiting now.

She took him in and stroked him with her mouth, and his masculinity filled her in more than a sexual way. It made her feel content, controlled, safe and warm. She devoted herself to pleasing him. At the same time that she worked her face up and down his erection she played her fingers around its thick base, swirling her tongue in small circles as she reached up and caressed his stomach then moved her hand down to his thighs, feeling his muscles, his exercised physique, and the tight roughness of his skin. As she sensed the five minutes coming to an end, she increased her speed, swallowing his hard-on faster and faster until the feel of his hand on her head told her it was time to stop. Stubbornly, she wrapped her fist around the base of his glistening cock and slid her other hand down to cup his balls as he laced his fingers through her hair.

"David, I'm so hot!" she panted up at him.

"Can you stand it for a while longer, Joan?"

"I can if you want me to…"

"Until next Friday?"

"Friday?" she exclaimed. "Please, David, I thought tonight we were-"

"No begging, Joan. I'm not asking you, I'm telling you. I want you to wait until then."

"I will…" The words where barely a whisper as she trembled with desire and frustration.

"Promise?"

"I promise."

"Tired of the floor?"

She nodded, her brown hair shaking softly.

He helped her up, then took off his shirt as he slipped out of his pants and brought her to sit next to him on the couch. As she ran her hands over his bare chest he kissed her face again and again, brushing wisps of hair from her forehead. "I'd like to take you to dinner then," he said.

"Yes, I'd love that."

He kissed her shoulder and moved down to her breasts, where he sucked her erect nipples one after the other until she was ready to cry out.

When he sat back, she gave his cock a few light strokes with her hand. "I'll finish it for you this way, if you like…"

"Just wait till you see how good it will feel a week from now." He rested a forefinger against her lips before she could protest. "Now it's time for you to get dressed."

"Yes, David."

He picked up the tray and the glass while she went upstairs and changed into an easy weekend dress and sandals. By the time she returned, he was fully dressed again and had put the coffee table back where it belonged.

"Just thought I'd help out."

"David, won't you come back and stay the night even if you just hold me?"

"That would be wonderful, but I've got the kids this weekend. I'm sorry, Joan. Just look forward to Friday, and I'll call you during the week. I'll introduce you to the girls after things have calmed down a little." At the door he held her close as he ran his hands up and down her back. She held him in return, and clung to him so tightly she felt like she was melting into him.

Later that afternoon, Joan poured herself a glass of wine as she relaxed on the back deck overlooking her verdant property. Her enforced horniness was difficult to endure. The fact that she was suffering on his behest turned her on all the more, but she could handle it; at least she would try. What moved her profoundly, she realized as she relaxed into the warmth and brightness of the day, was the fact that she had already fallen in love with him.

On Sunday afternoon she drove back to the city feeling wildly horny thinking about him every minute. She alternated between clear-headed control and a need so intense it was all she could do not to pull off into the woods, shove down her pants, and finger herself to an orgasm. She resisted the urge. *David owns me*, she thought happily. It brought her a strangely exhilarating joy to obey him, together with anticipating what he might have in mind for Friday night.

The investigation, she thought suddenly. She was going to have to call it off. She had already found out he was unmarried, and she believed in him. If he even got a whiff of what she'd done, she risked losing him. Pete had never been caught by surprise on one of her cases, but there was always a first time. That would be disaster, devastation, the longed-for Friday would never come…

She pulled over at the next parking lot she came to on the southbound highway and punched Pete's number on her cell. It routed her directly to a twenty-four-hour answering service.

"Call Pete now at home," she commanded the polite young man who answered. "Tell him to call it off. Tell him to call off the dogs immediately, to end the investigation. If there's anybody in the field, or anyone doing computer research, they're to desist at once. Is that clear?"

"Yes, ma'am." He read back her message verbatim, and promised to make the call the minute he hung up with her.

Pete phoned her later that evening. He told her he had called his detail man and done as she asked. "Found out one thing, though."

"What's that?" she asked with trepidation.

"Your man's not married. He's a regular pillar of the community up there."

No more information was needed, she told him. She would send him a check for everything he'd done. From here on it was clear sailing, as long as she could actually survive until Friday.

For the next several days, Joan immersed herself in work. Now and then thoughts of David crept in, together with a deep longing. The anticipation was delightfully maddening; it felt wonderful to be obeying him knowing she was bringing him enjoyment at a distance by staying faithful to his control.

"How are you doing?" he asked her Wednesday evening on the phone.

"I'm Managing."

"Have you touched yourself?"

"No," she said truthfully.

"I'm glad to hear you've been good, Joan."

"Sometimes at night I start perspiring thinking of you, David, and the way you're keeping me in suspense like this."

"I want you to know how much it excites me, Joan."

She imagined him sitting there calm, collected, in control. She wanted him desperately then, and not only in a sexual way. She wanted him to come to her emotionally, to tell her he wanted more than just excitement between them. She sat in silence, unable to speak she wanted him so much, in every sense. After a few moments of silence, a tear ran down her cheek, hot and salty.

"I had feelings for you when we designed your house, Joan," at last his quiet voice bridged the pregnant silence between them, "but with the way things were going at home, I wasn't… I just needed to get things straight before I went forward again. Then on Saturday, I decided to put certain sexual needs right up front because I didn't want it to be a problem later. You responded beautifully, and now the whole world is open before us." He paused before he concluded softly, "I love you, Joan."

"I love you too!" she sighed. "I always have, right from the start."

"Would you like to come over tonight?"

"I would love to, but I have to be in court first thing. I'm sorry…"

"Then no worries. I want you horny, but not pining away. Until Friday, then."

"Until Friday."

The last two work days passed in a dream-like blur as she threw one riposte after another across the courtroom. When Friday finally arrived, the two-hour trip seemed to fly by she was so happy. It was getting dark when she arrived at the house and time, now somehow cooperating, slowed down in a way that made every moment feel rich and clear as she slipped into a sleeveless black dress classically complimented by a single strand of pearls, and black heels half-an-inch shy of wicked. She deliberately didn't wear any panties.

When she saw his car pull up, she locked the front door behind her, then walked with regal slowness down the steps. He got out, and came around to hold the passenger door open for her. In the moonlight, he looked even better in a white shirt and black slacks than he had in his casual weekend clothes. She ran her fingertips up and down his tie. Then her hands were on his chest, and crooking one arm around his neck, she fondled his crotch possessively. He was hard for her and his erection was long and firm beneath the fine gabardine.

"Are you really all that hungry?" she asked.

"Nothing that can't wait." He touched the side of her face in affectionate, affirmative confidence. "We'll get something to eat later."

Without another word, they walked into the house. She turned on a set of low lights set against the back wall. There was a touch of redness above each of her cheeks. It wasn't makeup; it was need, emotional and physical, rising to the surface as naturally as water from a well. As he closed the door, she lingered at the edge of a rug where the backlight from the sconce lamps merged into darkness. As he approached her, she turned so the zipper on her dress was available to him. She felt it open, slow and sure, with a single motion. He kissed her neck, and the length of her back, as the zipper went down. He raised the dress, pulling her arms up as he did so. She didn't resist, nor did she assist him unless he moved her. He unclasped her bra, slid off the straps, and tossed it aside. Bare-chested, she turned to face him. He reached down and slipped a finger between her legs, applying a mild upward pressure.

"Oh," she said as she writhed upon that single, slender member touching her most delicate spot. She leaned forward, trying to squeeze his finger up between her thighs.

"Do you like being stripped?" he whispered.

"I do," she said just as softly.

"Louder, Joan."

"I like being stripped," she repeated clearly, still trying to get hold of his finger.

"Tell me you love it."

"I love it, David." Her head fell back and she took a deep breath. He slipped his finger away slowly, and she almost chased it as he stepped back. He took her by the arm, and guided her over to an ottoman. He seated her on it, and genuflected before her to remove her shoes.

"Take me upstairs," she begged. "Take me now, *please…*"

"You can last a few more minutes, Joan. You're likely to be very frisky tonight, so I'm going to tie you down. Go upstairs, sit on the edge of the bed, and wait for me."

"Yes, David." As she ascended, every step was difficult. The hunger for his company and his restraint was so intense that every moment away from him was a moment of loneliness. She went to the bed as he had told her to, and sat with her hands on her thighs, trembling a little as she waited for him.

Some of the skylights were open, drawing air though the bottom of the house and back outside so there was a constant light breeze, and Joan felt calmer with it caressing her. She heard the front door closing, then the subtle sounds of his moving around downstairs. Finally, his footfalls sounded on the stairs and he entered the bedroom carrying a small satchel.

"Have you ever been tied up, Joan?"

She shook her head. "I talked about it with Brian, but it never got past the talking stage." The words came out quickly, their haste designed to exorcise any memory of Brian from the room.

"Take the ropes out of the bag while I get undressed." He set the bag next to her on the floor.

Promptly obeying him, she was surprised by their silky smoothness as she unraveled the coils into long, white strands.

"Silk," he informed her. "You'll be wearing it in a few minutes."

As he removed his pants, she fished something else from the bottom of the bag. Seeing it, she turned away from him where he stood shrouded in semi-darkness. She was holding a red ball-gag with a leather strap that fastened with a buckle. She was taken aback at how large it was. "I wonder if this thing is going to fit," she mused out loud.

"Why don't you try it?"

Joan tentatively inserted the ball between her lips. It was a tight fit, shaping her mouth into a perfect O. As she reached back to buckle it, he sat down on the bed beside her. He moved to help her, but she gently shooed his hands away and fastened the buckle behind her head herself. With her mouth completely filled, she looked straight at him, ready and willing.

He was wearing light-blue boxer shorts, his body radiating strength as he ran his hands over her shoulders. It took her by surprise when he stood her up in front of him while he remained seated on the edge of the bed. She expected him to play with her breasts, but he moved higher, to the left side of her chest.

"Where you're heart is," he explained, kissing her there, his lips lingering against her skin. He broke contact gradually, then kissed her there again lightly and looked up at her.

She nodded and ran her hand down the back of his head to his neck, glancing expectantly at the bed.

"Yes, Joan, it's time." He rose and picked up the ropes. "Turn around." With his hands on each of her hips, he turned her to face the wall as he wound a long strand of rope around her waist, tying a knot against her left hip and letting the long ends trail to the floor. Then he slipped a second rope of the same length around her waist and knotted it against her right hip.

Joan observed that if she walked, the ropes would drag behind her like a long bridal train.

"Lie on the bed, right in the middle," he commanded quietly, patting the mattress.

She lay obediently down on her back. The ropes around her waist were comfortable because the knots were at her sides instead of bunched up beneath her.

He tied each of the long ends to the bottom posts. She turned her head to watch as he secured her right wrist, and it surprised her when he kissed it first. Then the rope went around it, was knotted, and looped around again to be knotted a second time where she couldn't reach it. He came around to the other side of the bed and did the same thing to her left wrist. She felt a welcome tightness as he fastened the ends to the bedposts and spread her arms wide. Because of the ropes around her waist she couldn't move her torso from side to side or inch up and down the bed. She kept following him with her eyes as he bound her right ankle in the same way, with a long strand knotted around it in the middle and long, trailing ends. He then raised her right leg up and pulled it back to tie one of the long end pieces to the top of the post above her wrist, using the ferrule around the crowning ornament to hold it in place. He did the same on the other side of the bed so both her legs were elevated and pulled back if in high birthing stirrups. Then he fastened the ends of the ropes dangling from her ankles to the bottom bedposts, likewise securing them beneath the ornaments. She now found herself helplessly available in the most receptive feminine position possible. She widened her eyes as he stood at the foot of the bed looking at her, and playfully wiggled her feet.

Judging from his broad smile, he found her gesture amusing. He tickled the sole of her right foot.

"Mm!" she moaned, shaking her head, but her eyes were lit up with fun. She was terribly ticklish, and she hadn't had the chance to tell him. She tossed her head back in suppressed laughter, her chest heaving.

"No?" he asked.

She shook her head vigorously.

"You look wonderful the way you talk with your eyes, Joan." He slipped off his boxers.

She looked down between her upraised legs and saw his erection standing straight up at the foot of the bed facing her. She wiggled her feet up and down, making the ropes dance like power lines in the wind. Even the air against her exposed pussy was turning her on; she simply could not stand the anticipation any longer. When he moved closer and kissed the inside of her thigh, she let out a shriek of delight from behind the gag.'

He laughed, and she tried to join him, her chest shaking with spasms of silent mirth.

He moved closer still, so close his face was almost against her pussy when he bent over. He touched the tip of his tongue to her slit, and she lurched against the ropes, uttering a muffled cry of pleasure. She was so aroused the opening between her legs felt like the centerpiece not only of the room but of the whole universe.

He kissed the inside of her upraised thighs as he had her chest, slowly and deliberately planting his lips against the same spot over and over again.

She pulled against the restraints, attempting to inch her bottom down towards him to increase the contact. She wanted him in her, she wanted him to lick her and suck her, but no matter how much she strained, she found she was struggling toward his face in vain.

He was holding a bottle of perfume in one he had picked up from the top of her dresser. Resting on one elbow, he held it up where she could see it. "Your favorite?"

She nodded, then dropped her head against the pillow. This was maddening! But she couldn't resist watching again as he poured a drop of perfume from the bottle onto his forefinger, and touched it to the right side of her pussy where it joined her leg. He caressed the fragrance downwards, and then did the same on the other side of her sex before drawing a line of perfume along the top of her bush to enclose it in a scented triangle. The sweet essence mingled with the odor of her musk and filled the room. He lingered over her, savoring the heady scents as he ran a fingertip along the ends of her pubic hair, and to her each follicle felt like a miniature clitoris responding to his touch. Her thigh muscles trembled as he searched for the real thing, and lightly rubbed it until tears of pure need filled her eyes.

She began struggling, pulling with her arms, but the ropes were inexorably tight. Her feet whirled in tiny, wild circles, and then suddenly he licked her pussy from top to bottom with the full length of his tongue. She stopped twisting and writhing and settled into the pleasure of having her labia massaged by strong, swift strokes. All her heat was concentrated in the liquid pressure of her pussy sending shockwaves of ecstasy through her body beneath each one of his hard licks. Finally, he thrust his tongue inside her. She twisted her hips in an effort to pull it in deeper, but he abruptly transferred his attentions to her clitoris, easily finding its swollen edge above her flooding sex. She shrieked into the ball-gag, taking deep breaths through her nose. She pulled herself tight with tension against the ropes, forced to hold the tortuous position, the knowledge that he could keep her here like this all night, teasing her to his heart content, threatening to drive her mad.

He kissed her clit, and then touched it with his fingertip again. She was emitting a constant low moan, humming her need, and the sweet beginning of the satisfaction of her painfully intense desire. He moved up, exploring her by kissing her stomach, inching up to the open space between her breasts. He suckled each of her tense nipples in turn, taking them in his mouth as they strained upward towards him. She opened her eyes wide and filled them with the love she tried to beam up at him, to show him all she felt through her gaze. At the same time his hard cock came nearer and nearer to her sex like an arrow closing on it's target. The instant the head of his erection touched her open and soaking lips, she felt waves of satisfaction flowing through her as he entered her slowly. He kept on sinking inside her, sliding patiently into her body. She desperately clamped her vaginal muscles around him, holding onto him possessively as he sank all way inside her and at long last began fucking her. He moved in and out, in and out, again, and again, in long, regular thrusts. Then he began taking her harder, rocking himself forward and back, pushing his cock into its thick base every time. Unable to move or to hold onto him except with her sex, she tuned in to the cadence of his thrusts and an orgasm shot through her in a great bright blinding flash of pure sensation. His face was nearly touching hers, and when she could see again, she looked straight up at him, directly into his eyes, as she felt his penis pulsing and squirting long streams of satisfaction deep inside her. She sought to take him even deeper inside her through vision alone as the two of them became one.

He pushed himself off her, sweating and smiling with satisfaction. Her perfumed musk was on him, his softening cock shining with her juices. He ran his hand over his forehead as she lay still, her eyes moving to the varnished wood of the ceiling. Never in her life had she felt anything like this. She had tried to, she had even faked it, but the real thing had never happened to her before until now.

"Hey," he said when he noticed her absorption. He touched her face, and she looked at him, saliva dribbling down out of the corners of her mouth. He wiped it away with the balls of his thumbs. "I really do love you, Joan." He leaned forward to kiss her cheek. "You were wonderful."

"Mm-hmm." She nodded with a mischievous gleam in her eye.

He left the bed, ducking beneath the rope, and walked over to a chair near the wall where he sat down facing her. His cock was smaller, but growing again, shining in the half-light.

Uh-oh, she thought. *Is this guy multi-orgasmic?*

He sat back to take a deep breath, and then perched on the edge of the chair, staring over at her with an amused expression.

"Mm!" She wiggled both feet up and down, her eyes narrowing as they glared the message that it was time to release her.

He laughed. "Okay, sorry." He returned to the bed and she raised her head as he unbuckled the gag. He took it out slowly, sensing the ache in her jaw. He freed her left foot, and then her left hand, tossing the ropes up over the baseboard as he moved to her other side. She stretched her legs luxuriously, and when she shivered, he lay down beside her and took her in his arms in a single motion.

She rested her head against his shoulder and ran her fingers through his hair.

He grasped her hand and kissed her palm, then each of her fingertips in turn.

"Stay tonight?" she asked softly.

"Yes, but in the morning, I've got to go home and let the dogs out, and even though I hate to work on weekends, I have to call my accountant. We've been auditing our books. It was supposed to have been wrapped up by today, so he promised he'd get it done."

"Why the delay?" she asked as a chill of fear made her tense against him. Had this accountant noticed someone nosing into David's affairs before she had time to yank the case away from Pete?

"He needed some files I thought we had closed earlier."

"No problems, then?"

"No, but next year I'll start earlier and get everything to him on time."

"That's good," she said with secret relief, and quickly changed the subject. "Tomorrow night I want to be on top," she informed him, running her hand down his arm. He made a sound she thought was assent, but she couldn't be sure. Soon he fell asleep, and she lay there luxuriating in his regular, heavy breathing.

The next day dawned as bright as the one before. They breakfasted on poached eggs and coffee, and during the short time he was gone she lounged on the deck watching the Saturday morning news. When he returned, she brought him another cup of coffee still wearing her satin pajamas. "Upstairs again?" she asked.

"First a question."

"Yes?"

"Did you have me investigated?"

"David, I... I started to, but I stopped it right away as soon as I knew what a mistake it was." There was no alternative but to blurt out the truth. If it had been anyone else, it would have been deny, deny, and deny again, but not with David; with him she had to be straight and clear. "It was reflexive," she explained. "Something automatic I always do. It comes from being a lawyer." She told him how she had felt, her change of heart, and how it had been an immense relief to call it off. She had found out he wasn't married, but that was all. "I'm truly sorry, David. It was ingrained cynicism, that's all. I was wrong. I just hope you can find it in your heart to forgive me."

"Do you know how I found out?"

"I have no idea…"

"I didn't find out. I guessed. When we first met, while we were designing this house together nearly three years ago, you mentioned you would do an investigation on anyone you became involved with seriously. So I just thought I'd ask."

"You have a good memory," she declared sadly. She picked up a magazine, leafed through it indifferently, and then tossed it aside. "What are you going to do?"

"I'm going to take you upstairs and have you ride me like you wanted to."

"You are?"

"Yes, but first you're going to get a spanking to erase the last of that lawyerly cynicism you tell me you're so sorry for."

"You're right, I *do* deserve a spanking, if that's what you want to do with me." She paused. "Thank you… not for the spanking you're going to give me, but for understanding."

"Like I said, I believe in you, Joan."

"Did you investigate *me*?" she dared to ask.

"No, because there was no need to. I saw you clearly back then the way I do now. I had a feeling things were right, and I didn't want to go behind your back. So don't try to turn the tables on me."

"David, I-"

"Don't explain, Joan. I already understand. Now, if you're truly sorry, go upstairs and take those pajamas off. Then put on the high-heels you wore last night, come downstairs, and sit on the couch to await your punishment." He wasn't threatening, but she could tell he wasn't kidding either. "What are you waiting for? Do as you're told, Joan."

"Yes, David." She walked quickly up the stairs. In the bedroom, she shed the silky pajamas in an instant, then slipped on the shoes. She came back down more slowly, assuming a deliberate, obedient pace. She sat on the couch, and he left her there to go upstairs himself. Watching him on the landing, she saw him use a chair to slide a rope over the main beam of the house before flinging it down to the first floor. When he returned, he instructed her to stand beside it, and then tied her hands, wrist to wrist, straight up over her head. It surprised her when he stretched her body out taut by fastening the rope to itself somewhere above her wrists. When he was finished, she was almost standing on tiptoe in her high-heels. She tried to move, but all she could do was step in small circles.

"I've got something special for you, Joan." He held up a fine ruler of dense, flexible wood resembling a yardstick but with finer numbers closely incised, the whole thing shiningly polished. "It was used to measure the fittings here, with close tolerance. I want you to know that." He ran the yardstick over the bare skin of her ass. "I believed you when you said you were sorry, and you're forgiven. I'm spanking you now for another reason. Can you guess why?"

"Oh, David please, I-"

Thwack!

The first smack of the ruler was light but stiff. It stung her ass so much she tried to step forward away from it, but the cord binding her wrists kept her firmly in place. As he raised his arm to swing again, she took desperate tiny steps to face him.

"Don't dodge me," he said with a smile.

She forced herself to stand still as he angled the yardstick to reach around to her bottom.

Thwack!

The second blow was as light as the first, but stung even more on top of it.

"You're punishing me for saying I wanted to get on top!" She guessed, speaking rapidly. "I was being too forward."

"Very good, Joan, you're learning fast." He spanked her twice more in swift succession straight across her tender ass cheeks. "And this will make you learn even faster. Now when I put you on top you're going to listen to every word I say."

"Yes, David."

"Good, because this ruler is long enough to reach around to your backside while you're up there. Do you understand?"

"Yes, David. Will you spank me while I'm riding you?"

Thwack!

"Not yet, Joan. You're being forward again."

"I'm sorry! Please forgive me! I'll wait."

"Yes, you will. You can wait right there while I read the paper and have another cup of coffee. Then we'll see about upstairs." He looked straight at her. He wasn't angry. He was so far from anger a smile softened his firm mouth. She saw into the future then, the way he would remember this foible of hers and take it into his heart, not as something to fester but as something endearing, something he had caught her at red-handed that would make him shake his head in wonder.

When he finally untied the rope, which was left dangling in a ray of sunlight as he carried her upstairs, she knew that, with him, she could spend her whole life learning more ways to trust and to love.

Staying Present

by
Ariel Graham

She waited for him to come home. The house was clean, the dishes out of the dishwasher and put away, the laundry done. There was nothing else for her to concentrate on. She hadn't gone into the lab. The day before she'd spent sequencing the same virus over and over; it felt like busy work and *he* was working to stop a new strain of virus that was killing puppies. His job seemed so much more worthwhile; more what she should be doing. She'd gotten into Virology to help people, not to map the same damn virus over and over again. Not that she wanted everything to be a level four biohazard, she was just bored.

So she waited. He finally called and said he was on his way. Her spirits plummeted. She had expected to see his headlights any minute. The lab was half-an-hour away. She poured herself a second glass of wine and played the conversation out a little further. The dress she wore floated around her, barely touching – certainly not rubbing – her nipples. She wore no underwear, per instructions. Nothing touched her anywhere.

She burned. She wanted something to caress her nipples, something to snuggle up against her crotch. She wanted to press herself against the edge of the sink, or run her hands down her hip bones and inward. She wanted to keep him on the phone. She licked the rim of her wine glass and said something to him, but he sounded tired and her spirits sank lower. Time to start dinner, then, something that could simmer on the backburner while they sat and discussed their individual days. Stew or chili. Something warm.

She padded barefoot into the kitchen, aware that every movement felt sensual, even the light dress she wore brushing against her mound, even the tendrils of long blonde hair escaping the clasp at the back of her neck and falling to stroke her shoulders and throat. All these things felt erotic. She bit her lip, enjoying the sharp sensation, and tried to lose herself in dinner. There wasn't anything else she could do. There were rules. Their rules, come up with together. What she could and couldn't do without permission. What she had to ask for. What she had to wait for. He liked her to be ready, hot and anticipating. She liked him to be in control. Most of the time it worked.

But lately, with the puppy virus making life miserable for him, no cures or vaccines in sight, she was hot and ready to no avail and the rules were making her crazy; desperate for him. She wanted his cock in her mouth and in her pussy, she wanted to be filled, held down and fucked. She didn't want to wait.

She was almost as tall as he was, five-nine to his five-eleven, able to lock hands and ankles at the same time when he lay flat against her, cock pressed against her belly, eyes laughing into hers in the moments before he relented and entered her.

She wanted it all now when he was at work, hard up against it, and wouldn't be home for lunch or home early. She had called that afternoon, called and asked. Getting through the receptionist and assistants had made her hotter refusing to leave a message, refusing to say why she was calling. The lab acted like Brent had security clearances. They acted like she intruded on their time with him. She had thought about telling them all what she wanted, but instead she simply said she needed to speak with him briefly, reminding each and every roadblock that she was his wife.

"Lily?"

"Hi."

"No," he said, with no preliminaries, no softening. No argument. Just the sound of her voice was enough to tell him what she wanted.

She thought about protesting, "You don't even know why I'm calling" but he did know, so instead she said, "Are you going to be home—?"

"Late."

She imagined he was smiling. A half smile, somewhat tired, mostly amused. He knew how she was feeling. He liked that no one else in the lab knew what they were talking about. She pictured him, tall, broad shouldered, strong hands that didn't look right for the minute, exacting lab work he did, buzz cut auburn hair, green eyes. *Tired* green eyes lately. "Late, and tired, I suppose." She sighed.

"Very. Move your legs apart."

They were pressed together. It wasn't helping, but she hated separating them. "I did."

"Where are your hands?"

"Both on the phone." She wanted to take the receiver and press it between her legs.

"Keep them there."

He was in a lab. He had a cubicle, but it was likely he wasn't in it. His colleagues were all around him, people he worked with, people she knew, people who knew her reputation in virology as well as his. He couldn't say much, but she knew he was smiling, and she knew if she didn't hang up now she'd have nothing left to work with.

She didn't hang up. That wasn't allowed either.

"You don't have permission," he said, and then, "For what? List."

Oh, God. He'd disallow everything. Her crotch throbbed, wanting, like a mouth longing for water. "To touch myself."

"Where?"

"Breasts. Throat. Mouth. Between my legs."

"Be specific."

She was alone, but her face burned. "My clit. My cunt. My ass. My lips. I need to sit on soft chairs or a pillow. I must keep my legs apart. I can't use–"

She couldn't use vibrators or dildos or hairbrushes or–

"You can't use anything," he said.

Her need rose a notch. To be filled. To be held. To be forced. And he was making sure nothing would even touch her. "When will you be home?"

"Be careful," he warned. It was a little too close to asking for something else. "Late. I'll call if it's past eight. Why aren't you in the lab?"

She'd been in the lab the day before. In her cubicle, doing paperwork, trying to ignore the tests she'd run that afternoon sequencing the virus hitting elementary schools, nothing more than a day of nausea per child. Boredom was about to send her screaming when Brent came out of nowhere. He leaned over, slid his hands down her shoulders and over her breasts, then circled them back up to hug her.

"What are you doing here?" She was too surprised to say anything else.

"There's a welcome every man loves to get."

From her vantage point he was upside down, his grin somewhat demonic. When he swung her chair around to face him, she automatically wrapped her legs around his calves.

"Careful." He grinned, that lopsided, ironic grin, the one that kept him from being a little too handsome.

"It's just a hug." But she'd released his legs and risen to give him a kiss and step back, properly respectable in her own cubicle. Around them people came and went, someone used the centrifuge, and several people typed, though *what* she couldn't imagine. They needed an outbreak, something curable but interesting. "I am so freaking bored!" she whispered fiercely.

"I wish I was." He ran one hand over his hair, which settled right back into place.

She cocked her head at him. "Why did you—?"

"Needed a break." He closed his eyes, rolled his head in a neck-cracking circle, trying to loosen the tension. "Just wanted to see you." He glanced at his watch. "And now that I have—"

"You're going back to it." She slid into his arms and smiled up at him. Their labs were a mile apart on the university campus, virology and epidemiology, one for humans, one not. The distance between them made for a nice walk when one needed to get away from sterile air and sterile work. "I could walk you back," she suggested. It was probably the most she was going to see of him for a while. She looked up at him, and caught the glint in his eye. "What?"

"You can't walk me back," he said, "because you need to take care of a few things."

And he whispered in her ear, walled off by flimsy cubicles and the sound of scientists typing, whispered to her to go into the bathroom and play with herself until she was wet enough to soak her panties. And speaking of panties, he didn't see any reason she should be wearing them, so she should take them off and put them in her purse. "You're not to make yourself come," he instructed, caressing her hair away from her face. "I'll take care of that tonight."

But he hadn't, not that night, and not the next morning, and Lily got hotter and wetter and wanted him even more watching his long legs disappear into jeans, and his chest vanish behind a long sleeved shirt as he kissed her and said, "Only coffee, and I'll take it with me. I love you." Then he was gone, exhausted, distracted, and she couldn't concentrate enough to make an appearance at the lab. Everything reminded her of sex. Sex she wasn't having.

She changed into a loose dress, one that tied under her breasts to support but didn't rub. She typed up old lab notes. She had lunch. She folded laundry. She read some erotica, but it didn't help; it made things worse. She thought about what she wanted to do with him.

Early in the evening she had a glass of wine. She had been reading, but her mind wasn't on the story and all she could think about was sex and wanting him. That was when he called to tell her he was on his way. That was when she gave up.

The rules were *their* rules. They had made them up together. Besides, he hadn't warned her about anything else when he called, and he wasn't going to be home for a while, and he wasn't going to be in the mood for anything when he got home anyway. By the time he wanted her she would be just as hot and ready as if she'd never touched herself in the first place.

If she thought about it anymore than that, she would have to admit she was doing it on purpose.

She didn't think about it anymore.

She checked on dinner. She kept her legs apart. She stood in the kitchen in her flowered dress with no underwear, wanting and needing, and reminded herself of the rules they had put in place together. She checked the clock. He had called fifteen minutes ago. He would be home soon.

She went into the bedroom and opened the bottom drawer of the dresser and just looked. There was the gym bag Brent called the "toy" bag when they went places. Sometimes he let porters carry it. It made her squirm and he liked that. The bag was flat, empty, everything spread out around it like an exploded sex shop, all the things she loved having used on her, all the things he liked to use on her. She knelt with her legs apart, just looking, checking the clock, but he wasn't due home yet. Her legs crept closer together and her hands folded and interlocked, tucked themselves between her knees, and started moving up.

I'm just looking, she told herself. At her favorite dildo. At the ball gag he had bought for her the last time he told her to keep quiet and she didn't. At the various internal and external paraphernalia.

Her fingers unlocked. She was still looking at the contents of the drawer, touching none of it, not using it, not even caressing it, but her hands were moving of their own accord, one index finger beginning to circle her clit, round and round. She was wet even there; her shaved pussy must be drenched. One finger circled, then pressed. Her other hand slipped lower, took hold of her sex lips and drew them up and out, opening and pressing. Her vision filled with accouterments, everything she loved to be touched with, played with. She let go of her labia all at once and three fingers slid into her very wet sex. Her circling finger stopped moving and pressed directly against her clit. She gasped, and moved her hand very fast, in and out of herself, three fingers fucking her, her mouth open, her eyes glazing, everything swimming around her as she climaxed, panting, her body trembling.

She didn't move as the last of the spasms ebbed. Her eyes were closed, and when she opened them she knew he was there, standing silently in the doorway, watching her. She didn't know when he had arrived and it didn't matter. He had seen the end of it, surely, and if he hadn't, she was still kneeling with her hands between her legs, her head hanging forward, her lips parted breathlessly.

When she turned and looked at him, he smiled lazily. "Was it worth it?"

She shook her head. It was never as good without him. She could tell herself what to do, give herself orders of a sort, but it wasn't the same. On the other hand, the look on his face said he was awake now, and that she wasn't finished.

"Take that dress off," he commanded.

She untied the ribbons beneath her breasts without hesitation, slipped the garment over her head, and let it fall to the floor beside her.

"Go hang it up. No sense getting the house all messy."

Unfair, she thought, noting he had already divested himself of shoes and jacket on his way to the bedroom. She could always follow his progress through the house by the breadcrumb trail of discarded clothing. She rose and hung the dress in the closet and came back to stand and wait.

He had gone into the bathroom to wash his hands and he took his time coming out again. She stood with her heart pounding in her chest and between her legs, the heat growing inside her again.

"You were studying that drawer pretty hard," he said, drying his hands. He deliberately dropped the towel on the floor, crossed his arms over his chest, and studied her.

"I was just looking." He made her feel defensive.

"At the toys," he agreed, but his meaning was clear. "I want you to look at them again. You need to get a few out of there."

Her pulse sped up even more.

He didn't move from the bathroom doorway. "Nipple clamps."

Lily took the alligator clips from the drawer, carried them carefully to the bed, and laid them on her pillow. Then she stood and waited again.

"Purple dildo."

She tried not to flinch. The purple one was large, the biggest they had, and it stretched her a little. She took it from the drawer, added it to the clamps, and waited.

"Medium butt plug."

She swallowed. So he was irritated. He had told her she couldn't touch herself and she had anyway. But this was the agreement they had entered into, what she had wanted – to be controlled, to be held in sway. It made her hot just knowing he could tell her to do anything or *not* do anything, and that she had agreed to unquestioningly accept his direction.

"Hairbrush."

"Brent..."

He raised an eyebrow. Clear across their master suite she could see that and she was sorry she had spoken. The smooth wooden hairbrush joined the collection on the bed. Only then did he cross the threshold, walk up to her, and kiss her on the mouth, his hands running down her back to her ass. He squeezed gently, then pushed her away from him, just hard enough that she lost her balance and sat down on the edge of the bed.

"Legs apart, Lily. Farther. Put your hands at your sides, palms up." He waited until she had arranged herself, then he moved one of the freestanding mirrors in front of her. Her breath caught at the sight of herself, spread open and waiting. He crossed to the drawer again, her image disappearing and reappearing as he moved in front of her. Two more items emerged – a knotted bandana and a handheld bell.

Her eyes flew to his face.

He didn't even blink. "I want to catch the news," he said, and slipped the knotted scarf into her mouth, tying it behind her neck. The bell sat at her feet. If she needed him, if something was wrong, she could ring it. "You're so beautiful." He leaned down to kiss her cheek, and then moved down to lick her nipples. He pushed her breasts together in his hands, squeezed them hard, and sucked their stiff points. He bit one, harder than she liked, tongued her soothingly, then bit her again. Then he straightened up and looked down at her, loving and stern. "Think about what you did, Lily. Think about what we agreed, and think about why, and think about what I'm going to do."

* * *

She could see the clock, just barely, from where she sat. Time passed exceedingly slowly as she breathed as steadily as she could through her nose, her pussy hot and wet, her hands aching to move towards it, her pulse fast and warm between her legs and in her throat and in her mouth. Her hair fell over her face and she tried to flick it away by tossing her head back. She *wouldn't* move her arms. Her body wasn't hers.

Think about what you did, he had said. *Think about what we agreed. Think about why.*

Why. Because she hated being told what to do, because she was independent and high-spirited and argumentative. Because nothing could make her hotter. Because she liked to be controlled and even liked to be hurt, liked it in a trusting relationship with a man she knew would never, ever back down and yet would never really hurt her, not permanently or more than she could stand. They had entered into their agreement because she had denied what she knew about herself, because she wouldn't tell him what she really wanted and was a bitch when she didn't get it. Brent was a natural Dom who knew how to control her, how to make her so hot she couldn't think of anything but sex for weeks at a time. He could make her come to heel, make her go to her job and do her work and reward or punish her at his pleasure.

For the two years since she had agreed to be his sub, she had flourished. Her work improved and she got a promotion followed by a raise. She concentrated better, got along with her co-workers better, and no one knew that when she went home she changed from leader to submissive. When she complained about her job, he listened. If her dissatisfaction was justified, he helped her work out a solution, if it wasn't, he punished her. When she bitched about co-workers, he listened for only so long before making her promise to take action before he had to. They celebrated her successes and commiserated her failures – unless they were her fault.

When they first met, after he found out what she liked before she even knew herself, he allowed himself to begin showing her what he was. He suspected the minute they got together that she was a natural submissive but that she didn't know what she wanted. He had been more than willing to show her. At first she had balked. She refused to admit she might want to be spanked, and that she even wanted to have days when she had to ask permission just to go to the bathroom. She wasn't going to let anyone tie her up, she didn't have much truck with toys, and she always ignored the excitement she experienced whenever she thought about things like that.

Brent refused to play along. He took her out to breakfast one morning. She was wearing a blue-and-white striped T-shirt that was quite tight, and jean shorts. When he finished telling her what he wanted, he said she had thirty seconds to decide if she was going to get up, go to the bathroom, remove her underwear, and bring it to him.

She got up, and it went from there. She was beautiful, but shy. She was used to being appreciated for her intellect. Brent – so in love with her his opinion should have been suspect – knew she was every bit as sensual as she was brilliant, and he set out to prove it to her. He liked it when other men looked at her. He liked to exhibit her. Once he told her to push her pants down in the car at night, her ass pressed against the seat, his free hand spreading her legs open. He drove a pick-up truck, and she cringed when they passed other vehicles, but her heart was pounding and she was breathless with excitement. Sometimes he made her remove her clothes in the car and walk from the garage into the house naked. By then the garage door was down, but there were windows and the lights were on. Inside the house she inevitably fell to her knees in the hallway and sucked him down as he stood above her, fully dressed and so much more in control while she was so much more naked because of it.

He began by tying her to the bedpost, making her endure so much pleasure she thought she would burst. At first he bound her with the belt from his bathrobe, then with silk cords purchased exclusively for the purpose, and finally he introduced her to metal shackles. He cuffed her ankles and wrists together, then to each other, and left her in vulnerable, crude positions. He brought home toys and tried them on her slowly. He blinded her with kitchen towels, then with leather blindfolds or a mask that covered all but her nose and mouth.

They both saw the changes in her, including the better work habits. She was just as bossy and demanding and sure of herself, but she developed an inner core of confidence that meant less fights with co-workers, improved performance and more fact-checking. She walked differently, less quickly and more gracefully, and she looked happier because she was. So his dominance of her expanded, moving out of the bedroom into other aspects of their life together. He respected her and she knew he would never embarrass her in front of her colleagues, but sometimes he called her at work and talked just long enough for her breathing to change as he described what was going to happen to her when they got home. If she sounded stressed, he ordered her to meet him for lunch, either at home or in the car; somewhere away from everything. He unbuttoned her blouse, unclasped her bra in front, and made her sit still and eat. Sometimes she argued a little, but mostly she was quiet. She liked surrendering control to him, even if it took her a long time to admit it.

One afternoon she came home in a rage about a co-worker who had dared to use her station. At first he was shocked, because her work was important and sensitive, but the longer she talked the more he realized the only thing the scientist had done was quickly write some notes on a pad provided by the lab. He tried to reason with her, because this was this kind of obsessive possessiveness that had lost her jobs in the past, but she didn't want to listen. Her work wasn't going well, she was frustrated, and the other scientist was a scapegoat. Finally he commanded her to be quiet. She snapped that he had no right to tell her what to do in real life, and he promptly informed her that he did, and that he would. That was when they hammered out their agreement, but only part of it, because she was unwilling to grant him permission to punish her for her behavior. It was silly, she declared, humiliating to even contemplate, and it didn't make sense. Granting him *permission* to punish her? Really!

"Oh, yes, Lily, this agreement between us is for all time, but renewable every year or every six months. We'll find a time limit you and I can both live with, but once you agree, that's it. And *yes*, you'll be granting me permission to punish you whenever you need it."

She looked snide. She was still annoyed by the incident at the lab and not thinking clearly. "And *you'll* decide when I need it?" She didn't believe him.

"Yes," he said seriously. He insisted she agree to be punished, and she insisted he tell her what he would do. He refused. In the end she swallowed her pride and agreed, and he actually drew up a written contract they both signed it. Then he told her he was going to punish her for her outburst.

She was appalled. "You can't!"

"I most certainly can." He was already towering over her.

"But that happened *before* we signed the agreement."

He was silent, his eyes boring into hers.

"What are you going to do?" she asked in a small voice.

"I'm going to punish you."

"But what–"

"You'll see. Now I want you to tell me the entire story again, everything you said and everything she said and how it all went down."

Still angry, and somewhat apprehensive now, she told him.

They went through it three times as he tried to make her understand how silly it was, how wrong she had been to fly off the handle, how destructive it could be to her career, while she refused to admit she was wrong, only grudgingly agreeing that perhaps she shouldn't have called the woman a bitch quite so many times, but at least she hadn't done it to her face.

"Get up," he said.

Surprised, she stood without arguing.

"I want you to go into the bedroom and get your hairbrush and bring it to me."

Her eyes widened and her lips parted as she prepared to protest.

He put a hand over her mouth. "I don't want you to say another thing until your punishment is over. If you do, I'll start again from the beginning. While I'm punishing you, you're not to make a sound. If you do exactly what I tell you to do without arguing, you'll get through this much easier."

She gazed up into his eyes trying to decide if he was kidding. He had to be. This was crazy. Yet she nodded, almost to herself, and turned to leave the room.

"Lily."

She faced him again.

"You have one minute to come back."

He was sitting in a hard-backed dining room chair when she returned. She handed him the brush without speaking. He took it from her, put it on the table, and pulled her around to stand at his right side. "Push your jeans and panties down to your knees," he commanded.

Her eyes got huge as she looked ready to protest again, maybe even run, and she shook her head a little, absolutely unable to resist arguing. For a few endless seconds she stood without moving, weighing her options as he watched her. She undid the button at her waist, unzipped her jeans, and pushed them down her thighs.

"Panties, too," he reminded her.

She hooked her thumbs under her thong, which she could technically have left on, but he wanted her naked; wanted her to fully understand she was being punished. She wriggled them down to her knees.

He admired her shaved pussy – she was so close he could probably smell her – then he yanked her down over his knees. Her hands went out in front of her as if she were falling. "Hold on to the chair legs," he instructed. "And don't let go."

That was unfair, to not let her have her hands, to not be able to make fists or flail at him. She grabbed hold of the legs.

He didn't wait any longer. With the flat of his hand he smacked her dead center on her bottom. "Spread your legs as wide as you can," he commanded, and that was the last thing he said. He began spanking her, alternating between her cheeks and hitting her along the crease of her ass and thighs then on her thighs as well so she could feel her skin getting redder and redder. Sometimes he struck the same spot over and over again, igniting it, landing four or five agonizing blows in the same place. She had breathlessly counted to twenty-five when at last he stopped. "Don't move," he said, and picked up the hairbrush.

She was certain she would scream if he spanked her with it.

Abruptly, he reached down holding a dish towel. "Put this in your mouth, because you truly do *not* want to make a sound."

She stared at the towel, then obediently stuffed it into her mouth and let her head drop. She was crying silently, the tears almost as hot as her ass.

He ran his hand over her flaming skin. "Ten," he said, and counted, slow and forceful, alternating his strokes, right cheek, left cheek, one each, and then again, and again. Afterwards, he held her while she continued crying, trying to be silent, still upended over his lap. His hands ran over her ass, not soothingly; more appraising and appreciative. After a minute or two he told her to sit up and helped her into the chair next to his. She reached down for her pants and underwear, but he yanked them completely off her before she could pull them up.

How long a journey from the living room to the bedroom? They didn't get there. Her hands fumbled at his fly, desperately unzipping him and freeing his cock. It sprang out of his jeans fully erect and she sank to her knees on the floor before it, forcing her mouth as far onto it as she could, and when that wasn't enough he pressed her head hard against him, his fist tangled in her hair to hold her steady while he pounded into her, fucking her mouth. She groaned and tried to take him in even deeper, but he slipped out from between her lips, showing more control than she had thought he could.

"Come here." He pulled her up by the wrists. He led her to a window and the armchair in front of it, making her kneel on the cushions. She could only be seen from the hips up by anyone on the street, but her breathing changed and her eyes closed. She loved the exposure, but she also wanted to hide within it.

"Stay here, Lily." He spoke sternly. "Stay present. Keep your eyes open." Standing behind her, he kept hold of one of her wrists and pulled her hips back a little with his other hand, forcing her to lean her weight on the windowsill. In that position, a little more of her might be seen from outside, but it was midday and there wasn't anyone on the sidewalks. Still firmly gripping her wrist, he slid his free hand over her red-hot ass, squeezing one of her cheeks along the way and subjecting her to a couple of light, reminiscent smacks that made her buck and moan in aroused protest. His hand slid lower, his fingers trailing along her ass crack and down to her pussy. She was drenched. Her breaths came fast and shallow. He stroked her sex lips, rubbing them, pushing them tightly together and then sliding a finger between them. She felt like honey, slick and sticky and thick with longing.

"Take off your shirt and bra." He was testing her. Pushing her. She knew he could see the side of her face, the dazed look of need and the fear creeping in.

The shirt slithered over her head, falling to the entryway floor. She tried to unhook her bra, fumbling with the clasp. He pulled it impatiently over her head, and a car drove by while they struggled with it.

He spun her around to face him, shoved her deep into the chair, and brought her legs up over the arms. She was spread wide, her pelvis tilted upwards. Her cunt was shiny, wet and smoothly shaved, her labial lips swollen and pulled open. She didn't have to look down at herself to know he could see straight into her.

"Pull your ass cheeks apart."

Sometimes she hated it, sometimes she loved it, having him look at every bit of her like this. Her fingers moved tentatively down the backs of her thighs, and she gasped when she touched the hot flesh of her punished ass. She pulled her cheeks apart, showing him her tight little hole, offering everything up to him. She was present, she was with him, staring up into his eyes, waiting and unafraid.

"What do you want, Lily?"

"Everything. I want everything. I want *you*."

Rearing out of his open jeans, his cock was breathtakingly hard, the swollen tip beaded with pre-cum. Her pussy was so wet he could slide right in and right back out again. He was still dressed, still in full control. He reached down and gripped his erection in one hand, running his fist up and down it, pumping himself while touching the hungry opening between her legs with his head, teasing her.

She jerked her hips at him, trying to take him inside her.

He laughed gruffly and bent over to kiss her. He sucked one of her nipples into his mouth, using his tongue and teeth to savor her stiff peak while she squirmed beneath him. He shoved a finger deep into her pussy, knowing it was nowhere close to what she needed, and fucked her with it for a minute before inserting another. Then he took them both away and abruptly shoved one finger up into her ass, penetrating the resistant ring of muscle and sliding it deep inside her.

Her whole body jolted from the shock. This was not something they did often, it was something she still wasn't sure of. She went perfectly still. She wasn't resisting, they were past that. He finger fucked her anus, thrusting two fingers into her sphincter as he knelt before her and brought his mouth down hard over her clit. She gasped his name, her hands grabbing at his shoulders, trying to pull him up. "Too much! Too much!" she breathed, or something like that, as he sucked her clit against his teeth, and then pushed his tongue deep inside her. She always thought it was too much, she couldn't take that much sensation, she fought it, she fought him; her hips bucked and she struggled. Yet one of her hands grabbed his hair as the other one came down over her clit. She stroked herself in front of him, letting go, giving into passion, falling hard into the moment. He lashed his tongue as deep into her slick pussy as possible, shoving his fingers into her ass as her fingers circled faster and faster on her clit, pressing hard, her hips moving rhythmically as he fucked her with his mouth and his hand. She moaned and let go of his hair to squeeze one of her nipples, emitting a sharp sound that sounded almost like surprise as she suddenly climaxed, her contracting muscles sucking on him and sucked by him.

He rode the contractions with her, her cunt and her ass pulling at him as he waited until her body went limp and soft. Then he pushed himself off his knees, yanked her body up towards him, and impaled her on his cock.

Her eyes flew open and she locked her legs around his waist, shoving her crotch against him and meeting him thrust for thrust until they came together and she gasped, "I love you! I love you!"

They went upstairs, and he made her stand in front of a mirror so she could look at the marks he had left on her body. There were imprints of his fingers where he had spanked her. She was shocked and slightly angry when she saw them. She wanted to shower and get dressed. She didn't want to remember that part of it.

He wouldn't let her do any of that. He made her stand there and face the marks, and he made her look at them again for the next few days until the light bruising faded. It made her truly angry the second night, at which point he took her over his knee and spanked her again, not as hard as the first time, but it was enough to let her know this wasn't the reaction he expected from her. Then he took her to bed and held her while she cried. She wasn't in the mood for sex, she was hurt and afraid of her own feelings, but he didn't want to fuck her, he just seemed to want to show her that it wasn't up to her, that everything was up to him. As she cried he held her tenderly. They slept cuddled close all night, and when she woke on the second morning after her first punishment, she wondered if she was crazy to agree to such a thing. Her ass was still sore, it hurt a little to sit down at work, but more than that she felt foolish, as if their relationship had changed to her disadvantage. Then she got a promotion and a raise, and six months passed before Brent felt the need to be punish her again. She would never admit it to herself that she almost liked it, or at least that she needed it. Things were different between them, but she no longer resented this because she could tell that they were, somehow, better.

After one year had passed, she did not hesitate to renew their agreement.

* * *

The evening he came home and caught her having an orgasm over the open drawer, he watched more than the news. From what she could see from the bed, the clock indicated he had been gone nearly an hour when he finally reappeared in the doorway.

"It's most complimentary that you can't resist touching yourself when you're thinking about me," he said, smiling as he approached her.

She had spent the hour alternately angry – because she was out of control, and because she felt like maybe he had set her up – and horny.

"You're thinking awfully hard," he observed, still smiling softly down at her.

She stared up at him, not bothering to try and talk through the gag. He would remove it when he was ready, and she didn't want to talk right now anyway. She was too excited. She wanted to be spanked and fucked and tied up. Most importantly, she wanted to be tied up. She wanted control taken from her, no choices to make. She wanted him to use the things she had laid out on the bed behind her, even the purple dildo that was a little too big. She lowered her eyes, and waited.

He leaned down and slipped the gag out of her mouth. "Unzip me," he said. "I want you to suck me."

She leaned forward eagerly and unzipped his jeans. He wasn't wearing underwear and she easily freed his cock, which was already hard. She dallied a moment, running her tongue over him, but he pulled her head back by the hair and slid his full length into her mouth. She swallowed him and began sucking, her head bobbing up and down as he held onto it.

"As I said, Lily, it's very complimentary that you can't keep your hands off yourself when you think about me. You're a very, *very* sexy woman, and I'm flattered." He paused as she swirled her tongue around him, then forced himself deep into her throat again. He wasn't taking up a rhythm – he wouldn't be able to talk if he did – but she could tell he was enjoying himself. "Nevertheless, we agreed you would ask for what you want, and today you called and I said 'no'. I told you I didn't want you to play with yourself. Maybe I wanted you hot for when I got home."

He looked down into her beseeching eyes, and had the grace to laugh. "Okay, yeah, this virus is kicking my ass, and I wouldn't have been very energetic when I got home, but I said 'no' Lily, and you did it anyway." He pulled out of her mouth and tilted her head up, looking expressionlessly down at her. "I said 'no' and you went ahead and did it. Did you want to get caught?"

God, she *hated* admitting it, but he would get it out of her eventually and then punish her for not confessing. Admitting she had wanted to be caught added humiliation to injury. Her cheeks got hot as she nodded, not speaking.

"Oh, I'm afraid that's not good enough, sweetheart." He stepped back. "Stand up and look at me."

She stood and met his eyes. She saw love there, but also the iron control of her master, the man she had signed an intensely binding agreement with. He was the other half of the equation. There was no reason to feel humiliated by what she wanted him to do to her. He was as much into it as she was.

"Say it, Lily."

"I want it," she whispered. "I want you to do whatever you want to me. I want you to do everything to me. I wanted it so badly today, and I knew you were going to be late, and I couldn't resist. I… I touched myself after you said I couldn't, and yes, I knew I was going to get caught."

He nodded, pleased.

"I don't want to know what you're going to do,' she added quickly. "I just want you to *do* it." She thought she might start crying. "I'm so hot!

He reached down between her legs and stroked her sex. "You're so wet." He turned her so she faced one of the mirrors. Her full breasts jutted out, her nipples long and taut, her pudenda visibly swollen between her slender thighs. Standing behind her, he brought his hands up beneath her breasts, cupping and squeezing them. Her nipples hardened even more, her aureoles flushing darker. He clutched her left breast and reached down with his other hand to thrust a finger up inside her. "You're so fucking wet!" He pulled out and slapped her cunt with his open hand, then shoved three fingers up inside her all at once.

Her eyelids fluttered as she gasped with pleasure.

"All right," he said harshly, "I won't tell you what I'm going to do. And I won't do it now." He let go of her.

Her eyes flew to his in the mirror.

"I put dinner in the fridge. Was that chili? It's a bit tired. You might want to throw it out tomorrow. Now put your clothes on, but no bra or panties. We're going out to dinner."

She closed her eyes, dreading hours of frustration.

He slapped her ass. "Hurry up. Aren't you hungry?"

* * *

It was a typical restaurant, people eating, small children making more noise than necessary, irritating people talking on cell phones. The tablecloth at the booth was long, and she was glad.

"Keep your legs apart," he ordered quietly, "and pull your dress up onto your lap."

She slid the dress to the very edge of her naked pussy. Their server walked over, and though she couldn't possibly see anything, Lily blushed. When dinner arrived, she kept her head down, her dress pulled up behind the barrier of the tablecloth.

Two hours passed before they were once more standing in the bedroom. She was completely naked again and he was still fully dressed.

"I won't tell you what I'm going to do, Lily, but you broke the rules and you knew there'd be consequences. You're not to ask a single question. You may respond, but not speak unless spoken to, or unless you're giving your safe word. What is it?"

"Red," she whispered, and didn't say anything else.

"Get on the bed and lie on your back with your hands beneath your head." He opened a window. Cold air wafted into the room and her nipples hardened even more. He approached her where she lay. He was wearing only his jeans now, his broad chest lightly furred, a trail of auburn hair snaking down into his waistband. He took the nipple clamps from the pillow beside her and fastened first the right one then the left one, connecting the chain between them and giving it a good tug.

She gasped, rising up against the excruciating sensation, but she somehow managed to keep her hands locked behind her head. Her eyes watered and her tongue ran over her lips. She closed her eyes.

STAYING PRESENT

"Stay present."

She opened her eyes again, staying in the moment, aware of what he was doing to her... of the fact that he could do anything he wanted to her...

"Get on your hands and knees and arch your back."

Her heart pounded. The purple dildo still lay on the pillow. Usually she was on her back to receive it because it was so big. But he still had the hairbrush, and maybe–

"Lily!" He slapped her pussy so hard her eyes watered. "I said get on your hands and knees and arch your back."

She scrambled into position. Her breasts swayed and the nipple clamps tugged, the chain swinging between them striking her as decadent and strange. She caught her breath at the sight, and suddenly he was behind her, pressing her shoulders down until they hit the bed, her head turned to one side, her elbows jack-knifed awkwardly upwards. He grabbed her wrists and tugged her hands behind her back, tying them firmly together.

"Look," he said, and she struggled to get her head up. He pointed to the mirror at the head of the bed and she saw one of the other mirrors behind her reflecting her to herself endlessly. She stared straight at the lewd image she presented – hands tied behind her, shoulders against the bed, her naked ass thrust up into the air, her pussy lips swollen and shining with moisture. He forced her legs further apart and she could see her wet cunt opening. His hands came down on her bottom cheeks, spreading them wide until she could even see her smaller, tighter hole. She should have been used to this kind of exposure by now, but she wasn't. Her eyes threatened to close and he gave her a hard smack on the ass, then another directly against her vulva again. She made a sound as his hand came down over her sex, rubbing, opening, penetrating her. He rocked three fingers swiftly in and out of her pussy, pressing down on her clitoris with the heel of his palm harder than she ever did. She pushed up against him, irresistibly moving her ass toward him. She felt tight and hot and desperately bottomless all at once.

The wooden brush caught her right ass cheek, along the top of her thigh. She cried out in pain as he said something she didn't understand. He dropped the brush and picked up the dildo and she closed her eyes as the thing pressed into her sex, slowly filling her. Then abruptly the rending purple erection slid out of her slick hole. There was the quiet sound of a bottle of lube flipping open, but she was wet, way too wet to need it... *No!* It was too big... *No!* She couldn't...

"I want you to relax, Lily, relax and trust me. Don't fight it." One slippery finger invaded her anus, thrusting past knots of muscle, fucking her. She gasped, violated, thrilled, scared...

"Ask me for it, Lily."

"Please..." Her voice was barely audible, not sure what she was asking for. The pain was instant, the pressure of something forcing its way into her ass. She bit her lip, trying not to pull away.

"Relax... relax and open up... let me in..."

The purple dildo was on the bed beside her. She looked up into the mirrors. Brent was holding her hips, his cock hard and straining for her gleaming wetly with lube, shiny, slick, huge, the head nearly as purple as the dildo. She gasped, bucking beneath him, afraid, but he pulled her to him remorselessly, using both hands to spread her open. She watched her bottom cheeks stretch apart and the head of his cock slip just inside her. There was an initial feeling of pleasure, and then a sharp stab of pain. She stared at her reflection and bit her lip over the word "Red". She said nothing, she didn't close her eyes, she didn't go away.

The end of his erection slid in, his head lodged in her ass just to the point where the shaft flared out again. She sucked in her breath, and he pressed forward remorselessly. She wanted to scream. It burned, he was too big... then the agony abruptly transformed into an unbearable fulfillment, a delicious fullness that left nothing to be desired. He was almost all the way insider her when he began moving carefully back and forth. She rocked her hips in rhythm with his, slowly taking him deeper and deeper inside her until she suffered the excruciating satisfaction of feeling his cock buried completely in her ass. When he began fucking her in earnest, the burning, rending sensation was so awful it had to be hurting her, she couldn't bear it... yet she didn't say her safe word or ask him to stop... her submissive moans were begging him not to stop, encouraging him to fuck her faster and harder, as selfishly as he wanted to, until gradually the terrible discomfort faded, giving way to an almost unbearable sense of fulfillment as she felt him shooting his cum deep into her bowels.

✱ ✱ ✱

The following week their labs merged, human and animal virology moving to a new shared facility. They would be working together unless they asked to be reassigned. They didn't.

The puppy virus passed and Lily's work picked up with a chicken virus that caused eggs to crack too easily. They worked in the same lab, and only occasionally did Brent whisper to her that she should go to the bathroom and play with herself. Sometimes he forced her to wear an anal plug beneath her lab coat until lunch, but most of the time work was work, the sex was vanilla, and their kinky contract appeared to be forgotten. Until their manager told them they were going to South America to chase mice that were spreading a fever.

They would have a team of assistants, and they were leaving soon.

Lily was terrified, of the shots, the plane flight, the job, the living conditions they would be forced to endure, everything. She had never been out of the country. Her confidence evaporated. She became shrewish, the person in the office everyone most wanted to avoid.

Brent was excited. He was trained in fieldwork and had been to South America. He understood her fear, but he didn't want her to dwell on it.

She wouldn't listen to his stories. His success – his survival – made her even more afraid.

He bought her books and videos. They watched improbable Sean Connery movies and dull-as-ditch-water documentaries. He showed her every tool they would use, bought her boots, snake bite kits, dinners out, and still her terror mounted until two days before the trip she was snapping at everyone, about to get herself fired and maybe him, too.

He signed them both out early. The manager said they didn't have to come in the next day. He seemed eager to see them go.

Lily didn't stop talking in the car. She was angry with everything and everyone. The lab was falling apart, she insisted. She had no back-up, no support. How the *hell* was she supposed to leave all her other research and go on a mouse hunt in South America?

"Lily" he said in the hard voice he used to enforce their contract.

She shut up immediately and stared at him, her eyes watering incredulously. "No, you can't, not now, Brent, please–"

"Are you breaking our contract?"

She opened her mouth, then closed it.

"Good girl." She was still wearing her lab coat and it was getting dark outside. "Lean your seat back and take off your shoes and pants."

She stared at him, mutinous, afraid of something different now.

They were at a red light, not moving, and he just stared back at her until she unbuttoned the coat and began the contortions of undressing beneath it.

When her jeans were on the floor, he raised his eyebrows at her.

She bit her lip, then slid her panties off as well.

"Good." He reached beneath the lab coat, and she sucked in her breath when he casually explored the entrance to her sex with his fingertips. "You're not very wet. Work on that while I drive and tell you about my field work."

* * *

When they got home, he told her to strip and stand beside the bed. He brought in some empty cardboard boxes, crushed them and scattered the entire contents of a bag of potting soil across them. He made her kneel in it, bound her hands to the bedpost, and blindfolded her. He put a tape of jungle sounds in the stereo, then dragged the old sun lamp out of the garage and set it on the dresser so it shone down on her. He pulled out his old field kit and unearthed a packet of sterile needles. He didn't know if he'd want anything else, so he kept the kit with him. He unplugged the phones, opened the windows, and sat down near her.

"We're in the jungle, Lily, spending everyday working with indigenous Indians. They're dying, Lily, and I know you haven't forgotten why you went into virology and public health. There's a virus here and we don't know what it is, and we can't be inoculated for it until we do, and we're the people they sent to find out."

Her head was up, her mouth open a little. The blindfold was a kitchen towel wrapped around her eyes and nose. He wanted her to breathe through her mouth, to alter her consciousness a little. He also wanted light to pass through the fabric as if she was bound outside in sunlight. A warm breeze wafted in through the windows and caressed her.

"We have to be careful, Lily. We have to do *what we love*. We have to admit that we *love* what we do. But we have to be so fucking careful, because just a little prick," he touched the tip of her finger with one of the needles, "can kill us." He reached over and pinched both her nipples hard. "We have to *stay present*, Lily. We have to be aware every minute. There's no room for…" He stopped. He wanted to see if she was listening, if she understood.

"Fear!" she breathed.

He kissed her. "Or anger." He leaned back, staring at her shaved pussy as her knees spread and pressed into the dirt. They were both perspiring beneath the heat lamp. "What *is* there room for, Lily?"

"Self knowledge," she replied in a clear voice. "Understanding why we do the things we do. Admitting what we love. Admitting what is only a defense mechanism or…"

"Or?"

"I don't really know what I was going to say." She laughed, self-deprecating. "It sounded good, though, didn't it?"

"This isn't a joke, Lily. This is your life. This could be your death. You have *got* to understand what it is you're doing. You can't react out of anger. You can't slam things around. This isn't a controlled laboratory, this is a field camp. And this," he pricked her right nipple with a needle, "is enough to kill you."

She shrieked, but didn't move, afraid of more pain.

"You've come so far, Lily, you've admitted who you are, what you want. You've done things you didn't believe you could do, things that had everything to do with sex and exhibitionism and being punished.

Things you knew damn well had nothing to do with anything except who you are and who you *could* be. You've overcome the fear of your own desires. Now admit you're afraid of this – of field work, the virus, of working with me in South America. Admit it so we can face it, so that you can go with me and be safe. Don't mask it with anger, don't make scapegoats of everyone else. Admit it, because I can't live without you."

She was perfectly still.

"That's *my* fear, Lily, losing you. One angry instant, one careless move, and I could lose you just like that."

When she started crying he removed the blindfold, untied her, closed the windows, and turned off the heat lamp. Then he settled beside her on the floor, leaning back against the bed, and held her while she sobbed and told him how mulch she wanted the trip, the field work, the mystery to solve, the chance to help, to cure, and especially the chance to work so closely with him.

She rested in his arms and listened to what he had done in Bolivia. He confronted and confessed his own fears, and held her while she openly admitted hers.

When she looked up into his eyes he made as if to get up, but she held him there on the makeshift jungle floor, the tape repeating the same bird sounds endlessly around them. He would say it was too dangerous, but she knew they would steal away and make love under the forest canopy, beside a stream, in the dirt. Anywhere was home as long as they were together. She could be herself and still be safe, still be present and aware.

The next day they packed for the trip. They had hired house sitters and the post office was holding all their mail. They took frequent breaks just to hold each other.

"Pack the toy bag," he commanded gently. "I want you to bring everything." Of course she couldn't, but she could bring a lot of it. He looked to see if she was obeying him. They would be going through a lot of airport security; her suitcases were bound to be opened more than once.

"And the contract," she said, reaching for the bottom dresser drawer. "Just in case we're there longer than we think. I don't want it to expire."

What It Means

by
Brooke Stern

I.

"You can use the bedroom if you want," he said. The voice was familiar, that of our host, a local radio personality. We woke up to his weather-and-traffic-on-the-nines every morning and now he was offering us some privacy. Maybe he was worried that our make-out session had gone too far—was it driving his guests away?—or maybe he just wanted us to be comfortable. Regardless, his offer, though kind, made me self-conscious and broke the mood.

"That's okay," I replied, sitting up and buttoning my shirt. "We really ought to be going."

He gave me a you-lucky-dog smile, looked at Ansel who blushed, and then told us to drive safe. When he was out of sight, I leaned back on the couch and took another sip of my bourbon.

"Come on," Ansel said, tugging on my arm. "You said it yourself. We ought to be going."

"God, you're in a hurry."

"Well…"

"You'd think you had something to look forward to."

As we found our way out of the house, she leaned into me and supported her body against mine. I should have said goodbye to my friends, but Ansel would have none of it. They would understand. We were a new couple and everyone was rooting for us. This was her first visit down here and all my friends had been excited to meet her. We had arranged it so that she would take a cab straight from the airport to the party and then we would go home together afterward. When we couldn't keep our hands off each other, the old couples stole glances at us and then at each other, hiding their envy behind isn't-that-cute condescension. Everyone knew that we hadn't seen each other in two weeks and this would be explanation enough for our rude exit. Little did they know.

We even had ourselves fooled. It was almost like we were just going home to fuck. It was almost like it was a normal weekend. It wasn't.

"It probably doesn't mean anything," Ansel said, buckling her seat belt.

I didn't say anything. It was a dark out in the country and I needed to avoid the other cars parked at odd angles in his yard.

"I'm a little drunk. Do you think I shouldn't be drunk?"

"I don't know."

"You're not drunk, are you?" she asked.

"I'm okay."

"Because if you were, we could just… I mean, it doesn't have to be tonight."

I made it off the yard and was focused on the road.

"You didn't say if you liked my dress."

"You look great."

"You can't even see me."

There were deer by the side of the road and I was ready to brake or swerve.

"How long until we get to your house?"

"Just a few minutes."

She was silent for a while as we drove into town.

"It probably doesn't mean anything."

It was the last thing she said. By the time we pulled into my driveway, the reality of what we were about to do had descended on us and there was no idle chatter about the house. I held her hand and guided her inside. We had talked about it constantly ever since we disclosed our shared secret and we had rehearsed it all countless times. It didn't surprise her when I took her straight to the bedroom and sat down on the bed; nor did it surprise me when she lay, willingly but a bit awkwardly, across my lap. It was happening just like we said it would. I knew what I was to do next, but I was insanely nervous anyway. I went to talk but nothing came out so I cleared my throat and tried again.

"You okay?"

"I think so."

This being my first time, I didn't know the words yet. What would, in the near future, evolve into an elaborate drama, complete with scripted dialogues and spontaneous improvisation, was a silent affair. I didn't know what to do other than start, so I lifted my arm and brought my hand down on her butt. It was a strange motion—not one I could remember ever having made before. It wasn't very hard, but not spanking someone very hard was still spanking them. I did it again. Her dress was thin cotton and her panties silk, but they seemed to turn each spank into a dull pat. I tried doing it harder. After ten times, I stopped and rubbed her ass, massaging her buttocks and pressing the fabric of her dress up between her legs. She was so wet that I could feel it through her dress.

I took that as encouragement and gave her ten more spanks, harder and faster this time. When I reached ten, I didn't want to stop. Something about it left me unsure—it went by so fast and I needed more time to think about how this felt. I could do what I wanted, right? Left cheek, right cheek, left cheek, right cheek. When my hand began to get sore, I stopped and lifted up the hem of her dress. Her panties had bunched up in her crack. I spanked her some more, aiming now for the skin of her hips and thighs, where her panties didn't obscure my view of the red handprints.

Even though she wasn't saying anything at all, I could tell it was hurting her. I could see her hands make their way towards her butt until she resisted her own instinct for self-protection and kept them in front of her. She balled her fingers into fists and then, when the pain became more urgent, she stretched her fingers out. I didn't know how much it should hurt so I stopped and rubbed her ass some more. It was really hot. I went to pull down her panties and she lifted her hips to help. Her cooperation felt to me like consent.

Spanking her bare bottom was what I had been waiting for. For the previous two weeks, whenever I masturbated, I had imagined her red butt and pictured the way her flesh would ripple with each slap. I knew it must hurt a lot more this way, though, and I didn't do it quite as hard. I kept going for a little longer and then took another break. I looked at the clock and it hadn't even been five minutes but it had felt like forever.

What was it like? Well, you have a lot of time to think when you're giving a spanking. You think about how it doesn't really feel like a fantasy come true, even though you know it is. It's not bad, it's just that doing it is different from fantasizing about it. You think about whether you're doing it the right way—should you do it harder or softer, faster or slower?—except it's not like fucking where you might be thinking these things but you're also thinking about how amazing it feels. When you're giving a spanking, it doesn't exactly feel amazing. You wonder if it feels like a fantasy come true for her.

I thought back to what she had said in the car, about it probably meaning nothing, and then I thought back to the conversation on the phone that started it all.

This is how that conversation went:

"Is there anything else you're into?" I asked her.

"Not really. What about you?"

"I guess not."

"There's something else, though," she admitted.

"What?"

"It's embarrassing…"

"That's okay. I'm fine with whatever."

"I've always been kind of into spanking," she confessed.

"Yeah?"

"Yeah."

"Me, too."

"Really?" she whispered.

"Yeah."

"You're not just saying it because I said it?"

"No. I've always felt weird about it."

"Yeah…"

"It's not like I want to hurt my girlfriends or anything."

"I know."

"I mean, I'm really into strong women. I don't do it to put them down."

"I get it. You don't have to apologize."

"Okay."

"Have you ever done it?"

"No."

"Will you do it to me?"

And that was it. We had been talking about it ever since, and that's why Ansel was so horny at the party and we were in such a hurry to leave.

I spanked her some more while I was remembering this, like it was something I did casually, daydreaming while smacking her bottom. I know she wasn't reminiscing like I was because I could tell it was hurting her pretty badly. I knew it was supposed to hurt and that she would be disappointed afterwards if it didn't, but I knew I should stop pretty soon. I didn't want to push it too far. The first time was scary enough. I hoped that there would be plenty of time for pushing her to her limits later. I don't know why the thought of pushing her limits turned me on, but it did.

I was kind of relieved when it was over. Doing it wasn't really like thinking about it. When I thought about it, I never had to worry about hurting someone real, but when I was doing it, there was Ansel, in pain because of me. This was particularly weird for me because I'm the kind of guy who made a special trip to the store to buy her the kind of pillow she preferred so she wouldn't have to suffer any discomfort in my bed. Yet here I was going out of my way to make her bare backside suffer a hard spanking. I had told myself a million times about us wanting it and consenting adults and all that stuff, but it didn't entirely solve the problem. Even how wet she was between her legs didn't make me feel like I was doing her any favors. I was hurting her. Every time I did it harder or did it in the same place or did it faster, it hurt her worse. And why? Because we wanted it, of course, but then there came a point where she wanted me to stop and I didn't, where I wanted it to hurt more and she didn't. It was my role to do what she didn't want me to do, all because that's what she said she wanted me to do. It made me nervous.

It's not like I didn't enjoy it, but her ass wasn't as sexy across my lap as it was when I was watching her walk naked across the room or when I grabbed it when we fucked. It was still, almost lifeless, the passive recipient of my spanks. I knew it was in agony, but the intensity was Ansel's alone. Except for her hands which struggled to stay in place, she gave almost no outward sign of distress. In my fantasies, there had almost always been squealing and pleading and maybe even tears. I felt lonely without her, like I had driven her away at the very moment we were trusting each other most deeply. Where was she? Did it mean I should have done it harder or did I do it too hard?

She got up slowly and cuddled up next to me without a word. I wondered if she would be mad at me because I had hurt her but it seemed to just make her feel closer to me.

"Ansel?" I said after a while of wondering what was going on with her.

"Yeah?"

"You okay?"

"Yeah."

But saying it seemed to release something inside and she got a little choked up. I dried a tear with my thumb.

"Did it hurt too much?"

"No. It's not that."

"What is it?"

"It's just... It probably doesn't mean anything."

"You keep saying that."

"Well, what if it does mean something?"

"Like what?"

"Like something bad."

I knew exactly what she meant but I was too scared to say it. Here are some of the things it could mean: There was something wrong with us. We weren't normal. We carried around crippling guilt (her) or a secret mean streak (me). We lived hidden behind a façade, too ashamed of our desires to share them with our closest friends. I was a hideous sadist or an angry misogynist. She was a self-hating anti-feminist or a guilt-ridden moral masochist. We were emotionally stunted, replacing a ritualistic fetish for a real, loving relationship.

It didn't feel like it meant these things, but it could.

"What if it means whatever we want it to mean?" It was a lame thing to say, but I couldn't think of anything else.

"What the hell does that mean?"

I think her anger wasn't about the question so much as it was about me blowing off her fear, like it was too small to worry about. But that wasn't it at all. It's that it was too big to worry about. Besides, if it was something big and serious, this was hardly the time to talk about it.

"Well, like maybe it just means that we like it. Some people like big tits and others like it doggie-style and some people like it tender and others like it rough. We just like spanking."

"Come on, David, you know it's not that easy."

"But maybe it should be. Maybe we worry ourselves unnecessarily."

"Maybe you're just not as fucked up as I am."

"Ansel, sweetheart. That's not what I meant."

"But you don't know what I want so how can you tell me not to worry about it."

"I know you like spanking."

"No, I hate spanking. It hurt like hell. I'm embarrassed as shit, lying there like a little girl—no, worse, like some woman who gets off pretending to be a little girl—while you beat my ass."

"Ansel..."

"Let me finish. It's not like I don't fantasize about it constantly. It's not like I don't want it. Hell, I want it again. I want it now. Why the fuck did you stop? Spank me more, but this time call me a naughty little slut, a sick pervert whose gonna get it because she's been bad and hit me harder when you say it."

"Ansel..."

"Stop saying my name."

"Hey..."

"Don't talk me down, David. I don't want another boyfriend who patronizes me when I get crazy. 'Look at cute little Ansel. She gets this way sometimes.' Not this time, David. Spank me and get it over with."

"Do you really-"

"God! I'm out of here."

She got out of bed and pulled up her panties.

"Hey. Wait. It's just..."

"It's just what, David? It's just that you don't want to feel guilty for this thing you did? Well, it's okay. I forgive you, okay? Now let me go. This was all a big mistake. I thought it would make everything better, but it doesn't."

I did think she was being shitty, but I was afraid to say so.

"You are naughty, aren't you?"

I regretted joking about it as soon as I said it. I really was mad at her. What was she so pissed off about? Where was her attitude coming from?

"No, David," she answered, "I'm just bad, and if you're going to call me on it, you'll have to do better than that."

I knew this was her way of asking for it—more than asking for it, demanding it, but I was still scared. I had seen her turn the corner and now all that was left to do was follow her.

"Come here, Ansel."

"No."

"Don't make me come over there and get you."

"Or else?"

"Or else you'll get ten more with my belt."

I made that up on the spot. I didn't know what else to threaten her with. I wasn't even sure if this was a game or not. Were we playing roles as a way to take it deeper or were we really fighting? How big a difference was there?

"I don't want any more spankings, David. This is stupid. You're as bad as I am."

I didn't believe her.

"Come here."

I unbuckled my belt and slid it through the belt loops. The sound made Ansel pause and look at me. The look on her face changed, softening from anger nearly to tears.

"You can't do it too hard. I'm sore from before."

"I'll do it as hard as I want."

"Please be gentle, David. I really am sore."

Talking like this terrified me more than the spanking had. Would she really have left? Was I doing the right thing? Was she running the show or was I? From the way she walked back towards me and lay over my lap for the second time in a half an hour, I guessed I had done okay.

I lifted her skirt and pulled down her panties like I had done it a million times before, like this was woven in the fabric of our relationship, not some risky experiment. I think the pretend normalcy of it turned us both on.

Her ass was red and blotchy, beginning to bruise in some places and still warm to the touch. I remembered what she had said about talking to her this time.

"Didn't get enough the first time, Ansel? Now I know what you mean. Something is wrong with you, you naughty slut. It has to be dirty for you, doesn't it? I was ready to hold you, cuddle with you, be with you after going someplace special together. But no, you couldn't have sweet and tender. You needed to get bitchy and fuck with me and threaten to leave just so I'd treat you like you wanted to be treated."

"Stop it, David."

"You told me what to call you, Ansel. Dirty slut. Sick pervert. You want to hear it. It's not like all your fantasies if I don't call you those things, is it?"

"Please, David. Stop."

I had started whipping her with my belt, but that wasn't what she was talking about.

"So, you can say whatever you want, but I can't? You can talk about how fucked up you are, but I can't? Well, you are fucked up. We both are. You're not the only one who wants it harder and dirtier. You're the naughty schoolgirl wannabe and I'm the bastard beating you with a belt. Fuck you, Ansel. Fuck you for making me beat you."

I was doing it hard, really hard. It must have hurt like hell, but she was just lying there, clasping her hands together to keep them from reaching back and protecting her backside. I didn't know how she could stand it. Her obvious agony might have made me feel sorry for her, but instead it made me wonder how much she could take. I did it harder. I aimed the belt so that rather than wrapping around her ass, it wrapped around one of her legs and whipped in between her thighs, grazing her pussy and making her gasp and squeeze her legs together in pain.

When she put her hand back and twisted her head up to look at me, eyes pleading with me to stop, I knew I had pushed her to the edge of her endurance, yet I also knew I couldn't stop just because she wanted me to. I would give her more. She would take more than she thought she could and afterwards that would make her proud.

"Ten more," I said, and I gave them to her as hard as I could.

Then I held her and we cuddled and it was tender. It was like it should be. We were spent by the intensity of it and were still in each other's arms as we came down from it. After a while, she reached back and began stroking her own ass, running her fingers over the ridges that bordered the welts. She reached between her legs and stroked her labia where the belt had grazed it.

"That one hurt the worst," she said. "You did it on purpose, too. You aimed for it."

I hadn't been horny until that moment, but something about those words—the aggrieved complaint, the flirty pout, the dirty detail—sent me into orbit. All the calm reflection disappeared in an instant and was replaced by urgent need. In her words, my sadism and her masochism met in a perfect kiss. I undid my jeans as quickly as I could, yanking my boxers down around my thighs as I knelt behind her and lifted her hips so I could fuck her.

I knew she would be wet—the spanking had caused a total flood—so I could fuck her without hesitation. I fucked her like I spanked her. I fucked her like the man who had hit her pussy with a belt on purpose, who had aimed for it. I fucked her selfishly, not reaching around to rub her clit, not stroking her back gently, but rather slapping her already sore ass and spitting on her asshole and prying it open with my thumb. Finally, I pulled hard on her hip bones and came deep inside her, slamming my thighs against her bruised bottom and then, in the post-orgasm come-down, wondered what the hell it all meant.

I had done it on purpose. I had aimed for it. I had fucked her without trying to make her come or asking her what she wanted. Was it really possible for it to mean nothing?

I came down afterwards as quick as I had risen up in the first place. I worried that it had gone too fast. We were a couple of steps beyond where we had talked about. We were curled up together now, both naked, as if it were your average post-coital cuddle.

"You okay, baby?" I knew I kept asking the same question, but it felt like the right one.

"I don't know."

Not a good answer.

"What's up?" I didn't want to sound too casual, but nor did I want to create drama where there wasn't any.

"Next time, can you fuck me quicker?"

"You didn't want it?"

"I want to please you, but the spanking kind of scared me. Then you fucked me like you were still the man who was beating me and I worried that you had changed. It's like now that you know about me, you'll treat me like a slut or something."

"I'm sorry, baby."

"That's okay. I know you didn't mean it that way. I've just never shown a man this part of me. What if you don't like me? Or what if you can only spank me and fuck me roughly?"

"What if you see me as some sadistic misogynist who can't see women as anything but an ass to spank or a pussy to fuck? What if you think I'm some Victorian headmaster wannabe pervert?

"Does that mean you don't want to see my girls' school uniform?"

I guess it was her turn to try to lighten the mood with a joke. I could have fucked her again right then and there.

"You have a girls' school uniform?"

"Yeah, bought it from a Catholic girl on e-bay."

"You're kidding."

"Of course I am. It's the real thing. I went to St. Mary's for a year when I was sixteen. Some crazy idea my parents had about getting me away from my friends. It's a size six and I can still fit in it."

"You were a Catholic school girl?"

"Don't look so happy. It sucked."

"You're cute when you pout."

"You're a bad man."

"You're a bad girl."

"What are you going to do about it?"

I slapped her ass and she squealed and we laughed and hugged and rolled around and kissed. It wasn't like before. I was hot for her and turned on by her red ass, but I felt overwhelmed by warmth and affection. Before, we were getting off on what we were doing. We were hot and bothered at the party because of what we were going to do, not because of who we were with. Now we were just happy to be with each other, happier even then before because of what we had done.

I loved her but it was too soon to say it, so I just stroked her tenderly until I felt her body jerk as she fell into sleep.

* * *

I woke up first the next morning, pleased to come into consciousness holding Ansel's warm body and then a little uneasy to remember the night before. What would it be like in the light of day? As a fantasy, it was spectacular—jack-off material for years to come—but we were beginning a relationship and I just wasn't sure what it meant to do it with someone I was falling in love with. She began to stir a few minutes after I did and we hid behind our grogginess until we had made coffee and contemplated breakfast. She was sitting on the couch in her robe, feet tucked up underneath her, paging through the newspaper without reading it. Was she thinking about it, too?

She caught me looking at her.

"Don't ask me if I'm okay."

"What *can* I ask you?"

"Tell me how *you* are."

"That depends on how you are," I said.

"It shouldn't."

"I shouldn't care about you?"

"No. It's not that. But you should have your own feelings, too."

"If you're okay with it, then it was great. If you're not okay with it, then I'm ashamed of it and wish it had never happened."

"It must suck for me to have that sort of power over you, David."

"I guess."

"What if *I'm* not sure?"

"Not sure about what?"

"Not sure whether last night was a good thing or not; not sure what it means to have bruises you gave me all over my ass; not sure if two people who do this can fall in love."

"I'm not sure, either. But here's the thing: it's just us—you and me—sitting here, and whether it was good or bad is up to us."

"No, David. It's not that simple. This morning it's you and me and this giant thing that we did last night. If you don't remember, then maybe you should take a look at my ass. I don't know whether it's sexy or scary."

"Can't it be both?"

"Yeah, I guess it is."

"Talking about it pulls me in two directions. Part of me wants to see your ass, wants to get off on what we did, wants to fuck you all day long. The other part of me wants to talk for hours, to be kind and hope to put your soul at ease."

"Can't you do both?"

"Yeah, I guess I can."

"I think if we start out talking, we'll end up fucking."

"We're already talking."

"So what are you waiting for?"

Would we ever be able to talk about it without getting horny? Not that I was complaining, but it was like even the serious part of it always got hijacked by the sexiness of it. Talking about it was a bit like two addicts talking about their high—all it did was make them want another.

It's like we had eroticized some of our deepest feelings—feelings of anger, guilt, shame, vulnerability, pain—and now when we went to talk about those feelings with each other, the words were overtaken by the urge for action. Somehow doing them was less scary than actually talking about them. At the fork in the road between sexy and scary, we chose sexy, but the scary wouldn't be quiet for long.

We had been making out, naked, in bed for maybe twenty minutes. I had gone down on her and made her come. I was kissing her, my mouth wet from her pussy. She licked her arousal off my lips.

"What were you thinking about when you were licking me?"

"What?"

"What were you thinking about?"

"Last night."

"More specific."

"Spanking you."

"You want to know what I was thinking?"

"Yeah."

"The same thing."

"More specific."

"I was thinking about being spanked. It made me come."

I began kissing her again and was ready to fuck her, but she wasn't done.

"What if I want it again?"

"To be spanked?"

"Yeah."

"I don't know."

I really didn't know. I couldn't imagine spanking her ass—it was really bruised and it was pretty hard to look at it and own up to having done that to someone I loved. But at the same time, I wanted it, too. Like her, the more I thought about it, the more urgent it became.

"I mean, it's like when I start thinking about it, I can't stop. I just want it so badly. But I think I must be crazy for wanting it again after last night. I don't know what to do, David. Will it ever be enough?"

"I don't know, sweetheart. I really don't know."

"Do you want to spank me?"

"Yes and no."

"Tell me how you would do it."

"I would do it hard. I would make you bend over this time, so that your bare ass was in the air."

"No, David. I couldn't stand being that exposed."

"You'll do as I say, Ansel. You'll bend over and grab your ankles. If you don't, I'll slap you hard five times on each cheek so that you remember to obey."

"Okay, David. I'll do it. Just don't give me any extra. It's bad enough already."

"I'm going to use my belt again, Ansel. It will sting your skin without doing more damage. But it will be hard, Ansel, harder than last night."

"Please, David. Last night was too much."

"If last night was too much, then you wouldn't need it again today."

"But I don't need it. I take it back, David. Please don't spank me. It really will hurt too much. It's not some erotic game anymore. I'm really scared. What if I start to bleed or something?"

We were just lying next to each other, whispering our words into each others ears, but the tears in her eyes were real. We had slipped into these roles. I was some stern disciplinarian who was to give her a punishment that would dissuade her from wanting future punishment and she was the poor girl, torn between her urges and the pain that they caused her. She was crying from the words in a way she hadn't cried from the spankings. I reached back and squeezed her ass, digging my fingernails into her bruised flesh.

"You naughty slut," I said as she moaned in pain, "You just can't get enough. Does this remind you how much it would hurt?"

"Yes, David. That's enough. I don't really want it. My thoughts got ahead of me. I just want to be with you. I just want you to fuck me."

"If I don't spank you, will you still be this hot?"

Silence.

"Will you?"

"No."

"That's a good girl for telling the truth. Now stand up and bend over. Let's get this over with."

* * *

That's how it all started. That last time I only gave her five. Tears streamed down her face the whole time, but it wasn't because of the spanking, which was pretty gentle. We held each other afterwards and didn't stop making love until the moment she had to leave on Sunday. We had turned a corner that weekend, but what it meant was far from clear.

II.

On the phone that week, we began each conversation as if nothing was new and then finally wound our way back to "what we did." At first, we couldn't even refer to it by name. Sometimes, though, after talking about it long enough, we would sink hypnotically into the memories and fantasies and I would begin to tell her about what I did to her and what I would do to her and I heard her breath as she touched herself and her voice crack with the occasional tear.

In between talk of spanking, we shared our lives, our dreams, our histories and ourselves. We developed our own private language of inside jokes and veiled references. We dreamt about trips we would take, houses we would live in, languages we would learn to speak and children we would have. Yes, we moved fast. We were in love and in no mood to hide it. But among all the topics of conversation, we always ended up talking about spanking. It was then that our voices went soft and we curled up on beds hundreds of miles apart. Spanking, not love, was the deepest intimacy we shared—a fortunate coincidence since we fell for each other before we knew that we shared it.

"What would you have done if I hadn't been into it?" she asked one night.

"I would have fallen in love with you."

"Really?"

"Really."

"Would you have ever spanked me?"

"I don't know."

"Would you have wanted to?"

"Yeah."

"But what if I didn't want to?"

"I still would have loved you."

"You would have gone your whole life without ever spanking anybody just to be with me?"

"Yeah."

"That's so sweet."

"What about you?"

"What *about* me?"

"What if I hadn't been into spanking?"

"I would have loved you anyway."

"But your poor bottom would never get spanked."

"I know. It would have been so sad."

"I'm glad I can make your bottom happy."

"Me, too."

This was how we talked—maddeningly, sweetly in love, with spanking as the icing on our relationship cake. It was easy to talk like this on the phone, too. We could take joy in our little fetish without having to do the act itself. Talking about it was sometimes easier than doing it, as we found out the following weekend.

III.

When she arrived that Friday, I was at a client dinner with some coworkers and buyers who had traveled to meet us. It was a friendly dinner and I told her she could join us when she got to town. She looked splendid when she arrived at the restaurant, the kind of girlfriend who would be a credit to any man. She had dressed up for the occasion, looking sexy and professional all at once—half advertising executive and half lounge singer. It seemed very glamorous to have a gorgeous girlfriend who flew in to see me for the weekend.

She was an instant hit. I introduced her and everyone was curious about her name. She joked about photographer parents and growing up with a man's name. She flirted with the men and whispered conspiratorially to the women; she undid her hair clip, letting her hair flow over her shoulders and shaking it out like she was in a shampoo ad. I couldn't believe she was mine, but she reminded me every time she squeezed my hand under the table.

Having breathed new life into the sagging evening, we ordered two more bottles of wine and speculated on a bigger deal than we had previously discussed. When the discussion turned to business, however, something funny happened. Ansel, with three more glasses of wine in her, began to demand the spotlight return to her. She touched the other men at the table and started demonstrating how she could tie a maraschino cherry stem in a knot with her tongue. I looked at her disapprovingly, and she turned away from me and pouted. When this failed to get her any attention, she began feeling my thigh and crotch under the table, massaging my cock and making it nearly impossible for me to think. I knew that this was every man's fantasy, but at that moment it didn't feel sexy at all.

I pushed her hand away but she put it back again, bringing her lips to my ear as if to tell me a secret and biting my earlobe instead. I knew she was drunk, and I even knew that she was doing this because she loved me, but the mood had turned sour and everyone took the first excuse to call it a night. On our walk out to the car, she began pulling at me and kissing me, grabbing my crotch again and delivering lines like "do me, now," in a breathy, porn-star voice. Who was this woman?

I began driving home silently, angry inside at what had happened and that some of our precious time together would be spent fighting. I was scared, too, that maybe Ansel wasn't as great as I remembered. What if the spanking thing had blinded me to who she really was? I didn't like her like this. It was ridiculous, but that felt like an illegitimate complaint when so much of what we did together would seem ridiculous to most everyone else.

Ansel acted like nothing was wrong and had my zipper halfway down before I pulled her head up and asked her what the hell was going on.

"I thought guys loved blow jobs."

"That's not what I mean."

"What do you mean?"

"What got into you back there?"

"I was wondering the same thing about you. You wouldn't even hold my hand. It's like you were some corporate big-shot jerk who wanted to show his friends that he's too cool for his girlfriend."

Things like this always left me speechless. I didn't even know what category to put it in: were these her insecurities talking? was she just drunk? was she making excuses for being obnoxious? or was she right?

I didn't know whether to offer apologies or explain my point of view or just tell her she was being ridiculous.

"What's wrong? Not so high-and-mighty now, Mr. Big-Shot?"

She undid her seatbelt and began climbing into the backseat.

"What the hell are you doing?"

"I'm going to sleep back here tonight. You're not sleeping with me tonight, Mr. Big-Shot."

By that time, we had pulled in my driveway and I opened the back door of the car. She curled herself into the opposite corner like a scared cat.

"Come on, Ansel. You're drunk. Let me put you to bed."

"No. I'm not drunk. Leave me alone. You can't boss me around, Mr. Big Shot."

When I finally got a hold of her and carried her into the house, the bottle of Xanax fell from her coat pocket and it all made more sense. The date on the prescription showed that she had just gotten it filled. She had told me about how she sometimes had panic attacks. This was probably the first time she had wine with the pills. I looked at her, still in her dress, asleep on my bed, and felt bad for her. Her words still stung, but I lay next to her and hoped that it wouldn't ruin our weekend.

* * *

Ansel awoke slowly the next morning. By the time she emerged from the bedroom, I had already read the paper, returned a few emails and was contemplating a work-out. She had taken off her dress and changed into pajamas. She looked adorably disheveled, with bleary eyes, smeared make-up and messed-up hair.

"What time is it?"

She was making a show of having just awakened and stumbling, half-conscious and not ready to face what she had done, into the kitchen. It was obviously a lie: she had taken the time to change out of her dress and into her pajamas before appearing. She was nervous, and so was I.

"It's 11:30."

"Oh. Do you have any aspirin?"

"Yeah."

"David?"

"Yeah?"

"I got these pills last week and I think…"

"I know. I found them. Do you remember what happened?"

"I wish I didn't, but I do. I'm so embarrassed. God, David. Please don't hate me. I'm so sorry."

I hadn't been sure how I would feel when I saw Ansel, but at that moment I loved her more than ever. I had been angry at her, even disgusted by her, but that hadn't been the Ansel that I knew. This was Ansel and I reached out to her and hugged her.

"Oh, baby. It's okay."

"No, it's not, David. It's not okay. I embarrassed myself; I made you look bad; and I might have ruined a business deal for you. It's not okay at all."

"It was a mistake, sweetheart. You're fighting the anxiety and it isn't always going to be easy. There are some things that are more important than a business deal."

"Do you mean it? Is it really that easy to let it go? I called you all those names and pretended nothing was wrong even when I knew I had fucked up."

"It's okay. It really is. I'm not angry."

And at that moment, it was the truth. Her small body was pressed up against mine and I wanted to protect her from everything bad in the world, even including herself. I couldn't muster any anger. She had already confessed to everything I would have accused her of and had already admitted to being in the wrong. It's like the fight was over before it could begin.

Good, I thought. We could get on with a nice weekend.

The ironic thing, though, was that it was easier for me to get over it than Ansel. She sulked through her cup of coffee and lay back down in bed afterwards. She said little and when she spoke, it was only to complain about her head or about how much work she had to do before she went back to work on Monday. She blamed her foul mood on her hangover, but she wouldn't even let me take care of her.

"Ansel?"

"Yeah?"

"What if it wasn't okay?"

"What do you mean?"

"When I said it was okay—about last night—what if it wasn't okay?"

"You mean you're mad?"

"Yeah, but it's because you're being so prickly today."

"Maybe I'm mad at you, too."

"You're acting like it. You were acting like it last night, too."

"I know. All that big shot stuff. I was making it up, David. I was making it up to get back at you."

"To get back at me for what?"

"For being so good. Last night I was mad because you weren't drunk like me; today I'm mad because you're acting like nothing happened. It's like you're too good to be mad."

"But why were you like that in the restaurant?"

"Because I was drunk and it felt like you were blowing me off. It felt like you were embarrassed by me, so I wanted to embarrass you."

"It's not okay, is it?"

"It doesn't feel okay."

"What would you like me to do?"

"Stop being nice to me."

"What?"

"You're either feeling sorry for me or you're still mad at me. I don't want your sympathy and I don't want your longsuffering patience."

"What do you want."

"What do you think?"

She didn't have to name it.

"Really?"

"No, not really. I'm not stupid. I know you'll do it hard and it will hurt like hell and I don't want it one bit. Plus, it's not fair that I get my ass beaten when I'm drunk and stupid and when you're drunk and stupid you won't get anything. But go ahead. I know it's what you're thinking about and we might as well get it over with."

She sure ratcheted things up fast.

"God damn it, Ansel. You're impossible. What am I supposed to do?"

"Stop asking me and just do something. I'm the fucked up drunk girl. Don't expect me to make your decisions for you."

"Go take a shower. When you get out, I'm going to spank you, but it's not for what you did last night. It's for shit like this."

"What the hell is that supposed to mean? I'm just being honest."

This wasn't going well. She was right. I didn't know why I was spanking her. Hell, I didn't even think I was spanking her until she told me that I was. I felt backed into making impossible decisions, decisions that stood to marry our first big fight with our newfound erotic life in a way that confused me.

"It can't mean nothing this time, Ansel."

"I know."

"What does it mean?"

"It means that when I'm bad, you're going to spank me."

"Is it really that simple?"

"We'll see, won't we?"

She was trying to sound smart, but she sounded scared. I wasn't sure I liked the idea of scaring her, but before I could say anything, she had turned on her heels and walked back into the bedroom. I heard her turn on the water for a shower and waited in the bedroom for her to be done. This wasn't like the previous weekend and we hadn't talked about this on the phone. On the phone, it had been fun and games, a painful but arousing form of foreplay; the previous weekend it had been a game where we could show our secret selves but also segregate those selves, keeping them in the bedroom and out of our day-to-day relating. Then it had been adjacent to sex, but fighting like this wasn't sexy at all. What sort of couple settles their fights the same way they get warmed up to fuck? I wondered if she was in the shower worrying about the same things.

* * *

More pressing still was the question of what to do when she emerged from the shower. Among the online spanking gurus whose wisdom I had at once scoffed at and been turned on by, there was a prevalent opinion that a couple could draw a clean line between punishment spankings and erotic ones. Erotic ones occurred when the mood struck both parties; they might involve an elaborate *mise-en-scene* that both parties got off on or role-plays or both. The anticipation of an erotic spanking is said to resemble the anticipation of lovemaking and may be prolonged for mutual enjoyment, much like what Ansel and I had done last weekend at the party that preceded her first spanking. During an erotic spanking, steps might be taken to minimize the spankee's distress, even as other steps are inevitably taken to heighten it. For example, the long and slow approach of an erotic spanking enhances the experience for all involved; for the punishment spanking, on the other hand, no concern is given to enhancing the experience except to the extent that an unpleasant and distressing experience may serve to dissuade the offending behavior in the future. In other words, a punishment spanking has only one concern: maximizing the spankee's distress for the duration of the punishment.

I had read that spankees typically hate punishment spankings, even if they are lifelong devotees of spanking in general. The idea that a beloved fetish could become something so hated confused me. Didn't spankings always hurt? Weren't they always to feel like punishment, even if they weren't? For some reason the twisted logic of it turned me on, but it didn't clear up what I should do.

I imagined how I might take Ansel unceremoniously across my lap when she emerged from the shower and begin with hard strokes on her bare ass, still warm and tender from the water. If I spanked her hard and without breaks, I was sure the experience would be brutally harsh for her. But was that what I wanted? Did what I want even matter?

The only clarity I could arrive at came from thinking about how bratty she had just been. She had been hurtful and mean-spirited, even as she had struggled to tell me some things that were difficult for her. She had pushed me away, which would ultimately hurt both of us. I was angry at her—the idea of spanking her freed me to be angry, freed me to feel the honest pain that her words and actions had caused me.

Where my feelings were muddied, I could spank her with clarity. I could express myself unequivocally, and my judgment of her transgression would stand, uncontested while she lay across my lap. It would take us to a different place, and anyplace was better than where we were now.

Ansel's words still rang in my head when I heard her turn off the water. "It means that when I'm bad, you're going to spank me." Did she feel like she had been bad? Was that why me saying it was okay didn't soothe her? Maybe it wouldn't feel okay to her until we had done this.

Whatever had occupied her during the shower, she emerged from the bathroom, naked and contrite. She hung her head, looking down as she walked over to me and awaited my instructions. I sat on the bed like I had last weekend and helped her over my lap. I looked down at her ass, the pale skin a bit rosy from the hot shower, and remembered the humiliation I felt when she had made a spectacle of herself with my colleagues. I raised my arm and brought my hand down with a resounding smack on her right cheek. The week before, I would have stopped to gauge her reaction, but I gave her another on her left cheek and then ten more on each cheek, nearly as hard as I could, before I even gave a thought to stopping. She bore it stoically, silently. She was at a remove, driven far away by the formidable pain and the emotional enormity of what we were doing. I knew I should have said something. I should have complimented her physical anguish with emotional reminders of her shameful behavior and the way shameful behavior begat shameful consequences, like lying on my lap getting a spanking.

Yet I just continued to spank her wordlessly, doing my best to insure that this woman I loved endured a lengthy and painful punishment. Words, even thoughts, if allowed to go freely, threatened to reveal the whole endeavor as silly, ridiculous, absurd or disgusting. Words like shameful and bad and spanking and punishment felt like role-playing words, words said in imitation of something we weren't. They were the words that gripped us in the throes of our fantasies, the naughty words that got us off, alone and with each other. This wasn't a fantasy, though. Or, rather, it was, but it couldn't be. For it to really be part of my anger and her absolution, we had to pretend we didn't fantasize about this. This lie was made easier by the fact that doing it didn't feel anything like the fantasy.

All the while, I was bringing my palm down on her bottom, feeling the ripple of her flesh as it received each blow and hearing the crack of skin on skin. It was like clapping but sharper, for hitting her soft, tender skin was very different from hitting one's own hand. If I had gone on for a while without pause or if the spanks came too closely together, I saw her hands begin to move involuntarily backwards to stop the onslaught, only to be willed back in place by her own better judgment. At these moments, her eyes squeezed shut and her fists balled up. I could see what a big thing this was for her. When she grimaced, I felt no pleasure in her pain. I simply felt obliged to give her an intense experience, far more than she would ask for but no more than she had imagined herself getting in a million tearful fantasies.

"Ten more," I said, and used my mercy to excuse letting myself do it as hard as I could. This was what made her bring her arms back all the way for the first time. She only had four left when she stopped me, but it took me a several more seconds to grab her wrists and pull her back into position. It was no way to end, and the four I had left were too few to make my point.

"Ten more, then."

She made no pretense of self-control then and struggled against my grip. But I could easily hold her still while I delivered my vigorous finale. She even kicked a bit. It hardly made a difference, but it inspired in me two opposite feelings—first, I found it cute, the struggle of a little girl whose small butt flexed when she kicked, causing it to feel that much more adorable when my palm cupped over its curves; second, however, was the feeling that this lovely young woman had been reduced to desperately kicking at me just to save herself the final moments of agony. I felt guilty about this, even though the struggle and the submission had always been integral parts of every fantasy.

When I finished, I loosened my grip on her wrists but I didn't let go, even when she tried to jerk her hands loose. It gradually became a gesture of comfort, of containing her distress. It was as if I was there to help her through her ordeal rather than causing it in the first place. I began tenderly stroking her ass with the hand that had just been spanking it. Then, too, my mind, which had previously been set on punishing her, became equally determined to comfort her. It was as if I had turned a hundred and eighty degrees, from one role to another. I helped her off my lap and onto the bed, where I cuddled up next to her, held her hand and stroked her hair.

"Aren't I supposed to feel better now?" she asked. "Isn't this supposed to make it better?"

"I don't know, Ansel. I'm sorry, but I don't know."

"But you did it. You must have wanted it to make things better, right?"

I didn't know what to say. Making things better wasn't what I associated with punishment, but neither was this.

"I'm scared, David."

"What are you scared of?"

"Will this work?"

"I don't know."

"I'm not even sure which would be worse—it working or it not working."

"What do you mean?"

"Well, if it doesn't work, then you just spanked me really hard for nothing, and if it works, then every time we have a fight, you're going to spank me."

"Neither sounds very good."

"I worry that every time we fight, you'll just say you're going to spank me and get your way. I always thought that submissives who did what others wanted lose part of themselves. I don't want this to take anything away from us."

"But doesn't it give something back to us, too? It's something we've always had to keep buried inside. Now we get to do it together."

"Come on, David. It's still a shameful secret. It's not like we're going to run off and tell all our friends about what we just did. We'd die if anyone found out."

"But with each other. Maybe it will take some time to get it right and to figure out what we like, but isn't it a relief to be trying?"

"It's not a relief when it hurts like hell and leaves you with bruises the whole next week."

"Damn it, Ansel, you've been fantasizing about a good, long punishment across a man's lap your whole life, and you check those bruises in the mirror every night, making yourself so horny that you can't go to sleep without masturbating."

"So? Can't I hate it, too? Didn't you want me to hate it when you did the last ten over just so it would hurt more?"

"You earned those last ten by putting your hands back. You don't get to stop the spanking whenever you want."

"You think I did that on some kind of whim? It hurt too, too much, David. I couldn't take it."

"No, you thought you couldn't take it. When I was holding your wrists, you took it just fine."

"Nothing was just fine about that spanking."

"Well nothing was just fine about how you acted last night, so I guess we're even."

There was a pause as we realized what we were doing.

"I thought the spanking was supposed to end the fight, not make it worse."

"I thought so, too."

The thought that we were farther apart rather than closer depressed us.

"Do it again."

"What?"

"You heard me. But talk to me this time. I feel so lonely when you're silent."

"Okay, baby. I'll talk you all the way through it."

The next five minutes were as you might imagine them: another spanking, harder, more painful, with words and tears. But this time we curled up afterwards and were able to come out of it together, emerging on the other side of our fight and freed from our bad feelings.

With that, we learned something essential: it always took two spankings for us to feel better. The first forced it all out to the surface—all the tensions, anxieties, grudges, guilt and bad feelings. The second one put us back on the right track—our weird little track, unlike anyone else's. This was our cycle. Ansel always knew she was in for two spankings and always knew she would be glad for it afterwards. That didn't make it hurt any less, but it made it easier for both of us.

We kept wondering what it meant and how it would affect our love, but we just kept doing it and kept loving each other. Slowly, we stopped worrying so much and became more comfortable with who we were and what we wanted to do. It's not like we hadn't lived most of our adult lives with a spanking fetish. For all that time, we had managed to hold down jobs, have relationships, be decent citizens, and love puppies and kittens. The only difference was that we were doing it together.

Our relationship wasn't perfect—whose is?—and spanking didn't solve all our problems (not even close), but the bond it created between us didn't hurt (or, as Ansel was always quick to point out, it didn't hurt me). We never did come to any real conclusions about what it meant. Sometimes it felt like a shameful secret; sometimes it felt like red-hot erotic play; but most of the time it just felt like it came from those murky regions deep inside where our bodies and minds find themselves inexplicably drawn to the strangest things.

Did it indicate some emotional darkness inside us? Did it reveal us to be haunted by past wounds or damned by our imperfections? Well, yes, but who doesn't have an emotional dark side, past wounds and imperfections? The pressure we felt to be normal and the shame we felt about our secret were endlessly more hurtful than the secret itself. As time went on, we were able to accept ourselves the way we were and this has always been the greatest strength of our love. Even now, years later, whenever we immerse ourselves in our fetish world, playing the roles we love and doing the things that set us off, we are thrilled to have each other.

Necessary To Her Good

by
Marilyn Jaye Lewis

At first it was not sexual. Not overtly. I was too young. It was more my erotic imagination at play, my fingers furtively between my legs. I was touching my clitoris – although I had no word for that place yet. Did not know the word clitoris. I touched myself there without fully knowing I was doing it, feeling ashamed of myself because I'd been punished and yet delighting in my shame, reliving my punishment with my fingers between my legs until it seemed more than I could stand. The shame blossomed in me so exquisitely that I felt as if I needed more and more of it, until I was drowning in delicious shame. It shook my legs. That was an orgasm – though I had no word for it yet, either. The only word I knew really was 'spanking.' I'd been spanked. The secret damage was done, a lifetime's worth.

She somehow learns to drive a car. She graduates from school. She is an adult. She does adult things. Yet she never feels like an adult. She doesn't remember growing up because she didn't; she simply got older. She merely 'behaves' without recognizing her behavior. All she's after is the eroticism of it, of her behavior – the sexual payoff. The orgasm.

She craves her punishment. She wants it repeated. Her father is dead now, he died long ago. By anyone's definition the spanking had ended. But not for her. In her mind, it had never stopped.

Her humiliation has never stopped. It is why she is willing to do so many seemingly degrading things. Why she wants it up the ass. *I am always secretly begging for it 'up the ass.'* It's her punishment on a grander scale. She has fantasies of it, thrilling pictures in vivid colors: her rape. Her rape up the ass. She wears fancy clothes for her rape. She imagines the finery of her surroundings in detail. This way, when it is forced up her ass, she is even more unlovely in comparison to her surroundings or even to her clothes. Her degradation is somehow *enhanced,* made more degrading, by her lovely clothes.

NECESSARY TO HER GOOD

When she meets him she is without guile. Everything about her is straightforward. It is why her belly flutters so. She has met him unexpectedly on the street. She hasn't time to toss up that false image of herself, the one she comfortably hides behind.

He takes her by the arm. He is so cavalier now. *What happened to that private detective? Why is it no longer a concern?* "Come on," he persuades her. "Let me at least buy you a glass of wine."

The wine tastes unusually seductive. She is horny now. Horny for him. He will walk her home. He will want to come up. For old times' sake. To kiss her, he says. And she will betray herself, her lust. There is always that lust for him. Even while she tries to keep it buried.

In a wooden box, down deep under the earth with only a small hole to slip a straw through to the surface. That is how deep I have buried away my lust for him.

And almost without realizing it, she is out of her clothes in her gloomy apartment, bending over for him and clutching the edge of her bed, letting him slick her asshole with Vaseline because it's handiest, feeling his finger working it in, getting her ready. He fucks her up the ass while she grunts like the lusty animal she is.

The degradation is good. She orgasms from it. She kisses him on the mouth. Her passion is burning hot. *Am I thanking him for defiling me again?* He must hurry or 'she' will suspect; he must run home to have dinner with his wife. By now she is likely waiting, glancing at the mantel clock, food laid out on their expensive dining table.

After he is gone, she sits alone in her room, feeling little but she is an adult, betrayed by her lust. *I am floundering in shame and lust. I cannot resist either of these feelings.*

He's gained the upper hand again. What is she supposed to do, not walk down the street? Always be on her toes and expect that he will be around every corner?

***

She remembers wondering: *How long have I been holding my water?* It could have been yesterday, she recalls it so vividly. The pressure is tormenting her. She won't let go until he tells her, "Let go." She knows better.

Why won't he look at me? Has he forgotten about me, that I'm squatting here, my knees spread, exposing myself? I know he could not have forgotten about me. He's only ignoring me.

She looks down at where her bladder bulges beneath her tight-fitting tee shirt. It actually bulges, it is that full. She is naked except for the tee shirt. *I don't know how much longer I can hold it.*

At last he remembers she is alive. He comes over to her. He is still fully dressed, immaculately dressed. He squats down in front of her. But he doesn't say, "Let go." He inserts two fingers up her slick hole instead and kisses her full on the mouth. His fingers feel roughly around inside her and she is delirious from the exquisite pressure, her bladder is so full.

"How do you want it?" he asks quietly.

She wants to say *over your knee*. She always wants to be over his knee. She feels safest there. Instead, she says, "However *you* want it. That's how I want it."

He commands her onto all fours, like she is a bad puppy. He swats her bare bottom hard with his open hand. Then harder still. She endures the smarting blows and won't let go until he says, "Let go."

When he tires of swatting her, the torture continues. He commands her back to the squatting position, her knees spread wide. In this position, it is hardest to hold it. He walks away and ignores her again.

She silently counts the tiles on the floor, keeping her mind occupied, her thoughts off her bladder. She can hear him in the kitchen. He is preparing dinner. When he re-emerges, it is to set the table.

He is opening a bottle of red wine. "Are you ready to be honest with me?" he calls out to her.

She looks up at him. He is standing next to the table. Isn't she always honest with him? "Yes," she says.

He sets the bottle down. He comes over to her. He squats down in front of her and looks her in the eye. She exists once more. "How do you want it?" he asks again.

She wants to say *however you want it* until she realizes that this is not true. He is waiting on her reply, for her to be honest with him. *I love you*, she wants to say. "Over your knee," she says.

He smiles. He helps her to stand.

This is her favorite thing and she so rarely gets to experience it, to be over his knee, to be spanked – just like a little girl. Only now she will have to endure it while tormented by her near – bursting bladder.

He leads her over to the table that is set for their dinner. He pulls out a chair and sits down. Then she is over his knee, her bare bottom square in his lap. In this position, the pressure on her bladder is extreme and he is wearing expensive, tailor-made trousers. She will have to be vigilant.

She waits in his lap, eager to feel the force of his hand, to delight in her punishment now that she's in her favorite position. But he doesn't strike her. He doesn't touch her. Of all cruel things, he says instead, "Let go."

No, she thinks frantically. *I won't do this. This is too humiliating.* She doesn't think it's fair that she should have to feel vulnerable like this, in this un-erotic way.

"I don't want to tell you twice," he says. "You know better."

She does know better. She won't be told twice. She let's go, she soaks his expensive trousers. The release is not a relief so much as an utter humiliation. Her ass, untouched now, feels exposed and unappreciated. She wants to shrink from his gaze. She knows he is watching her, looking at her "relieving" herself in his lap, ruining an expensive item of his clothing. It would take her a lifetime of scrupulous saving to buy such handsome, tailor-made clothes and here she is, pissing on him.

He has achieved his goal for the evening. She has done everything he's asked, to the letter, and all she feels is ashamed of herself. *Touché, my love.*

* * *

That's how he always was, honing in on what would humiliate me most and then forcing me to endure it because he knew I would. I wonder if he's changed? She's foolish to think he might ever change. What would be the incentive for him to change? He claimed that he was "never this way with his wife," that he saved this behavior especially for her because he knew she craved it – the humiliation, the surrender, being punished.

These are things she remembers: The phone ringing in the late afternoon. She is tempted to not answer it but at the last moment, she does.

"I'm downstairs, on the corner. Let me come up."

He sounds rattled – not normal for him. He is always cool and collected.

In her apartment he kisses her with a great measure of passion. He does not take off his coat. He holds her in his arms and kisses her. He clutches handfuls of her hair as he kisses her. He might devour her; he is kissing her so ravenously.

His wife has hired a private detective, he says. He will not be visiting again.

Their good-bye, their parting is so brief, so fleeting as to seem fragile, delicate, unbearable. In a heartbeat, he's gone. There is emptiness to take his place, but an emptiness that brims with shadows, ghosts, the overwhelming specter of Eros. An emptiness that mocks how *un-penetrated* she remains for months. She masturbates. It is incessant – that urge. She masturbates and she remembers and it is never good enough.

Finally, she doesn't even touch herself and the days go on.

* * *

This is how we first met: through a mutual friend. We were having espressos and Italian pastries in a small coffee house in the East Village. It was late in the evening. I remember it was fall. There were several of us gathered around the small bistro table. The conversations were lively and inane, but good-natured. We were all having a pleasant, easygoing time.

At one point, he got up from his seat across the table from me, pulled up a chair right next to mine and sat down. "I'm Armand," he said. "I don't think I caught your name?"

"I'm Elisa."

"Elisa," he said. "How beautiful. And not just your name," he clarified quietly. "*You're* beautiful." He said this like a confession, like a personal plea for my ear, my undivided attention.

"Thank you," I said.

He asked for my phone number. I saw the gold ring. I knew he was married, still he asked for my number. "We could meet for a drink?"

he asked. He was handsome but I was reluctant to say yes.

When our little crowd was dispersing, saying our goodnights, he said, "Elisa, let me walk you home. It's late."

It was late and it was also a clear, inviting night. A night that would have only been enhanced by an agreeable companion, a handsome man to walk with for those few blocks to my apartment. "Okay," I said. "Sure, Armand. Let's walk."

As we walked, he held my arm. We made the usual small talk. He was charming and he had an engaging smile, perfect white teeth set off by his olive-toned skin, his black hair and dark eyes.

When we reached my building, he asked again for my phone number. I sighed. "Armand," I said. "I know you're married, okay? I see the ring. Why would you want my number?"

"Oh, I can think of a few reasons," he replied, coming up close.

I didn't move away. His looks were appealing to me, married or unmarried. "And what might those reasons be?"

"There's the ever-popular 'we could meet for a drink,' as I tried half-heartedly before."

"Or?"

"Or, if you're looking to make a considerable chunk of tax-free cash, I know of something you'd be perfect for."

I was quietly astounded. "Excuse me? Is this an illicit job offer?"

"It could be. Do you do scenes?"

I had no idea what he meant. "Scenes? What kind of scenes?"

"Rape scenes," he said. "Play-rape. A small group of us pitch in a good chunk of change and hire a girl to come out to the beach with us for a night and we rape her," he said. "No safe words, but nothing too brutal. It's just for play. And then we drive her back to the city before the sun comes up."

"Are you out of your mind?"

He looked amused. "No, I'm not out of my mind. I take it you don't need the extra cash?" I couldn't tell now if he was serious or not. "We pay extra," he added cagily, "if she's agreeable about taking it up the ass."

How disgusting. "It doesn't seem like 'being agreeable' and 'rape' belong in the same sentence."

He laughed. "Elisa, I am only teasing you. I swear."

I wasn't sure I believed him. Now he seemed almost dangerous.

"It makes meeting for a simple drink seem a lot less complicated, though, doesn't it?"

"I don't know about that."

Then without asking me if it would be okay, he kissed me. No tongues or anything, but it was right on the mouth. "Come on," he urged me. "Let me have your phone number."

I felt overwhelmed by Armand. I couldn't decide if I wanted him to have my number or not. He pulled out a scrap of paper and he was searching his coat pockets for a pen. When he found one, I made my fateful decision. I gave him my number and we said goodnight.

I went up to my apartment alone. Of course I couldn't stop thinking about Armand, he'd made a unique impression on me. I had the profound feeling that he'd been serious about the rape scene, that he'd only passed it off as a joke once he saw how I'd responded. I wondered who were these girls that were being paid to go out to the beach, to get so mercilessly used by men for an entire night? Were they procured as casually as Armand had tried to pick up me? And what had made Armand think that I would ever be amenable to a sick scene like that in the first place?

Later in my bed though, with the lights out, in the safety of the familiar darkness the idea re-surfaced in me vividly. I saw it all from a less selective point of view, from the perspective of my clit. I saw Armand and those faceless men and I *wanted* to be that girl. It suited my fantasies perfectly, didn't it? To be defiled? For a few unbridled minutes in my head, I was that girl. I took the money, went out to the beach and let the men have me savagely for an entire night. When I had my orgasm, I came quickly to my senses. I shoved that dark idea as far away from me as I could, refusing to claim it. I turned over in my bed and wondered if Armand would really call. I realized then that I hoped he would.

He did call, a few days later. And when he did, I got wet just hearing his voice on the telephone. We agreed to meet, even though he was married. When we hung up, I felt vaguely ashamed of myself.

* * *

Armand had a *pied à terre* near Sutton Place and that was where we'd usually meet for our illicit trysts. It was where we were when he forced the confession out of me at last; he was the first man to succeed at it. Frankly, he was the first man to even try. At that time, we'd been meeting secretly for only a couple weeks.

We were sharing a bottle of red wine in the afternoon, expensive wine, the kind of wine I could never have afforded on my own. He said, "I want to try a little experiment."

I wasn't sure I trusted that unusual tone in his voice. "What kind of experiment?"

"I want to tell you a story," he said. "A story about you. And I want you to sit quietly and listen. Will you do that?"

"All right." I had to admit, I was self-involved enough to be very intrigued.

"And when I'm done telling you the story, I want you to take off your panties and give them to me. No questions asked."

That seemed weird. "Okay," I said.

"You're sure?"

"I'm sure."

"Okay," he said, pouring us each a little more wine. He handed me my glass. "Once upon a time," he began, "there was a young woman named Elisa."

I sat next to him on the divan, sipping my wine, sliding into the comfort of his hypnotic voice. The living area in the *pied à terre* had one wall made entirely of glass with sliding glass doors set into it. Outside those doors were a rock garden with a high privacy wall, and a shallow pool with a modest fountain. A stone walkway bridged the pool and led to a magnificent modern bedroom with a connecting bath. That area, too, had one wall of glass. The living area and the bedroom looked across the pool at each other; there were no drapes of any kind. Up above the stone wall, I could see the tops of trees, their autumn leaves amber and crimson, and above the trees, I could see the tops of skyscrapers looming in the waning afternoon light.

"Our young woman, Elisa, has a secret," Armand went on. "It's a magical secret, in that it acts as a key to an inner kingdom that nobody knows exists."

I think I smiled pleasantly, I'm not sure. I only know I didn't feel alarmed. It seemed like a harmless story, maybe even a pointless one.

"It seems like it must be a powerful secret, doesn't it? Seeing that it's capable of unlocking a door to an entire kingdom that nobody knows about?"

It took me a moment to realize he wasn't being rhetorical, that he was waiting on my answer. "Yes," I said without thinking. "It must be very powerful."

"Do you want to know what Elisa's secret is?"

I sipped my wine. It tasted seductively complex on my tongue.

"Yes," I said, going for the bait. "I want to know what her secret is."

"Can you be trusted to keep it a secret? It's something Elisa is ashamed of – she wouldn't want it bandied about in the wrong sort of crowd."

I smiled. "I can keep a secret," I assured him. Although he seemed to be asking me, in a convoluted way, to keep my own secret a secret...

"Okay then," he began. "Here is her secret. Under cover of darkness, without anybody knowing, Elisa accepted the money and went down to the beach one night."

That brought me up short. The wine glass was at my lips but I didn't take a sip. My mind was riveted instead on Armand. He had my complete attention. His eyes seemed to be taking careful note of this new expression that I was certain was on my face.

"That isn't even the worst part of her secret," he continued. He took my wine glass away from me and set it on the coffee table. He scooted closer to me on the divan, his eyes never leaving my face. "The worst part is that she even took the extra money, ensuring that she would be very agreeable, even with her ass. That's a pretty disgraceful secret Elisa has, isn't it?"

Yes, I thought, although I couldn't say it.

"Shall I go on? You want to hear the whole sordid truth about Elisa?"

This time I nodded my head, yes.

"I picked her up in my car and drove her out to the beach house where the other men were waiting. Now, Elisa is very shy. She's the kind of woman who's always vaguely ashamed of the thoughts that are in her head – have you ever known a woman like that?"

I didn't reply.

"Well, Elisa is that way, so when we were finally at the beach house, she was too shy to speak to anybody. We were reduced to having to read her mind. We had to figure out – without any input from her, mind you – just how rough she wanted to play. After all, we didn't want to send her out over the edge, did we? This was about satisfying a need. It was not about a trip to the psych ward at Bellevue. So we had our work cut out for us. For instance, we had to decide if Elisa was the type of player who preferred to take off her own clothes or have them stripped from her. I'm curious," he said. "What do you think her response would have been in that situation?"

I looked at him uneasily, reluctant to take part in his story, to add my two cents. But he repeated the question. "What do you think her response would have been? I'm just curious. It's just for the sake of argument."

I entered the fray of my psychological turmoil haltingly. "I suppose," I said. "Well, I think she would have…"

"Yes?"

"She would have chosen to be undressed by the men."

"To keep it real?"

"I suppose so. Yes, to keep it real."

"I see," he said, barely even blinking. "We misjudged her on that count. We had her undress herself. But we watched. We watched every move she made. And how do you think we had our way with her? What would be your guess?"

"I don't know what you mean."

"Sure you do."

"No," I insisted quietly. "I really don't."

"Well, for instance, once she was naked, did we toss her out in the middle of the floor?"

I could scarcely catch my breath now, he'd honed in on me with such precision. "I suppose so, yes."

"Did we go at her like a pack of wild dogs? Or did we each take our time defiling her?"

I didn't want to answer. He was asking too much of me. I wanted my wine glass safely back in my hand. I wanted something to distract me. I stole a quick glance out the giant glass window and noticed the sun had sunk down considerably in the late afternoon sky. And yet he waited. Was it for me to feel comfortable with my answer? I could feel his eyes studying my face. I finally found my nerve to reply. "They took their time with her," I said.

He said, "You know? That's what I guessed, too. That she would want her debasement to be methodical. That we needed to be thorough with a woman like Elisa. You know what else I decided? That it would be best if she were tied in some way. Now how do we tie a girl like you? What's the best way?"

Suddenly everything had shifted, he had gotten personal. I couldn't reply. Not only because my mouth was too dry but because I'd never been tied. I knew nothing about it.

"I'll tell you," he said, having mercy on me. "This is what I chose, this is what we did to Elisa. Tell me if you think the punishment fit the crime. When she was out there naked in the middle of the floor, we had her turn over. We tied her wrists, one to each of her ankles, and we propped her up on her knees, her head down and her lovely ass in the air. You get the picture, I'm sure. She was quite helpless in that position. Then we went at her, one at time, any hole we pleased since she'd agreed to it before hand – she'd already taken the money. We went at her all night, we really had our way with her. What do you think she did?"

"I don't know," I said almost inaudibly, swallowing hard, unnerved by his uncanny assessment of me and my secret fantasies. How could he know this? My wonder bordered on panic. I'd never breathed a word of it to anybody. How could he have unearthed a secret I'd kept buried so deep?

"Did she scream?" he asked. "Did she cry and try to take it all back, to get us to see reason? Did she beg us to untie her and let her go? Did she tell us we could have the money, anything, just as long we stopped violating her and gave her back her clothes? Or did she enjoy herself?"

"I don't know," I said again.

"Well, think, Elisa. Use your imagination, your best judgment. If you need to give it some serious consideration, that's okay. I have all the time in the world."

There was no beach house. There were no other men. There was only Armand and I, secluded in the *pied à terre* in the busy heart of Manhattan. Somehow I found my voice. "I suspect she did all those things. She cried, she screamed, she begged for mercy, to be untied…"

"And then what?"

In a near whisper, since I didn't even want to hear myself saying it, I finally confessed. "I suspect she came."

"Really?"

"Yes. When they ignored her pleas, when they kept going, I suspect she had an orgasm in spite of her misfortune."

He seemed impressed with my answer. "I suspect so, too," he said. "In fact, right there in front of all of us, she had an orgasm during her misfortune, as you put it. We knew, but we kept her little secret. End of story. Let me have your panties."

It was plain why he wanted them – as proof that I knew he had me pegged. My panties were soaking. As far as proof went, soaking panties were as good as having had a detectable orgasm. I reached under my skirt and peeled them down. I handed them to him.

"Well, in light of our little story, are you still going to spend the night?"

"Yes," I said.

"Interesting," he said, tossing the panties on to the coffee table.

* * *

Welcome to Elisa's secret inner kingdom, I thought. For once, I didn't feel ashamed of myself. Instead I felt mesmerized by the thoughts that were in my head – or, more, by how my thoughts had sounded coming out of Armand's mouth. I spent the night with Armand and, to my dismay it passed without incident. He didn't make love to me, although every cell, every square inch of me, craved his contact. I never felt comfortable making the first move with Armand, so there I lay beside him the entire night, unable to sleep while he lay next to me, sleeping soundly. I felt as if each of the tiny nerve endings throughout my body were exposed electrified wires, culminating in my aching clit. *Was that all there was to it*, I wondered? *He knew this secret about me and it wasn't meant to be more than that? Why didn't he want to make love to me? What was he waiting for?* I was trapped in a cycle of unanswered questions, wrapped in an invisible blanket of arousal and wet between my legs all night.

A week later, when Armand was back in the city on business and staying at the *pied à terre*, he called me on the telephone, inviting me to come over, to stay the night. For me, it had been a tortuous week. Thoughts that I'd normally kept locked away until I was alone in bed at night were now hovering at the surface of my mind, screaming out for my attention even in broad daylight. I was driven to distraction by the unsavory nature of my constant desires.

I arrived at the *pied à terre* early, without realizing Armand might not be alone. "Come in," he said. "I'm just finishing up some business."

I followed him into the living area and encountered three men, all wearing suits and ties, the expensive kind. Clearly they were successful businessmen, just like Armand. He introduced me simply as 'Elisa' and then told me to have a seat and wait.

I did as I was told, not listening to their conversation, wondering instead if the beach house had ever really existed and if it had, then who were these men? How well did they know Armand? I asked myself secretly, what if it were these men? What if they offered me money to be very agreeable for an entire night? What if they even tied me, ensuring that I couldn't change my mind?

Four – including Armand. I felt I could survive it. I wondered if I would ever be asked?

Within the hour, Armand and I were alone. "You look especially pretty today," he said. "What's on your little mind?"

My mind felt enormous, expansive, vibrant – anything but little. "Nothing," I said.

"Nothing?" He seemed disbelieving.

"Nothing unusual," I clarified, hoping that at the very least he would tell me another story about myself. A story my thoughts could feed on for another tortuous week in the event that, once again, we were not going to make love.

"So, Elisa," he started in.

"Yes?" I said. He was going into the kitchen and I followed him.

He perused the contents of the small refrigerator, seeming disinterested in what he found there – perhaps even disappointed. "We have a maid, you know," he informed me, closing the refrigerator door. "She gets the day off when you're coming over. But I always leave her specific instructions on what I want in this refrigerator before she takes the day off. You'd think it wouldn't be too much to ask of her to get it right, wouldn't you? It's not like we're even here everyday."

For the first time, I found myself resenting that he had a wife, that he considered himself part of a 'we' or that she in any way inhabited the little *pied à terre*. And now I hoped this maid I was hearing about was an overweight, middle-aged German woman of little humor and a thoroughly uninviting disposition. It was envy that I was feeling, and it was not just a trickle but more like a deluge.

"I guess we're going to be ordering in," he said. "Elisa, what should I do with a maid like her? Settle it the old-fashioned way and take her over my knee?"

"I'm sure I don't know," I replied, feeling a little surly. "I've never had a maid."

He smiled at me. "You've never had a maid – have you ever been a maid?"

"No."

"You're a little testy today, aren't you?"

"Not especially. I just don't know anything about spanking a maid."

"Do you think I do? Is that what's bothering you?"

I didn't answer. It was such a stupid question; I didn't think I needed to. He stared at me and I stared right back at him. He didn't speak. We stood in the small kitchen silently staring at each other, until I finally said, "You're not really expecting an answer, are you?"

"Actually, I am."

"Why would I care if you spank your maid?"

"Oh, I can think of at least one good reason why you'd care – the same reason why you'd care if you knew I spanked my wife."

That I definitely did not want to hear about. I was fuming. It was too late to act uninvolved in what he was saying but it didn't mean I had to keep speaking to him. I left the kitchen and went into the living area and plopped down on the divan.

He followed me into the room, then stood in front of me, musing, for all I knew. His hands were casually in his pants pockets while he considered me. "I take it you're ready for the rules to change," he said.

He seemed so calm compared to how I was feeling; my newly unleashed envy was galloping through me at a wicked speed. "And what does that mean?"

"How about another little experiment?"

I tried my best to act uninterested.

"I don't spank my maid, Elisa. And I don't spank my wife. You can calm down."

I managed to look in his direction. "And that's the experiment?" I didn't want to give him the satisfaction of knowing that I felt relieved.

"No, that's not the experiment."

"Well, I'm all ears."

He came closer. "You're in such an unattractive little mood right now, Elisa. How would you feel about getting punished? It might help you get over yourself."

My heart leaped at the sound of his words, but I couldn't say what I was thinking, I couldn't answer him.

"Come on," he said. "Let's go." He pulled me up from the divan. I followed him out through the sliding glass doors, across the little stone bridge over the shallow pool and into the bedroom. I felt extremely excited. No one had ever done this to me before. No one had so much as suggested it. I knew I had his undivided attention and I was quietly reveling in it, and in the thought of my impending punishment.

***

The days go on and she manages to subsist. It's only a pale reflection of life that goes on around her. Her mind is disengaged. Nothing suits her. Dating is out of the question. The notion of dating is absurd and ridiculous. What is dating? Dinner and a movie. When all she wants is Armand commanding her, defiling her, exposing her from the waist down and then ignoring her.

That was my first taste of his kind of punishment. I wanted the old-fashioned kind; I wanted to be spanked like the maid. Instead, I was told to remove my shoes, my stockings. I was told to lift my skirt and lower my panties. I did as he asked and it was exhilarating. He told me to kneel down in front of the bench at the foot of the bed, to bend over the bench and I did. He made sure my skirt was raised up high; he spread it out just so. His foot nudged my knees further apart. He adjusted my panties, lowering them a mere fraction of an inch more down my thighs. The touch of his hand going briefly between my legs was thrilling. In that exquisite position, I awaited my punishment – my idea of punishment. What I got instead was his.

He stops speaking to her. He changes out of his business suit into more casual clothes. His cell phone rings. "Hello?" he says. "Sure, sure. Not a problem. Come get it. I'm here."

She is speechless, appalled. Who is coming over? Whoever it is will surely see her through the giant windows, through all that glass.

On his way out of the bedroom, he makes eye contact with her. "You're not to move," he instructs her. "I mean it."

Now she is delirious with her desire to please him. She rests her head on the bench and takes comfort in her ridiculous pose. She gets wet, thinking of how exposed she is. She hopes that whomever it is who comes over, sees her without any difficulty, that he gets a good look and secretly sodomizes her in his imagination.

Who was it, she wonders now. *Who saw me like that?* She had her suspicions but she never learned for sure.

There was a brownstone on the Upper East Side, just off Central Park. She remembers the entryway, the foyer, the grand staircase that led them up to an imposing library on the third floor. After that, she saw nothing. Armand had blindfolded her, tying the blindfold tight, then he helped her down to her knees, helped her bend over the leather chesterfield. He sat next to her the entire time, speaking very quietly to the man who had joined them in the library. It was this man – the man whose hands went up under her skirt and tugged down her panties, the man who mounted her, whose thick cock filled her vagina then forced its way up her ass, causing her to cry out until Armand had to cover her mouth with his hand – it was this man who she suspected had seen her on display that afternoon in the *pied à terre*.

Armand and the other men – all of it is over, she knows this and she knows she has to accept it. She understands that Armand chose his wealthy wife over his common whore. But she also knows there will be no replacing him. Understanding the void is one thing. Filling it with anything else – it's an impossibility.

The secret is staying out of his way forever. Merely seeing his face again, let alone having a quick fuck…This business of running into him on the street – I won't survive it.

She turns over in her bed and faces the wall. Empty. Thoroughly empty, and ashamed of herself now for so many complex reasons. She no longer bothers to answer the telephone. When she hears it ring, she doesn't stir.

✱ ✱ ✱

That day when the rules changed, that was when my life changed. That was when I realized I'd never known what feeling fulfilled meant, or what it meant to feel happy. My mistake was believing that Armand was in love with me, but beyond that, I started my existence over that day, I began living in a newfound bliss. A new life that demanded strict obedience to boundaries. It required deprivation and surrendering at last to my punishment. Above all, it necessitated opening my body without fear, turning it over to Armand as an empty receptacle for him to fill with his fertile imagination. In my new life, with the new rules in place, I was happier than I'd ever been. I still believe that Armand was happy, too – uniquely content. And I want to believe he loved me, even if he didn't choose me in the end.

By the time he told me that the beach house was real, I already considered myself his canvas. My holes belonged to him, my mind was his domain. I trusted him to know what would make a woman like me feel fulfilled.

"You don't have to do anything you don't freely want to consent to," he explained to me one afternoon over lunch. "I'm not suggesting you go. I'm just letting you know you have the option. I know you. I know it's something you still think about."

He was right, as always. At first, I was only curious to know who the men would be.

"The only way you'd learn that would be to accept the money. If you're the kind of girl who wouldn't want to be paid, you won't ever know who they are. You'll be blindfolded. It's different when the girls aren't paid. It's a different arrangement, a different type of power exchange."

I wondered how many girls had there been to necessitate different arrangements? Still I kept the question to myself.

"And it's reasonably safe," he assured me, as if it were a mere afterthought. "Not that there are safe words, I just meant that everybody wears condoms."

It was at least another month before I got up my nerve to ask to be taken to the beach house, to rise to the surface of my fantasies rather than be submerged in their inscrutable allure for the rest of my life. I told Armand that I didn't want to be paid, but I made him swear not to leave me in the house alone with the other men, and I made him promise to be one of my ravishers.

It was not so harrowing an experience as I'd feared it might be. There were only two distinct points where I felt I might panic: when I was first blindfolded and someone was stripping me out of my clothes, removing my last vestige of false security, and then again late in the night, when a man untied me and moved me to a different room. I became disoriented then and it became immediately clear that several men would be enjoying me at once, overwhelming me with too much stimuli. The rest of it was an experience that suited me. It suited my temperament, my bottomless pit of sexual need and my unfathomable desire to be used as an instrument for sexual pleasure.

In the beginning, I was tied in the way Armand had suggested. By now, I was familiar with being tied in this position. Armand had already introduced me to it at the pied à terre. It was a position that profoundly excited me – my wrists tied to my ankles, my ass in the air – because it kept me at the mercy of my tormentor. It kept me from being able to change my mind. It presented me as strictly an object to be taken. The simple thought of how wide open my most vulnerable parts were – that alone kept me wet, kept me aroused, so much so that I enjoyed every man who took me in this position regardless of how they made use of the holes that were being offered; the men who were rough, as well as the men who took their thorough gratification in my ass. I enjoyed each gradation of my predicament. I enjoyed the sensation of being bound in utter darkness while being probed, penetrated, stretched open and filled, then mercilessly pounded while conversation went on all around me. I lost track of how many times the men took me. There were chunks of time where nobody used me at all and I drifted into a sort of sleep, my knees, my face, my shoulders impressed in the rough carpeting. Each time Armand went at me, I knew without doubt it was him. He had a habit of opening me first with his fingers, whichever hole he was selecting, feeling me up avidly before sliding his cock in and taking his fill.

In my ecstasy, I did not know which pleased me more, being taken by Armand in full view of strangers, or having strangers take their pleasure in me while being observed by Armand.

I preferred that part of the night to those final hours that came after I was untied and moved to another room. What I learned about myself was that as long as I was tied, I was in a type of erotic trance and all of the fucking appealed to me. When I was untied, I felt at odds with myself and at odds with what the men wanted from me, even Armand. When several of them held me flat on my back and spread me, pinning my arms and forcing my legs apart, displaying me obscenely while another one took full advantage and fucked me – even when I suspected the man fucking me was Armand, I had to fight against my urge to struggle, to get free of the assault. I wasn't entirely successful, either, as the intensity of what they took from me had heightened, a sort of 'final frenzy' that seemed to signify the end of the evening. It bordered on being brutal, although it was never pain I was feeling but extreme vulnerability and utter immodesty, complete emotional exposure.

When the dawn finally came, the men left and Armand removed my blindfold. I was allowed to shower and then he drove me back to my own apartment. He came upstairs and stayed for an hour with me, lying next to me on my bed.

"Tell me what it was like," he said. "Tell me every detail."

As I told him every detail of my exquisite captivity and debasement, he gradually undressed me, he removed my clothes. When I spoke of how it had felt to be tied as opposed to untied, how it had felt to be randomly penetrated and probed for hours, to be blind while filled by so many strange cocks, his mouth was between my legs and I held my thighs open for him. His tongue licked my clitoris with such deliberate attention, I could hardly keep track of what I was saying. When his fingers went in me, investigating the swollen depths of my still eager vagina, I bore down hard on them. I came with his mouth ardently sucking me and his fingers deep in my hole. Then I fell sound asleep. I didn't even remember Armand's leaving. I hadn't had time to thank him for his incredible gift, for showing me to myself, for leading me to the tempestuous waters of my imagination and then encouraging me to drink.

The very next evening he invited me to the *pied à terre*. Explaining, "Now that we've explored your capacity for boundless pleasure, we'll explore your capacity for deprivation."

To my surprise, the idea was equally arousing to me. I reveled in the severity of the deprivation he administered. It seemed to be in perfect balance to what I had yielded to the night before.

Armand took me into the small study – a room I hadn't stepped foot in until now. He told me to undress. As I did, he took each article of my clothing, folded it neatly and put it into a drawer. Even my shoes went into this drawer.

He opened the door to a small closet and told me to sit down with my back against the wall, my knees up and my thighs open. I did as I was told. He left the room briefly and I waited, without moving, for him to return.

When he came back, he tied my wrists to my ankles once again, only now I was in a sitting position and now a thigh spreader was fastened between my thighs, keeping my legs forcibly spread. For the first time ever, he gagged my mouth. Then slid two tiny earphones into my ears. They were plugged into a micro cassette recorder that seemed to be playing the audio track of a porn loop. It was the sound of a man and woman having unbridled sexual intercourse. Soon enough, I determined that it was a tape recording of Armand fucking somebody, somebody that I suspected was his wife. He didn't blindfold me. However, before leaving me alone in the dark closet, he attached a small, weighted clamp to my clitoris. The clamp had teeth that held snugly to my clit, keeping it securely in place without causing me too much outright pain. The tiny lead weight was there solely to torment my clit, to pull on it and create constant movement. The clamp ensured that I would only be incessantly teased and not reach an actual climax until the clamp was removed and the natural blood flow to my clit could resume.

Once I was trussed in that manner, Armand closed the closet door and left me there in the dark.

At first, the inescapable sound of Armand fucking his wife perturbed me. There were snippets of sex talk peppered throughout the recording that made them sound like comfortable lovers, at ease with their bodies and their sexual needs. There were moments when Armand called his wife dirty names – a cunt, a whore – which only increased the pleasure she was so obviously receiving. There were times when he instructed her to turn over, or to assume different positions that I could only guess at without the necessary visuals to accompany it. There were moments when his wife begged to be fucked harder but most of the time, she simply exuded lusty and – ultimately – very arousing sounds.

I was in a state of agonized desire. Even the smallest movement of my body sent the tiny led weight shivering, pulling on my swollen clit. I was aching to masturbate but could do nothing, really, except listen to the two exuberant lovers. I couldn't help but try to picture how they were pleasuring each other, the positions they were in as they fucked, how their naked bodies related to each other, what their mouths were doing. I was even forced to listen to their orgasms before the tape would loop over and start again, and all the while I was unable to escape the idea that this was the man I loved making love to his own wife. And it surprised me – just how badly my eyes wanted to see it, to see Armand fucking his wife.

I lost track of how many times the tape looped before he came back and opened the closet. When he did, my gag was soaking with my own spit and my vagina was so aroused that the slippery wetness had gradually oozed from me and collected in a tiny puddle on the floor.

The first thing Armand did was remove the earphones from my ears, then he took the clamp from my clit. The rush of blood to the tip of it was both delicious and painful. His fingertips rubbed it vigorously and I felt like coming on the spot, but before I could, his fingers were up inside me instead.

"God, you're wet," he said quietly. He had knelt beside me in the dark closet. As usual, he was still fully clothed next to my utter nakedness. "I feel like I could slide my whole hand up you without any effort at all."

I moaned deliriously into my gag, loving the exquisite sensation of his fingers moving inside me, my clit freed at last. I felt like I *could* take his whole hand at this very moment, but all he gave me were two fingers. I pushed down on his fingers. My hole opened wide to accept them.

"You must have loved that, huh? Eavesdropping on me during something so private?"

His fingers pushed relentlessly against my swollen G-spot.

"Listening to me fuck my wife, you loved that, didn't you? You've completely wet yourself."

I groaned some more. I was helpless, the fluids began to gush out of me, his fingers would not let up on my G-spot. I squirted all over his hand several times. The release was exhilarating. Still it embarrassed me, I made such a soaking mess on his closet floor. I wondered what he would tell the maid.

* * *

The specific punishment she so craved did not take place in the *pied à terre*. Instead, it took place in the familiar surroundings of her own apartment. They'd had a light supper out together. The summer evening was stifling. Her apartment was not air-conditioned and all her windows were open wide.

Without her knowing it, he watched her ass intently as she climbed the stairs to her apartment – remaining a few steps behind her. She had a full, round ass that always delighted his eyes, regardless of the position he would see it in.

"I love your ass," he told her as she was putting her key in the front door. "I really want to spank you, right now."

She was afraid to get too excited. So far, his spankings had been administered with a ruler, a hairbrush, the bottom of his Brooks Brothers bedroom slipper – never his hand. And she was never over his knee, either. She always bent over something else instead; a dresser, the table, the arm of a chair.

She didn't reply at all to his remark. She opened the door to her stifling apartment, they went in and she waited for his instructions.

He said nothing, though. He took her by the hand and led her to the one bedroom at the back of the flat. It had two large windows overlooking a small courtyard and another apartment building. Everywhere along the courtyard, windows were open wide onto the thick, unmoving humidity of the summer evening.

He sat down on the edge of her unmade bed. "Come here," he said. And suddenly she grew very excited. Finally. He indicated that he wanted her over his knee.

I am always craving to be over his knee. I feel like I have craved this my whole life.

And in fact, she has. She has craved this very spanking for her entire life. It is her first erotic spanking and she suddenly feels alien to herself – she's trembling, she's too excited.

When she's over his knee, he lifts her summer dress. The thin material of her pale, silky panties is clinging to her cheeks, making her ass look even fuller, more round. At first, he keeps the panties right where they are and he spanks her bottom with his open hand – no warm-up spanks, either. He just starts spanking her.

She is certain the sounds of the smacks are resounding in the quiet courtyard. She is reluctant to cry out, even though the spanking immediately stings, for fear of piquing any prurient interests of nosy neighbors. What she doesn't understand, though, is that he wants her cries to be heard by nosy neighbors. He wants her to be spanked in public, and for now, this is the next best thing. They are at cross-purposes: she is trying not to cry out, and he is trying harder to elicit her cries.

Quickly, the spanking becomes more brutal as they lock wills. He doesn't tell her, "I want you to cry," because then she would obey him and the thrill of the hunt would be snuffed out. Instead, he simply spanks her more severely. He tugs her panties down her thighs now, which arouses her secret inner world acutely. Each of her senses is heightened by this simple gesture of having her panties tugged down. She is soaking herself with arousal but her face is beginning to sweat from the agony of the pain.

It is now the flat of his hand against her bared ass. Rapidly, she succumbs to the irrational power of all-out lust. He is striking her very hard and she cries out now in a thick mixture of pain and desire – an unmistakable sound, she fears, but it's too late. The sound is out of her, drifting out the open windows and suffusing the still evening air out in the courtyard.

Now he wants to hear more of her cries, he wants the sound of her distress saturating his ears and not just filling the world of her room, or the world outside her room. Her hands inevitably have come behind her to shield her bottom from the severity of the blows. He clamps his arm tight around her waist, trapping her hands, and delivers more of the smarting blows to her already bright red cheeks. The sight of her reddened flesh, bouncing under each blow he delivers, stimulates his eyes and the sight shoots straight to his cock. His erection is rock hard underneath her. He knows she is a helpless prisoner to her lust now. He can tell by how she is squirming. He can tell by the pitch and fullness of her cries. He is making her suffer, he is the cause of her tears, of her pleas that are wrenching out of her so unattractively and yet so enticingly, and he is certain that if he were to feel between her legs this minute, if he were to shove his fingers up her hole, she would be hot and swollen and wet there, she would be writhing against the intrusive fingers in a heartbeat.

She is in her bed alone now. Armand and all of it is over. It is months and months later now. It is many spankings gone now, it is a lifetime ago. She faces the wall and she remembers. The first spanking. *It was right here in this very room, on the edge of this bed.* She looks now at the very spot where it occurred. She remembers her delirium. She remembers her embarrassment when, without warning, he tugged her panties all the way down and roughly shoved his fingers up her hole, discovering how wet she was. She remembers how her legs parted quickly for him. How badly she wanted just those fingers, she didn't even need to be fucked, didn't need his cock although he gave it to her moments later. It was those fingers her legs parted for, her smarting ass arching up, betraying the utter depths of her lust. And the sounds she made – those sounds that filled her room and rushed out into the night. She was certain that no neighbor could have missed them. That every window along the courtyard held a rapt listener as she half-cried, half-growled on his rough, intrusive fingers.

Then I was right there, bending over the bed and getting his cock. Grunting like crazy on that thorough cock, my ass stinging, my heart on fire...I'd been spanked. Finally.

She is going to masturbate again. She hates this about her life, how she masturbates instead of having fresh experiences.

And always the phone rings.

She finally answers it. "Hello?" she says.

"Please," he says. "Just come downstairs. We'll find some neutral territory. We have to talk."

"About what?" she practically spits. "Having a glass of wine? Fucking my ass and then taking off again?"

It's unthinkable and yet she's done it. She's slammed down the receiver on the man she wanted to hear from most.

* * *

My problem is that I don't want to go back to being the woman I was before Armand. It isn't just the punishment I still crave, it's the boundaries; the psychological, emotional, and physical boundaries that I enjoyed. I want those back. I thrived on being held accountable for my choices, for my actions, for my tiniest infractions of the agreed-upon rules. It meant I existed in the world, that I made an impression on it, that there was someone reacting to my behavior at all times, reflecting it back at me. With Armand there was incredible sex but there was so much more. There was an ecstasy that felt ethereal when I knew I had obeyed him to the letter, or equally, when I was subjugated to my humiliation because I knew I deserved it. My punishment was necessary to my good, but I also understood my good for the first time in my pathetic life.

No other man but Armand has understood me in this way. He understood me long before I understood myself. He pointed me in the direction of home and then he made the journey with me. He led me there by exploring me and challenging me to explore myself, regardless of the unexpected worlds my exploration would then uncover.

* * *

Obviously he knows now that she is home. He rings her number again and again.

She masturbates even while the phone rings because she knows for certain it is him. It's a delirious feeling, knowing that she's once again connected to him if only through these ringing bells. She pictures his fingers going in her. She remembers herself tied, exposed for him, and his fingers going in her. Up her ass. Until it is his cock she remembers going up her ass while she's tied, blindfolded, lost in the same pleasure she feels him succumbing to in her. She doesn't stop masturbating until she has brought on the orgasm she craves.

The phone has not stopped ringing. The ringing drowns out even her bitterness. At last, she answers the phone again.

"Don't hang up," he shouts. "Listen to me, Elisa. I'm sorry, okay?

I'm sorry. I know it sounds like too little too late, but I want you with me. I mean it. I want you with me."

He begs for at least a chance to plead his case in person, to explain that he's left his wife. That his settlement will include the beach house and the *pied à terre*.

Their memories will be part of his settlement, part of his permanent departure from his wife. He surrendered a lot to secure those two things before leaving.

She's almost afraid to believe it but there is nothing she would rather believe instead. "Come up," she says. She is ready to be amenable.

After all, she decides, there is only life to be lived and so little time even for that.

Comfy

by
William Gaius

held the disintegrating newspaper in my hands and approached the ragged, one-story house. Only one of the circled ads in the folded paper was not crossed out. I looked at it again.

> *FOR RENT – Comfy basement apt.,*
> *4 blocks from NIU, suitable 2 females.*
> *Share bath. No lease. $800, 1 mo. sec.*
> *dep., 1414 Spring St., after 6.*

It was last on my list. The rent was exorbitant, and the ad had specified 'female', which should disqualify me right off. Only the word 'comfy' had kept me from striking it. Whoever had placed the ad had paid extra to put in that word, 'comfy'. In a college town, students were expected to sleep just about anywhere; they didn't need 'comfy'.

The house itself didn't look comfy. The asbestos siding was dirty. The screen door had come off and was propped against the side of the house. The lawn might not have been mowed all season. The two-year-old Camry in the drive seemed in decent shape, but needed washing. Yet I was at the end of the list now, and if I didn't find a place to stay, I was going to have a hard time in two months when the semester started.

The unkempt house did not prepare me for the tall woman who answered the door. I had to look up to meet her eyes, which were deep brown, Hispanic looking. She was in her thirties, I guessed. Her face was tanned and smooth, her lips full. Black curls cascaded over her shoulders. I did not want to be rude, but her height made it difficult not to look at her breasts. Without actually staring, I could tell they were full as they strained gently against her blouse.

"I'm here about the room," I said.

"I only rent to women," she replied. "That *was* in the ad, right?"

"Yes, but I'm getting desperate. Every place I've looked at is taken or too decrepit or dirty to live in."

"And you think my place will be different?"

"Sure," I said. "If you only rent to women students, you're trying to protect your property, right? Guys will trash the place and leave food around and bring in vermin, right? I can't handle the noise and commotion in the dorm. I'm neat and clean and quiet. I'll respect your property."

She looked into my eyes for a long moment. Then she stepped back and looked *me* up and down. I had been consciously forcing myself not to look at her body, and here she was, minutely examining mine! I exercised and lifted weights for up to an hour every morning, and I knew most women liked what they saw.

"I'll show it to you, but that doesn't mean I've agreed." She turned and walked ahead of me back into the house.

I finally had a chance to look her over. She wore denim shorts and a plain white blouse. Her hips were broad but tight. Her legs were tanned and free of blemishes. Her calves were muscular and their skin was as smooth as her face. Nice.

"You'd use the side entrance," she told me. "You'd have your own key, of course." She led the way down the steps into the basement. The stairway was paneled and the stairs carpeted. She opened a simple hollow interior door and showed me into a small sitting room with an easy chair, an old couch, a kitchen table and chairs, and a little sink and stove in the corner. Nearby was a half-size fridge. The TV cable hung limply from a wall.

She watched me as I wandered through a short hallway to the large bedroom – two single beds, without linens, two unmatched dressers, two desks, and two bookcases.

"They're pretty simple digs," she said, "You have to use the main floor bathroom, but you do have your own thermostat. There's air conditioning and heat ducted down here. My husband put all that in five years ago."

"Why is it eight-hundred dollars?"

"You showed up to look at it, didn't you? Even though the ad clearly said eight-hundred? That meant you had some idea you could pay it. I charge that much because someone *will* pay it. In any case, for two students, it would be only four-hundred each."

"I need a place for myself," I insisted. "I need to get out of the dorm this year."

"Then you'll have to keep looking," she said, looking a little disgusted. I supposed I had wasted her time. She moved to herd me toward the steps.

"Wait! Is there anything I can do to work off part of the rent? Paint? Mow the lawn?"

"I need the money more. I'd like to get the house fixed up, but I can't afford it."

I must have looked like a whipped puppy then, because the tone of her voice changed. "Look," she said gently, "I've been widowed for two years, and it's awfully hard to scrape by. I'm just glad I have no kids to support, too."

"I'm sorry..."

"Don't be sorry for me. My husband was an asshole. He got himself killed riding home from his girlfriend's. He was on a motorbike, and drunk. He'd cashed in all his insurance and run up the credit cards on his girlfriends. Then there was a lawsuit. I may not be out of debt before I retire."

"I'm still sorry," I said even though I had not wanted this tidal wave of personal information. "That shouldn't happen to anyone."

"It's my own fault. I knew what he was when I married him." She seemed to shake herself. "Well, do you want the room or not? Seven hundred dollars."

"*Seven*-hundred? Sure!" I said quickly. How the hell was I going to pay that?

"Another thing – you've got to take it right away. I can't afford to leave it vacant until September."

"I…" I pondered. How much could I scrape together? Would it pay me to stay here? I'd be closer to work than at my parents' place in Aurora. It would save me an hour's drive. That would save two-hundred a month in gas and maintenance, too. But what about the cost of food and telephone? At least I'd have a place for the fall semester so I wouldn't have to stay in the dorm. With my own place, I could bring girls back here. "I'll take it."

"One more thing," she smirked. "No women."

Shit! Well, every rule gets broken eventually. If I paid regularly, and if I was quiet and careful, I'd be able to get away with the occasional transgression. Even the primmest landlady would forgive anything if the rent check always showed up on time. If I could manage that… "Okay," I said. I wrote a check for two month's rent. I made it out to Rose Ann Hardy.

Seven days later, I closed the door on my own place. Comfy? Hardly. I had brought my thirteen-inch TV from home, and hung a couple of tiny pictures in the middle of a big, blank wall. These only served to make the place more depressing. I had twenty dollars' worth of food in the cupboards and the fridge. I still needed a carpet. It was bleak, but I would fix it up more in a few days.

The bedroom was a little more welcoming. I had made up one of the beds to sleep in that night. I'd also had the foresight to bring a matching spread for the other bed so I wouldn't have to stare at a bare mattress. A couple of movie posters hung on the wall – I had been careful not to tape or tack them to the paneling. I had set up my computer on one desk, and arranged my writing blotter on the other. The telephone would be connected tomorrow. Two empty suitcases stood in the open closet.

I heard a sound through the little window, set high on the wall at ground level. I could see the landlady's marvelous calves, then her thighs, as she dragged a Weber grill onto the back lawn. Its legs pulled apart, and the bowl tipped onto the lawn. She kicked uselessly at it, then bent and began assembling the pieces.

Without conscious decision, I ran up the steps and out the door. I came around the back of the house just as she failed in her attempt to reassemble the grill and it fell over again. She had ashes all over her arms and blouse.

"Let me help," I said, and she backed off while I grabbed the pieces and sorted them back into order.

"It always falls apart on me," she complained. "Then I have to fight with it. There's got to be a better way."

I laughed. "I've done this a hundred times with my parents' grill. Some genius should invent a way to keep the legs from dropping off." I picked up the bag of charcoal and shook some into the grill.

"No," she said, "I can take care of that."

I ignored her and began arranging the damp briquettes with my fingers. She let me, and watched as I built an intricate pyramid. I grinned at her and picked up the can of charcoal starter and squirted it liberally on the pile.

She grabbed the matches. "At least I know how to do this part," she declared, just as the head snapped off the match. She took out another one, and attempted several times to strike it. It sparked, but wouldn't ignite. "God damn!" she muttered, while I grinned. The third match struck properly, and the flames soon billowed head-high over the grill.

"Yet another triumph of American engineering!" I pronounced.

"Oh, just never mind! But thanks."

"Anytime." I started to turn away. "Well, enjoy your supper." I hoped she would stop me.

"At least you could join me," she said quickly.

I spun all the way around to face her again, and nodded okay, perhaps too enthusiastically. "Only if you let me cook."

She brought out a cheap lawn chair and lounger from a dented tin garden shed. The chairs did not sit evenly in the calf-deep grass. I set up a folding table while she brought out the meat and a couple of beers.

"I'm only twenty," I told her, waving away the beer.

"No, you're not," she winked and pushed it into my hand. "You're twenty-one. For now, at least."

"I never argue with a woman," I said, taking a short swallow. I had not drunk alcohol since before going to New Mexico, a year before. Alcohol was forbidden on the Reservation, and this regulation was most easily enforced on outsiders.

She had brought out four potatoes wrapped in foil, and I set them in a corner of the grill where they would cook, but not burn. The steak was cheap, but she had marinated it, and it cooked up tender and spicy. With a little butter and steak sauce, everything came out just fine.

I watched her with pleasure as we ate and talked. She carried her plate to the lounge chair and kicked off her shoes. Her bare feet were strong and graceful. She supported her plate on her thighs and handled her knife and fork with long fingers. Her lips were mobile and delicate, and gave me erotic stirrings. Her dark eyes were enigmatically bright in the rays of the setting sun. Her voice was musical and it made me feel relaxed listening to it. There were so many things about her that reminded me of Star.

When she handed me a second beer, I picked up the faintest odor of female sweat, and it made my belly surge with adrenaline.

By the time the grill had burned out, it was almost dark. The mosquitoes came out in force, and we collected the dishes and retreated indoors. I set the dishes on her sink, beside stacks of more dishes crusted with food of unknown vintage. I started to run some hot water to wash them.

Rose Ann went into the bathroom. From the kitchen sink I could scan nearly the entire upstairs. Her living room was furnished with older but substantial pieces and a large TV. A treadmill and exercise bike stood in one corner. A wrinkled towel over the treadmill arm indicated she actually used it. That would account for the sleek, muscular legs.

Two bedrooms let off the kitchen, and the doors were open. Her bed was unmade, and a pile of laundry lay near the door. Another bedroom held a desk and bookcases filled with academic tomes and paperback novels. An ironing board and baskets of laundry covered much of the floor. That would once have been her husband's office.

Rose Ann came out of the bathroom, and was flustered to see me washing her dishes. Over her protests, I continued washing them. I wanted to stay in her company a little longer.

She picked up a towel, but I made her sit down. "You bought dinner," I said. "Anyway, feed me beer and I'll do any chore." She laughed too hard at my bad joke, as though she hadn't enjoyed a good laugh in a long time. She sat down and I had her tell me more about herself.

When I finally went downstairs to my new apartment, I knew Rose Ann had to be thirty-four or thirty-five. She had been raised in

Chicago, and studied comparative religion at UIC. When she graduated, she married a young assistant professor of history and moved with him to DeKalb. He rode a motorcycle. It had been his wildness that first attracted her, and then made her life a misery after the wedding. Now she worked as an office manager in an academic department.

I still wasn't bruised by life, which I suppose means that my grand mistakes – and we all make them – were still in the future. I had told Rose Ann that I was studying chemistry, with plans to go on to medical school. I had carefully mapped out my future. But all maps are plotted with the best of intentions, and a mixture of realistic estimates and unrealistic hopes. I had no real financial means to deal with medical school. My parents would do their best, but that would not be much.

In despair after freshman year, I had taken a year off to work in a medical clinic at an Indian Reservation in New Mexico. I wanted to build a history of working in the medical field to increase the chances of winning a rare scholarship.

I did not tell Rose Ann how, during that year, I lost my intended, my girlfriend since high school, or how I was initiated into the private life of Star, the head nurse at the Reservation clinic.

I turned out the light. It was my first night in my own place. The image of Rose Ann buzzed in my head. I was acutely aware that a beautiful, breathing female slept in the same house. More to the point, was it possible she could be like Star? Could I teach her to be like Star? Star, who taught me new ways to pleasure a woman. It had only been two weeks since I was allowed into Star's bed for the last time.

This thought, and the fantasies that came with it, kept me from sleep until well toward morning. My shift in the *Jewel* store dragged. Stocking the shelves with cans and boxes gave me a headache, and the day never seemed to end. I wanted to go back to the apartment and sleep. Also, I could not get Rose Ann out of my head.

I parked in the drive at five-thirty. Her spot was still vacant. I took a can of Coke from my refrigerator, put on some shorts, and sat in the lounge chair behind the house. In the warm sun, I relaxed into a dream state where memories of Star replayed themselves.

Star had targeted me from the first day. By the end of the week she had seduced me during a long picnic in the hills. By the end of the afternoon, I crawled like an eager puppy between her legs. She had come many times that day, while I did not. I was so distracted by her energy that I barely noticed, or cared, that she had done nothing for me.

After that first time, she had me come to her room. She left the door to her room unlocked on certain nights, but she would never tell me when. Each night, I would steal through the hall of the hospital dormitory. I would try her door, overjoyed if the knob turned easily, devastated if it remained unyielding. If it were my lucky day, she would pretend sleep or indifference as I stripped and slipped into her bed and kissed her from her neck down to her belly. Then she would come alive and push frantically at my shoulders. And always she left me unsatisfied, but after a time, that didn't matter any more.

Soon she had me bring breakfast to her room each morning. Sometimes she wanted a relaxing orgasm to begin her day. Often she had little chores for me to do – sewing on a button, ironing her clothes, sweeping under her bed while she read a book. Later, she let me – let me! –wash her undergarments in *Woolite* and hang the frilly little confections on a line over the tub in her private bathroom.

Before a month had passed, I understood her method. Always demand, always push limits, but rarely reward. It worked for training dogs, and it worked for training men. Knowing her method did not release me from my bondage. Less than a dozen times that year, Star rewarded my efforts. She would slide down over me and kiss a trail over my chest and belly and do for me what every teenage boy dreams of...

"Young man, you're going to get sunburned." Rose Ann's voice woke me.

I opened my eyes and squinted into the light. My cheeks tingled, but I was also aware of the fact that I was painfully erect and my shorts were tented; I could feel a damp spot had formed.

I looked at Rose Ann, who smiled and said, "I have some sun block, if you want it" as her eyes flickered to my crotch.

I was embarrassed, but managed a lame, "I didn't intend to fall asleep. Thanks for waking me up."

Her glance swept over my shorts again. "I feel like pizza tonight," she said. "But I hate to order one just for myself."

"I'll split it with you," I offered quickly. Oh God, she wanted to spend more time with me!

"I'm going to exercise now. You can watch TV with me while we wait for supper or stay out here."

Was she kidding? Sit out in the heat when I could watch her work out? I followed her into the house. I ran downstairs and took a couple more Cokes from the fridge.

"Call the pizza place, would you, Tim?" she said from behind the bathroom door. "The number's by the phone. Mushrooms and sausage on my half!"

I ordered a large mushrooms and sausage, and went into the living room. She had changed into brief shorts and a halter top. Her long thighs were every bit as trim and muscular as her calves. Her abdominal muscles were defined in a way that made my heart ache. The hips that had looked merely broad now looked like a robust cradle for the bearing of big, healthy babies. What a shame she didn't have any.

The TV was on the country music network. "Hey," I said, "another country fan! I developed a taste for it out west." The old couch creaked and moaned as I sat down. I pretended to watch TV but surreptitiously watched her instead as she stretched her long, muscular body, first standing and then sitting. Finally, she mounted the treadmill, and I watched in delight as the precious mechanisms of her legs began to work. I had always thought of the human body as a miracle, it was one of the things that drew me towards medicine, but her body was more of a miracle than most.

She walked five minutes, then broke into a trot. The treadmill's rumble swelled and drowned the TV out, but I preferred to watch the gentle bouncing of her breasts. The pizza arrived before she finished, and I paid the boy, who stared past me at the jogging woman. Envy flickered in his eyes.

Go away, sonny, this one's mine, I thought.

She began to cool down, slowing the treadmill to a walk. My chest ached as I watched the beads of sweat shining on her body. Star loved to have me lick the long day's sweat from her skin. I began to grow erect again and fussed with the pizza to distract myself.

She drank from her water bottle while I found a knife and two forks and plates. She laughed. "Who eats pizza from a plate?" she asked. Well, I did, usually.

She sat and picked up a slice with the tips of her fingers, and brought it to her mouth. It collapsed suddenly in the middle and fell into her lap, spilling tomato sauce and cheese. "Oh, shit!" she swore, knocking the limp slice from her lap. She shook her hands in the air to cool them, and clawed at her crotch. "Help me! It's burning!"

I leapt to my feet and scraped the steaming paste from her thighs and shorts with my fingers. The slice had fallen dead center, and I had to get down on my knees and draw my fingertips across the crotch panel to get at all the hot topping. It was burning me; it must have hurt her.

I grabbed her water bottle from the table and poured some in her lap, saving some to cool her inner thighs. I trickled the water there, trying the make the best use of the last few ounces.

"If you cool the skin right away, it won't leave a burn," I said.

"Thank you, doctor. It doesn't hurt."

I looked up. I was on my knees in front of her. She had that look in her eyes, Star's look.

"You've still got tomato sauce on your legs," I said. My heart hammered in my chest. My belly was taut. Could this be happening so soon? What had I done to deserve this kind of luck?

"What are you going to do about it?" Her voice was low and husky and controlled. Those eyes!

I hoped she meant what I thought she meant. Faint heart ne'er won fair lady. I bent down and licked at the tomato sauce on her thigh. She gasped and gave a little cry. I licked again, and tasted tomato and female sweat. Please, God, don't let me climax in my pants!

She rested her hands lightly on my shoulders, without pressure.

Encouraged, I licked more enthusiastically and pursued the tomato paste wherever it was hiding. She let out a satisfied "Mm!" which encouraged me to search under the hem of her shorts. The intimate taste of her! Not at all like Star's. It was an exquisite, individual taste. *Her* taste! I had noticed long ago that different girls' kisses tasted differently. I guess it held true for everything about their bodies.

"I like that," she murmured.

I paused only long enough to say, "Not as much as I do."

I felt her tremble. She said, in a whisper, "You can do more."

Now I was shaking, too. I could barely coordinate my fingers as I slipped her shorts and panties over her wide hips. She pulled me to her, enveloped me, smothered me in her powerful female scent. She sucked the energy from me and focused it on herself until she erupted in a shouting, crying climax. She clutched at my hair, as her hips bucked and writhed. The couch squealed. When finally she collapsed, her arms thrown wide, I moved up and kissed her neck. I wanted to kiss her lips, but I didn't think she'd want to taste herself on me.

After her breathing slowed she said, "I guess you'd like me to do something for you?"

I thought a minute, remembering what Star had taught me. "Only if you need to do it for your own pleasure. I'm okay."

"Really?"

"Really. That does for me what the regular thing does for other men."

"Mm!" she purred against my ear. "You sound like a lady's dream come true."

Already I dared to hope it would be *her* dream.

"Still," she said, "I feel I have to do something."

"You can let me do it again." My face was buried in the soft curtain of her hair. I could have died happy right there.

"I couldn't handle that now."

"Then you can let me sleep with you tonight."

"I said I'm really not up to anymore."

"I mean really sleep. At bedtime, like a normal couple."

"You know, we're not a normal couple. I'm thirty-five and you're practically a teenager."

"According to the books, that puts each of us at our sexual peaks."

"We just did something impulsive. That doesn't mean it should be a long-term thing."

I mused on this a while. I had always dated girls my own age, until

Star. Star had taken me and used me for a year. She confided that she had selected me from a dozen applicants, mainly on the basis of how I might fit her sexual needs. She needed a sex toy, she said. She could tell me this with impunity knowing I was beyond turning away from her. I was utterly in her thrall. Next year, I guessed, she would choose another and initiate him as she had me.

"I'd like to at least give it a chance," I said to Rose Ann. "I've never quite been swept away like that. It felt good and it felt right."

That was almost a direct quote from what Star had said to me a year ago while catching her breath, naked on a blanket under a mesquite bush. It had been a lie, of course. Star had seduced me with skill and precision and spent the next months honing my training to a fine edge. In the end I told her I loved her and begged to stay with her on the Reservation permanently, but she sent me away. "If you love me," she said during our last night together, "you will remember what I've taught you this year. Teach those things to a woman and be a worshipper of that woman. If you worship her, she will become your goddess."

Rose Ann did not answer me. At some point, in our few moments of passion she had muted the television, and now she turned the sound up again. While she pulled her panties back on, I covered the soaked spot on the couch with towels. We ate the lukewarm pizza, then I lay my head on her lap, inhaling her odor, and she stroked my hair as we watched TV.

At nine o'clock, I told her I had to get up early in the morning. "Where will I sleep tonight?" I asked, trying to look more like a lost little boy than a lusty young man.

She looked down at her spread fingers. There was no sign that she had ever worn a wedding ring. "I don't want to get so involved so quickly," she said.

I slid off the couch to my knees and took her hands in mine. "Please? I've never had a feeling so intense for any woman." I was still lying, but my desperation was very real. I would not sleep if I had to sleep alone.

"You silver-tongued devil!" She stood up. "Tonight. Just tonight. No promises for tomorrow. If I say 'no' tomorrow, I want no argument from you. Understand?"

I nodded gratefully. I went downstairs, vibrating with excitement, and brushed my teeth. I washed her essence, and a trace of pizza sauce, from my face, and put on my pajamas. I went up the steps. My heart was pounding again. She was already in bed, covered up to her neck. She turned the hastily arranged covers back for me.

"You won't need those," she fluttered long fingers at my pajamas. "If we're going to do this, we'll do it my way. I'm the one who'll wear the pajamas."

I slipped mine off. I was very fit and tanned after a year in the desert, and I gave her a moment to look my naked body up and down.

"I can't believe you don't have a girlfriend." She gazed at my erection.

"I did, until I went to New Mexico. There it was all work, work, work." I ached for a time when I could stop lying to her, but I could never tell her about Star.

I got into her bed. The sheets probably needed laundering by ordinary standards, but what mattered to me was that they were saturated with her personal odor. It was strong and distracting, and powerfully erotic. I moved close to her, intending to put my arms around her, but she took me by the shoulders and pulled me to her bosom. She opened her two top buttons, exposing just enough silky flesh to rest my head against.

"Sleep," she commanded. I tried to settle down. After a few minutes of lying quietly she said, "Stop shaking." I tried harder. Eventually, the softness of her breasts was calming rather than exciting, and I fell asleep.

I worked the next day in a fog of fatigue and distraction. All I could think about was Rose Ann. How could I win a long-term invitation into her bed?

When I arrived back at the house at around four o'clock, I was assaulted by the sight of the unkempt lawn. I went to the tin shed and pulled out a cobweb-covered lawnmower. The gas can looked intact, but I poured a little into a glass jar to make sure it had no water or dirt in it. I took off the carburetor bowl and rinsed out the dirt. Ten minutes later I had the motor running and started working on the grass.

Rose Ann pulled into the driveway at six just as I emptied the grass catcher for the last time. The cuttings made a pile three feet high in the back corner of the yard.

"Whoa," she said. "I hope you're still not looking for a rent reduction." She saw the mock-hurt look on my face and smiled. "Or does a little bit go a long way with you?"

"How about I *liked* fixing the lawn for you? You're a beautiful woman, and I want to do things that please you. Do you like it?"

Her smile deepened as she led the way into the house. I watched the finely tuned movement of her leg muscles and the wonderful tilting of her hips as she walked. She was the distilled essence of female, and I wanted her again. But right now, patience was paramount.

I insisted that tonight I would cook dinner for us again. I had brought home a couple of decent steaks, some potato salad, and good charcoal. I lit the grill.

"You're spoiling me," she accused later as she cut into her steak. It was tender as butter and spiced simply with garlic and pepper. Once more we sat in the yard until dark. When it was time to go inside, I nervously asked if J could sleep with her again. She said, "Oh, I hope so."

It was different tonight. For one thing, it was Friday night and neither of us had to be out the door first thing in the morning. I saw she was as anxious to get started as I was, and we went to bed at about nine-thirty. There were no pajamas tonight. I lay against her bosom as before, but her hands were more active this time. She steered my face across her breasts. I found the nipples and sucked them gently to rigidity, but she quickly lost interest in that. She bore down on my shoulders, and I was soon kissing her belly, around and below her navel. Hard muscles moved ceaselessly under her silky skin and the pressure on my shoulders was unrelenting. I knew by that point that things were going to turn out just fine.

She came violently, crying and gasping for breath, her hips surging against me. Her hair was soft against my cheeks and lips and her honey soaked my face. This was not enough for her, and she demanded another orgasm before either one of us had completely recovered. Her second climax was as energetic as the first.

Afterward, my head rested lightly on her thigh as we caught our breaths.

Her voice was cautious as she asked, "Tim, do you always intend to let me call the shots when we make love?"

"*Always?* I like to hear you say that. It means you think there's a future for us."

"I'm a little surprised at myself. Being in control is very exciting. Unexpectedly exciting. My husband and I, we always did things the way he wanted whenever *he* wanted. This is so different."

"I'm glad I can please you."

"I'm thrilled when I think of making you go without. Am I perverted or something?"

"I don't think so. I'm a willing collaborator, aren't I? If you think about it, *I'm* the perverted one not wanting what the typical man should want. But it's quite an ego trip, you know, to give a woman that much pleasure." Thank you, Star, for that lesson.

"I got all frothy at work," she said, not seeming to hear me. "I was thinking about making you do me, and then telling you that you can't have anything for yourself." She became hesitant, about to reveal something very personal. "I, um... at one point, Tim, I... I had to go in the bathroom and relieve the pressure so I could concentrate on my work."

"You're embarrassed!" I laughed. "Don't be. I find it just as exciting to think about you controlling me and using me for your own pleasure. Some men are just made that way. It's also exciting to hear that you got all overheated thinking about me."

"I'm getting horny again talking about it like this."

I smiled happily. "This time you won't have to run into the bathroom."

"Don't bother with the slow seduction," she said. "Just do it." She sighed and arched her back and opened her thighs and waited for me. She didn't have to wait long.

Saturday morning I found some eggs in her refrigerator and cooked breakfast for us. I had reserved a pressure washer at U-Rent, and by three in the afternoon the house looked as though it had all new siding. Apparently, Rose Ann felt guilty sitting in her lounge chair watching me work, so she went to do something in the kitchen. Soon she was scrubbing and bleaching the filthy counters and soaking the hardened food from the dishes.

When I came back from returning the pressure washer, she did not hear me come into the house. I stood back from the kitchen doorway, watching as she dried the dishes. Her muscular body moved with an exquisite grace. Her long black hair rippled and waved over her shoulders, and her calf muscles bulged each time she stretched to put a plate on the top shelf. It was the most mundane work, but she made it a graceful ballet. I ached inside, wanting her again. The more we made love, the more intense my desire for her became.

Watching her, I had another thought, foreign to me until then – I wanted to have children with this woman. I wanted to see her belly swollen and heavy. I wanted to hold a baby in my arms we would create together.

That evening she wanted to make love as soon as the supper dishes were cleared. She came twice in her bed. We got up to watch some television, and we made love again on the couch.

Sunday morning, I woke up to her gently shaking my shoulder.

"I need to talk," she said, sitting on the bed. She wore only a loose bathrobe. "I've been lying here for two hours, thinking."

This did not sound good, but she had made coffee and a steaming cup waited for me beside the bed.

"Every day I'm finding myself investing more in you, Tim. Emotionally, I mean. We really have to settle some things before this goes any farther."

"The age thing?"

"Well, yes. That's one thing. The main thing, I guess. I mean, I have friends and bosses at work. If I were a faculty member, I'd be in deep trouble for cohabiting with a student. I'm only a staffer, and I won't lose my job over this, but I have to be able to deal socially with my coworkers."

"People will stare and talk," I agreed. "There's no doubt about that."

"I think I can put up with it. People will talk, but I know they'll secretly envy a middle-aged woman on the arm of a buff young man.

But what about you? You're something of a hunk, and I don't really think you'd have trouble getting girls your own age. Am I right?"

"I've had a lot of girlfriends." Including Star, who was probably older than Rose Ann. I figured that Star may have been as old as forty-five. Of course, every junior nurse and probably some of the doctors knew about Star's hobby, but in the gritty atmosphere of the Reservation hospital we dealt with the products of domestic violence and road accidents and alcoholism and venereal disease. Nobody concerned themselves with something as trivial as dalliances amongst the staff, let alone an age difference.

"Do you understand me? Sooner or later my coworkers and friends will know about you, and that will be okay with me. But if you get lured away by some woman closer to your own age, the humiliation will be more than I can handle. I'd have to leave my job."

"I won't leave. I don't know how to make you believe that."

"Then why did you choose me?"

"You're an exotic beauty. You're sexy, you're smart, you're experienced, you're adventurous…"

"And conveniently available?"

"Rose Ann, if I wanted a woman my own age, you know I could find one, but I want you. The age difference doesn't matter."

"How can that be? How can it not matter?"

"Who knows why we're attracted to other people? If you want specifics, your age had nothing to do with it. It was your height that got to me first, then it was your eyes, and then your legs, then it was watching you work out. Tall, athletic women are very sexy. I love the graceful way you move and I love the sound of your voice and your laughter. And there's dumb luck. If the pizza disaster hadn't happened, I might still be downstairs sleeping alone. But it *did* happen, and the rest is history.

"For the record," I added, "I'm mature enough to know I'm not in love with you. Not yet. I'm infatuated, sexually entranced, totally absorbed by your body. I think love will come in time, but neither of us can predict it any more than we could have predicted the pizza folding up."

"Have you ever been in love? Would you know what it felt like?"

"No, and no. Have you?"

"I don't know. What I felt for my husband felt like love, but it went sour faster than it grew."

"I suggest we not worry about it. The question, 'are we really in love?' is kind of self-defeating. The fact that anyone has to ask the question at all implies that the answer is 'no'. Doesn't it?"

She looked at me with something like amazement. "You don't talk like a twenty-year-old."

"Ten points for me, then," I grinned. "Get back into bed."

"What will happen when your parents come to visit, or when your friends show up and want you to go bar-hopping with them?"

I stared stupidly into her eyes for several seconds. "I don't know," I said finally. "I'm trying to visualize introducing my mother to you. My mother is over forty, but she's very young looking. She could adapt, though, but I'm not sure about my father. He's old-fashioned."

She threw off the bathrobe and got back under the covers with me. She put her arms around me.

"Does this mean we're through talking for now?" I asked.

She giggled, a strange sound to hear from her.

"We don't have to settle everything right now," she said. "But you're still a mystery to me. You know quite a lot about me, but I don't know as much about you as I should."

"Besides what I told you Thursday night? I didn't tell you about my family. I was raised in West Aurora. I did okay in school. My dad's kind of an authoritarian…"

"I guess I need to know all that sooner or later. What I really want to know is your love life. Where did you get all the skill for someone your age?"

I had really hoped this subject wouldn't come up so soon. "I was taught," I admitted, "by every girl I ever knew."

"But where did you learn how to treat a woman like a spoiled princess?"

"Was that what I was doing?"

"Most men are pretty selfish, and good-looking guys like you are usually more so. Who taught you to be so different?"

"You did."

"I'm serious. Who taught you those things?"

I thought I was ready to tell her about Star, but I chickened out. "You have a commanding presence. You're not one of those willowy, giggly college girls. You're self-possessed and comfortable in your own body and your own power. You're the sort of person I want to make a life with."

"And how's that going to happen? I want children while I still can, but you're a college student. We wouldn't be able to start a family for years."

I hadn't really thought all this through, and I realized I'd steered the conversation into a dangerous new area. "I've got to get through medical school, but before that, I've got three years of college…"

"Any idea how you're going to accomplish that?"

"I can do it. Lots of people in worse circumstances than mine have done it, and I can, too. The relevant thing is that I can't get married before medical school. No med school will admit me if I can't show them that I can afford to finish. I can only do that if my parents are supporting me. If I'm married, they'll expect me to show I can do it on our own resources. "Anyway, it's kind of early to be thinking of a family, don't you think?"

"Tim, I'm *always* thinking of that. I'm thirty-five and running out of time."

"You'd be thirty-eight by the time we were able to marry. Still time for two or three children. A woman in your physical shape should be fertile until forty-five or more."

"Tim, you've just asked me to invest a critical three years just *to find out* if we're suited to each other. I'm not sure I can afford that."

"Can you afford another mistake?"

I had argued her into a corner. "No," she conceded, reaching out and stroking my crotch. "Next time, it's got to be right. Now make love to me again."

But as I moved toward her, she spread her fingers over herself, almost covering the wild patch of her pubic hair and blocking my way. I hungrily kissed the backs of her fingers, waiting for her to stop her teasing.

"First you have to tell me who taught you these things, Tim. The whole truth this time."

I told her. I knelt on the floor and lay my head on her belly, where I would not have to look in her eyes, and murmured the whole tale of my year with Elaine Yellow Star, the head nurse. I included everything this time – how I shaved her legs, did her errands, and knelt before her and massaged the soles of her feet. When we were together in private she had called me her 'slave boy' and I had called her 'Mistress Star'.

As I confessed these things to Rose Ann, I was sick with worry. How would she react? In the worst case she would send me away in disgust. The best I could expect was resigned acceptance. I did not expect that, as I spoke, her belly would begin to heave. She breathed hard and her hips began to writhe. At the end of my tale she was breathless with excitement. She pushed me down between her thighs.

"Tim, you will be *my* slave boy now. I will work you and treat you badly and you will pleasure me and come back for more."

After only a moment she climaxed, and so did I. My seed sprayed onto the floor while her hips churned and bounced against my mouth and she cried out her ecstasy.

After she calmed down, I told her what had happened to me. "I've *never* climaxed without being touched," I said joyfully. "I've never been that excited. You did that to me!"

The rest of that Sunday was lost as far as work on the house was concerned. Rose Ann was obsessed with trying out her new slave boy. She had me draw a hot bubble bath for her. She ordered me to strip and kneel beside the tub in case she needed anything. Before she got out, she had me get her razor and soap and shave her legs. She giggled with glee as I soaped her skin and went to work. I became excited all over again, touching and following the curves of her smooth legs, raking off the minute stubble of black hair.

I offered to shave under her arms, where a dark fringe had gained a foothold. "Would you like it if I let it grow?" she asked.

I nodded. Among my other secrets, I had told her that Star let the hair grow under her arms where it would capture and hold the sharp and exciting scent of her sweat.

"Then we will let it grow," she purred.

She got out of the bath and stood with her fingers laced on top of her head while I dried her body, carefully blotting and rubbing each part with a fluffy towel. When I had finished, she drew me to her and kissed me. It was an assertive kiss. Her arms were strong, and she squeezed my naked body against hers and pressed her lips tightly against mine. She left me a little dizzy.

"Now I require a proper massage, slave boy." She smiled and stretched out on the bed.

I searched in a dresser drawer where she indicated, and found a bottle of baby oil. I drizzled it on her back and carefully rubbed it into her skin, working at the knots of muscle. She murmured her delight and shrugged the muscles loose as I kneaded from her neck down to her buttocks, moving down to her thighs and calves. She turned over and I worked more oil into her skin beginning at her feet and finishing with her breasts.

The prolonged fondling of her body had aroused her again, and when I finished her massage she required another climax to relieve the tension. After that her imagination failed, or perhaps she'd simply had enough for one day. She wanted only to cuddle under the covers with me. I fell asleep until she woke me. She had prepared a supper of spaghetti with meat sauce and garlic bread.

No sooner had I cleared the dishes than Rose Ann led me back to the bedroom.

"I see you didn't get me up to make supper for you," I said.

"I don't really want a full-time slave boy." She smiled pleasantly and reached for my belt buckle. "It was fun, but it would be too exhausting for both of us to keep the fantasy going all the time. Even your Star became distant and professional when on the job, right? I want us to be a real couple, talking together and going places together and sleeping together and enjoying each other. But maybe you can be my slave boy when the mood strikes me." She pushed my shorts and underwear to the floor.

"Yes, Mistress Rose Ann," I said with a grin. "Your merest whim will be my command."

"Well, I have one last demand for today." She smiled slyly. "Something I have not done for a long time. My husband insisted on it, and I hated it, but with you, I *want* to do it. In fact, as your mistress, I *command* you to let me do it." She made me sit on the edge of the bed while she knelt on the carpet and took my cock into her mouth.

Life that summer was a beautiful dream. Each day my shift at *Jewel* passed in a flicker and I arrived back at the house with my heart full. I was healthy and strong and bursting with energy. I resumed my running and weight training, and I thrilled to the look in her eyes when she stroked and squeezed my muscles.

We shopped for groceries together and began going to movies and baseball games. Then came the inevitable invitation to a backyard barbecue, where she nervously introduced me to her coworkers. All there were younger than Rose Ann and, to my surprise, they took to me immediately. One woman whispered to me, "The office is a much nicer place since you came along. I've wondered for weeks who it was got the boss out of her funk."

When we returned to the house, Rose Ann was giggly and a little drunk. As we prepared for bed, she pulled a little card from her bedside drawer and waved it at me. It was a month's supply of birth control pills, and several were already gone.

"I should have talked to you first," she said, "but I need more from you than I'm getting now. Meanwhile, while we're waiting for these to work, you know what I like. I want three good ones, right now."

"Order up," I said, reaching for her.

With the end of summer came registration for classes. My obsession for Rose Ann had increased, if anything, but new elements began to intrude. Friends began to look me up as they returned to DeKalb for the Fall semester. Soon they began dropping by, bearing pizzas and six-packs of beer, often at strange hours and always uninvited. I had been gone for a year and there was much catching up to do.

By now I had repainted the apartment and put a carpet on the floor, making it look much more 'comfy' than it had when I first saw it. Soon, as I feared, I was under pressure to share the place with one or another of my classmates. These were invariably the guys who were not invited back by their last years' roommates or landlords or had waited too late to search for a place to stay. They were, in other words, the losers, the deadbeats, and the slobs.

One Friday night in late September, I was awakened by a pounding at the front door. I looked at the clock. For crying out loud, it was three a.m.! I got up from Rose Ann's side and peeked around the living room curtains to see a large shadow standing against the rain. It was Andrew, a particularly foul and obnoxious jerk. He had attached himself to me in our freshman year. He was oblivious to hints, snubs or even a direct 'fuck off'.

I felt Rose Ann behind me, and I whispered over my shoulder, "If I answer, he'll just barge in. Just tell him I'm home in Aurora tonight."

She looked at me severely, and waved me out of sight.

"Where's Tim," blurted Andrew. He sounded drunk, but then he always sounded drunk.

Rose Ann repeated what I had told her.

"It's alright," he bellowed. "Tim said I can stay here if he's not home." He pushed past Rose Ann and strode into the living room, where I stood in my underwear.

"You son of a bitch!" he shouted. "What's your problem? I'm kicked out of my place and you tell your girlfriend to lie for you and leave me out in the rain!"

"She's my landlady, Andrew," I said through my teeth, "and I expect you to be polite to her." I turned to Rose Ann. "I did not give him permission to use my apartment. I would tell that to no one without your say-so."

"You fucker!" he yelled. "I'll get fucking pneumonia." He tottered where he stood for a few seconds, and a faraway look came into his eyes. "Tim, I'm going to be fucking sick…"

Rose Ann and I both reflexively jumped back as he pitched forward onto his hands and knees and vomited onto the living room carpet. He toppled on his belly into the stinking pool. He lay there and started to cry. "Oh, God, I feel so awful. I've made a mess of your place. I'm such an asshole!"

I looked at Rose Ann, and she glared back at me. "Do you understand now why I only rent to women?"

I tried to move Andrew to the bathroom. He was fat and limp and it was like hauling a huge, sloppy bag of water. Rose Ann brought a small carpet. I managed to roll him onto it, and used it to drag him to the bathroom. I got him into the tub – a virtually superhuman task – and turned on the water. In New Mexico, I had learned about the effect of sudden physical shocks on alcohol poisoning, and I made sure the water was lukewarm before turning on the showerhead.

He barely noticed; he leaned against the wall under the torrent of water and began to snore.

Rose Ann went back to bed while I got a bucket of water and a sponge and cleaned up his reeking mess. I called Mike Postman, his roommate, waking him up at four in the morning. He told me he had thrown Andrew out when he came home drunk and refused to stop shouting and singing. No, he wouldn't come and get him. I left Andrew sleeping in the tub.

When I woke up again it was to the alarm clock. Now that the semester had started I had a new schedule and worked at the *Jewel* store on Saturdays. I couldn't leave for work with Andrew still sleeping in the tub, but he wouldn't wake up. I didn't want to disturb Rose Ann, either. She was already angry enough. I shook him, to no effect. After I had gone downstairs and dressed, I shook him again until he stirred.

"You're the only person I know who's got extra room," he begged when he finally came to his senses. His face was flushed and he chewed on a piece of dry bread I gave him. "Tell your landlady I'm okay, Tim. Last night was just the one time. I won't do that again soon, not the way I feel today."

"Andrew, you've been like that ever since I've known you. My landlady's already mad enough to throw me out after last night. She usually rents only to women, and I had to talk her into renting to me."

He looked up at me with red-rimmed eyes. He was still sitting in the tub, and still soaking wet. "You and she came to the door together, didn't you?" he accused. "In your skivvies, too. You're fucking her! Isn't she a little old for you?"

Now was my time of decision. If Andrew knew, all my classmates would soon know. Since several came from my neighborhood, it would be a matter of days, or perhaps hours, before my parents would know, too. I could deny the relationship, or commit myself to her now.

I sucked in my breath. "Yes, I *am* living with her and no, she is *not* too old for me. Now get out!"

Somehow I got him out the door in his damp clothes, although it cost me a cup of coffee, a sandwich, and ten dollars. He said he'd keep quiet about Rose Ann, but I knew he was full of shit. He'd been a bigmouth since I knew him. He would tell the first person he met, and that would probably be Mike Postman, whose parents were my parents' best friends.

After work I was back at the house at three-thirty. I found Rose Ann sitting with a cluster of K-Mart bags. I looked at the cheap blouses and slacks she was sorting. I thought forward to the day she could sit like this among boxes and bags from *Nordstrom's* and *Nieman Marcus*. She deserved to be the contented wife of a successful physician, not a desperate widow or the wife of a dissipated, adulterous history professor.

She looked at me sharply.

"He won't be back," I promised. "I read him the riot act." My inflection said I had more to say, and she watched me patiently, waiting for the rest.

"My parents will know soon. The shit will hit the fan."

Her voice was icy. "What do you plan to do about it?"

"I don't know. I can't make it through college without their help, and I can't imagine my father agreeing to my living with any girl, let alone…" I stopped. This was taking all the nerve I could muster.

"With someone my age?" she finished for me. There was no smile.

I waited a long time before saying, "Yes."

I'd had a day to think about what I would say to her, and now was the time.

"Rose Ann, I want to live with you more than I've ever wanted anything. I will do anything, give up anything, to be with you."

"If your parents don't buy into this arrangement, where will you be?" She was in full serious mode now, and very businesslike. "You'll be out on your ass in the snow and I'll have the apartment up for rent again. Where's the future in that?"

"Hear me out on this one, Rose Ann. If I moved upstairs with you, you could rent the downstairs to two women, couldn't you? I've already shown I can fix the place up. You can come home every day to supper and a clean house, but there'd be no reason for my friends to keep hitting on me for a place to live."

She looked at me. Her eyes were still hard, but did I see a glint of interest there? I spoke quickly, "Don't you like having a nice warm body next to you in bed at night? Don't I treat you with consideration? I've sincerely tried to be everything you want. Please,

Rose Ann, don't make up your mind too quickly."

"I want you to sleep downstairs tonight," she said.

Her words hit me like a plunge into ice-cold water. I hurt in my heart, a big hollow ache. It didn't get any better when she let me sit with her while she exercised. I watched her lovely body stretch and move and sweat, but it was like looking through bulletproof glass. She let me cook supper for her and wash up afterwards. As I went down the stairs at eight-thirty, I waited for her to call me back, but she didn't. I got into bed and started to cry. I couldn't help it. I cried quietly, so she wouldn't hear, but something had been ripped from my soul.

I lay awake, feeling sorry for myself, until sometime around two o'clock. The next afternoon I was expected at dinner at my parents' in Aurora. I had hoped to talk Rose Ann into coming with me and meeting my folks. Now I would go there alone and I wouldn't have an appetite and my mother would get anxious and want to know if I was sick.

"Tim?" It was a gentle whisper.

"Rose Ann?"

Her voice came out of the darkness. "I can't do it. I can't send you away. I want you beside me. I want you inside me. Come and make love to me." In the near-darkness, I felt her approach and saw the faint outline of her naked body as she reached the bed.

My heart leapt. "Oh, Rose Ann, I love you!" I knew now that it was true, and I hoped she would grow to believe it, too. I leapt from the bed and embraced her in the darkness. I stood on my toes to kiss her cheek and her neck and her lips. She pulled me closer and her hot breath thrilled in my ear.

"I want you to come with me in the morning to Aurora," I whispered. "I want you to meet my parents."

"What if they don't like me?"

"Not possible."

"I mean the age difference."

"Rose Ann, I can't leave things like this. I have to resolve it now. I've decided I want to be with you, regardless of the consequences. You know how resourceful I am. I can bull my way through medical school. When the time is right, I want to marry you and have children with you. Perhaps I can do all that without alienating my parents, too."

Her voice relaxed as she said, "We'll bring them grandchildren. That'll win them over. I guarantee it."

Arms around each other's waists, we walked up the stairs together.

Pony Penning Days

by
L.A. Mistral

We don't need time machines. We already have them and we just don't know it. A certain sight or scent can instantly transport a person to another time and place. It's not just *remembering* another place and time. It's like actually being there with all your senses intense and intact. That's how I remembered Geraldine.

That's how I remembered even now. Seeing her after all these years, it all came back to me so immediately and palpably. Her auburn hair flew behind her like a battle flag as she rode. Her red shirt with the pearl snap buttons pressed tight against her. She sat straight and sexy in the saddle, her ass surrendering to the stern, muscled leather. She was a flair-hipped, spear-nippled, apocalyptic Amazon.

Her ass bounced in the saddle like a church bell. Its sound woke me up again. It woke me up and brought me back twenty-two years to when Geraldine and I were in the full-fledge of our hanging out. I woke up to her lucid skin, so pale it was almost translucent; her flesh was so pale it seemed like the alabaster treasures dug up with the rest of King Tutankhamen's loot, the likeness of the boy king outlined in gleaming alabaster and onyx, a dark shadow over his luminous body. Geraldine's skin seemed like a body of light to me. Not just how she stood with her provocative, full hips and her swaggering looks. Her light came from how she moved her body as well.

My own body reached back into Geraldine's body, scent and soul. Each cell of my body touched her again. We started hanging out after our eighteenth birthdays. We knew we each liked to ride and had swapped horse and riding stories a few times.

We grew closer over time. Then one day we agreed to ride together.

That was how we were back then. Geraldine held my heart inside her alabaster skin. I wondered if our skin still held the prophetic gift.

PONY PENNING DAYS

We each knew we'd tease, please, and squeeze out the fortune of each other's body sooner or later.

We joined in the Chincoteague round up every July. Wild ponies grazed along Virginia's Eastern Shore, that knotty wand of land south of Maryland. Since the sixteen-hundreds, English shipwrecks spilled horses onto the narrow beaches. Some of the horses survived on the skimpy beach grass and sea oats that grew along the windy shores.

These hearty ancestors gave birth to generations of fast and clannish horses now protected in the Assateague Island National Seashore and the Chincoteague National Wildlife Refuge. These descendents have few natural predators, but are rustled into auction every July. This keeps the population down and keeps the rest from starving. The horses are sold and the profits donated to local firefighters and EMT squads in what the locals call the "Pony Penning Days."

Geraldine (I called her Gussy) and I always helped out with the penning part. We helped corral the horses, give roping lessons to the locals, and gathered strays. Gussy's hair sailed behind her like a map of the universe. She smelled like horseflesh, oiled leather and her inexhaustible hair.

Gussy and I grew up in the same part of southwestern Virginia. It was horse country, not English style either, like so many places near Charlottesville or Arlington. We wore blue jeans and boots, not top hats and britches. But we liked the riding crops.

Other guys called us "hicks" and "hayseeds" even though they lived only a few miles away from us. We wore our work jeans and our straw cowboy hats to classes with the brims broken down exposing a dark band of sweat.

Some of the other girls chewed tobacco and spit into Styrofoam coffee cups, but that's where we drew the line. It was cool for the guys back then, and they took pride in spitting contests and how the cans of tobacco wore pale holes into their back pockets.

Generally, though, we were outcasts. Some others girls had the nerve to tell us that playing with horses was a kid's game and we should've grown out of it a long time ago, but that was only part of it. We were always clean, our teeth brushed and our hair washed. But our jeans smelled of horse soap and hay and our hands smelled of lanolin and horseshoe salve. Our fingernails were always cut and polished – you'd never know where we'd put them.

Well, that's not exactly true… my fingers were always up my pussy. I used to worry about being addicted to masturbation as I stretched my cunt open, my clit like the pommel of a soft and scented saddle. I would have rubbed and ridden it all day long if I'd had the time. Just thinking of Gussy's jeans stretched out along her thighs, her pussy mound slapping down hard against the curve of the pommel, started me rubbing my own thighs together. I loved the squishy feeling between my legs. It felt warm, like the breath of some goddess was whispering oaths and incantations there.

My hand did the rest. I got better. That means I became less timid and less scared of myself. I began slapping my ass and thighs just like I wanted Gussy to do. I imagined Gussy slapping my pussy. Her palms stung me and her palms soothed me. She slapped my ass like she urged on her horses and I liked it that way.

Gussy and I liked the hard-muscled, animal spirit smell of the ride. It was an old wives' tale that women lose their virginity when they ride horses, that's why they used to ride side saddle. Truth be told, it was my imagination that popped my cherry. I popped my own cherry with the lusts I made up in my own head. My skin couldn't get enough of her skin, but it was more than that.

I loved her even then. I even loved her hair. Gussy's hair was always thick and dark-red, almost black, but when the sun shone on it you could see streaks of red. When I brushed the mane of my own darling roan, I imagined I was combing Gussy's auburn hair.

She always said her hair was like me, myself.

"People need to cast light on you," she said, "to see you like you really are."

I loved her and I loved even the sweat of her. The dirt and sweat smell of the horse and her own animal smell put me into a swoon. I'd sometimes stand real close while she spoke. Not to hear her words, but to smell her. She smelled of horseflesh and sunlight. The smell settled in her hair, nestled in her clothes or spiced up her alabaster skin. I wanted to feel her pale moon muscles, all of her way up inside me.

Of course, we never spoke about it. We never had the words. Our words were as awkward as our actions. We bumped into each other, we didn't caress. We blurted out things, we didn't whisper. Our feelings burned somewhere between our clits and our tongues. The mystery of our feelings gave them a life of their own, even a body of their own. Lust became a separate entity. The sweaty gravity between us was as real and palpable as the horses we rode.

And did we ride! Almost every weekend, rain or shine, hot or cold. When we were in the saddle, we lost all our awkwardness and all our inhibitions – almost.

I always rode behind Gussy. Her ass slammed up and down like a throttle in the saddle. It stretched out her jeans across her ass and thighs, so tight I could almost see the crease of her crack. I imagined my fingers there, spreading her ass wider, moving forward in the wet surf to the damp delta of her pussy, my fingers and my tongue up her cunt.

In my mind, my tongue was the saddle horn. I felt the zipper of her jeans against my raw skin. Her legs spread wide over the saddle and I could see the lips of her pussy flipped open like the robes of the Virgin Mary. She smelled like ripe apples and white licorice and I wanted her to smear her smell all over me. I wanted her to form and to storm me with her tight ass and her taut belly.

I didn't know she liked it so rough – at least, not then.

I didn't know I liked it so rough then, either.

She was my rider and I was her horseflesh. I liked how she commanded me, firmly and respectfully. Her conquering me was my only salvation.

My parents said we were hanging around each other too much. They said I should broaden my horizons. Gussy's parents didn't care what she did, so long as she didn't do drugs, get pregnant or land in jail.

I mostly kept to myself and read the ancient stories of compulsive love and killing. My favorites were the Mesopotamian epic of *Gilgamesh* and *The Iliad*. I imagined myself the war booty of some Trojan prince, splayed out on the Troy's walls as a ransom for the hungry Greek army. Maybe I was the one lovely who could satisfy the blood lust of their hands, tongues and swords. They lay down their armor in honor of my nakedness. They removed their helmets to better suck on my nipples. They bit them and twisted them. The hands that killed Achilles and Agamemnon pried my pussy open. They said I was the new Helen. They would sail a thousand ships if I would let them slip into me. The army that slit the throats of their Trojan enemies licked my slit in revenge and reverence.

Or maybe I was a priestess of Inanna, the love goddess of ancient Sumer. An eclipse darkened the sun and I was their chosen sacrifice. They tied me to the top of the great ziggurat of Ur with leather chains. The priests extracted favors and the cruel pity of the gods. They ravished me with the ends of gold scepters and raised welts on my thighs with filigree whips. Their exquisite lengths cut the orbits of stars and constellations into the curves of my breasts and on the insides of my thighs. The priests opened me again and again with their urgent and brutal batons. My body became beautiful, the sacred hematoma.

My body was the oracle of the planets. The priests' pleasure was the pleasure of the gods.

* * *

Anyway, that was the truth of my heart. It did not come true right away. My body had to wait. We both attracted and repelled guys. Gussy wore her body, especially her jeans, easily and aggressively. The boys saw that immediately. She was slender and her jeans drew tight across her hips and her raised mound. The boys got a lump in their jeans as well. But Gussy didn't seem to care. She was a horsewoman. If they looked at her cross-eyed she'd kick their asses with her two-toned, pointy-toed mink-oiled cowgirl boots. She sent the guys flying with one long-legged kick. But she liked the attention. I tried to copy her, but I was too shy.

You guessed it. Everyone said I was the smart one. That meant I was the nerdy one.

You guessed it. Gussy was the sexy one.

Guys would call out, "Hey, there's cow shit and cutie pie."

Guess who was who.

Gussy would shoot back, "That's horseshit to you, asshole. And if you ever want some of me, you better know the difference."

We'd laugh and she'd put her arm around me.

Sometimes she'd yell back, "All hat and no pony!" then hack up a big lougy and spit it at them.

I asked her once what she meant. She told me it was an old rodeo expression meaning that a cowboy was all show and no talent. They called me the smart one, but all along I knew it was her.

After a while the guys did start calling me new names. They'd call me "shelf" and say, "Nice shelf" as they walked by.

I was embarrassed to have to ask Gussy what they meant.

"It means you could balance a bar tray on your breasts," she said. I was too embarrassed to laugh. "You hadn't noticed?"

"Not really."

"Liar."

I winced with embarrassment, but of course I *had* noticed. I was a late bloomer, but the harvest was full.

Some other guys called me "The door."

My whole body shrank from the insult.

"That's good," she said. "That's a compliment."

I looked up, brightening. "What do you mean?"

"They call you 'the door' because you have great knockers. Come on, your titties sprouted up overnight. You know it."

She was right. We were both surprised, and relieved. For almost nineteen years I had waited for them, hoped for them and even prayed for them. I didn't know of any patron saint of nipples, but if there was one, I would have been on my knees on a very thick rug.

I even tried pinching my nipples into blooming, like I was pruning them or something. I'd take my hand and pull and twist my nipples and stretch them out. I wanted to pull, prod and placate them into shape. That was at first. After a while, I began to pull and twist them because I liked how it felt.

But nothing happened. I consigned myself to absence and oblivion. I didn't talk much and dreamed about being more like Gussy. I dismissed myself and admired Gussy. Maybe that will make me more like her, I thought.

She always told me her hair reminded her of me. She said that when she unbound it and let it loose behind her, it reminded her of how I might be.

"Let life spill out of you," she urged.

"How do I do that?" I whined. "Look at my mousy, brown lengths," I complained.

She stopped in her tracks, turned around and looked me right in the eye. "Stop it," she said. "Stop running yourself down or I'll hog-tie you."

"I wish these ropes were lassoes," I told her. "I'd bull-dog you down for sure."

"You already have," she said. "Pretty soon your body will catch up to your imagination. Your knockers already have."

It was not only spilling out. It was gushing out.

The reality only happened once, a few months after our eighteenth birthdays. We celebrated in our own way. We always went riding. We rode out into the fields, to the end of our property. A stream flowed there, the boundary of my parents' property.

I remember the firm fingers of fire beneath me as I rode my darling Sheba – a roan of thirteen hands or so. I was riding behind Gussy, her hair and her hips teasing me. My ass was being caressed by the hand of the saddle as I rode up and down. The fire flared up inside me like my body was dry wood.

We stopped to eat in a high, dry patch of grass beneath a locust tree. Gussy dismounted and I loved watching her stretch her thighs over the saddle. She took her rope, but I didn't think anything of it at the time. She won awards for her roping. She could lasso a steer at full gallop eight times out of ten. She won ribbons at the Wise County

Fair and the Virginia State Fair three years running. Her rope was woven so tight it seemed lubricated, and the noose knot slid effortlessly up and down it. It was thick, too, nearly as thick as my wrist. Gussy looped it out of the saddle horn and lay down with it.

We both leaned back on the blanket. My blouse rode up to my midriff and you could see the tiny hairs of my pussy as my jeans sank down my hips. The sunlight danced with warm feet all over my stomach and hips.

As I lay beside her, she opened her arm to me. I slid into Gussy and leaned against her shoulder. I could feel her mouth on the nape of my neck. She started to kiss me there and I unsnapped her blouse. We slipped off each other's blouses and bras with ease. Our lust made our bodies more lithe and graceful.

Not knowing if that's what other people did, I moved my hips back and forth, shy and delighted at the same time. We were both leaving our town, our horses, and each other soon. We knew it and our bodies knew it. Each in our own way, we craved comfort. Our bodies sought security in each other's bodies. We were crossing the boundaries in a new country. We huddled inside each other like refugees.

She undid my fly and unzipped my jeans. I lifted up my hips so she could pull them off. As I opened my legs, I could smell how wet I was. It was the smell of moss and chamomile just after a rain. I smelled of thickness and wet and I took two of her fingers and guided them along the entire length of me, from my clit to my anus. My own smell rose up to me in waves evoking rosehips and lilac. Then, like taking the bit into my mouth, I dipped them into me, cooing to her, begging for more and more of her. Love made me speak things I had only thought. Our hands and mouths, our entire bodies, became articulate as poets. The lyrics within my skin let loose.

"Ride me, rider on the Clouds!" I cried, "Ride me like the Bull of Heaven!"[1]

I closed my eyes, then felt her fingers come out of me. There was an absence there, almost an emptiness. I thrust my pelvis up to her. Soon I felt something hard and curved against the mouth of my pussy. I looked down. She was pressing the coil of the rope into the cleft of my vulva. It felt hard, not rough but good. My clit bucked and so did I. I closed my eyes again, took her hand, and helped her press it deeper against the length of my damp channel. Then she entered me. I could feel it – like a rose-studded shaft of sunset. I pressed back into her hand so it would go deeper into me. I was a well and I wanted to know how deep I could be. It made me feel powerful and proud. I shifted my hips to take in her fingers, the scent of her roan hair, her fierceness, her wide mouth – I wanted them all inside me.

Gussy bent over to pick up something, so I waited and let my legs go loose. Soon it felt like she was feeding something into my cunt. It felt rough against my walls as it stretched me out.

I looked down. My pussy was as wide as a red hibiscus. She was pressing one end of the rope into my pussy, inch by inch. By now I couldn't stop her – I didn't want to stop her. It felt like her love entering me, length by length. Anything she loved me with was love itself. Anything that came from her would be welcome inside me. She kept her mouth close to my ear whispering, "I want you. I want all of you. Is this all right? Can I go further?"

My hips said, "Yes!" and I pressed my cunt into the lengths of the rope. "I want all of you, too," I said over and over again.

I thought I was ready for anything – but I wasn't.

She reached around with the rope and poised the coil over my ass. Then she spanked me with it. She started slow at first and I raised my bottom to meet the sting of the rope. I'd seen her do it to her Frenzy.

I felt sleek and slender as a racehorse.

But as the intensity of her strokes increased, I tensed. I was unprepared for my secret desire to come true.

I hesitated. Even though her spanking was exciting, this was an intensity of intimacy I did not expect. It wasn't that I didn't like it. It was that I felt I shouldn't like it. The things I wanted most were the things I most feared – and I feared I liked it too much.

We shrank from each other. We unwound from each other. Gussy smiled. It was her embarrassed smile. She started to hiccup. She always did that when she was embarrassed. She withdrew her hand and let the rope drop. I knew things would never be the same again.

At that time, neither of us knew the difference between the kind of fear that is attractive and the kind of fear that is repulsive.

I touched her hand, pleading for something… I didn't know what. She just hiccupped and took a long drink of soda. Gussy looked away from me.

***

My hesitation haunted me then. It haunts me now. When I got home that afternoon, I pulled my jeans and panties down and saw the red blossoms. If I could have, I would've taken pictures of the crimson splotches of skin because they looked just like the lovely, purple cloaks of the Virgin. While the bruises soon went away, the lust of their memory bit into my skin like a stigmata.

My regret fed my fantasies. The scene played in my mind over and over again. Like an artist repainting the canvas over and over with each new inspiration, I recast the scene with greater elaboration and intensity. My mind dropped the needle onto the same record. It played again and again, with more elegance with each repetition. The deeper the groove, the more vivid the fantasy. Sometimes a vivid fiction trumps an obscure reality, but my skin itched for the real skin.

Sometimes I would slap myself on the ass with something she touched. I slapped myself like she spanked me, as if the repetition of this vicarious act would somehow put my regret to rest.

Yeah, as if, I thought.

When I saw her again, I would seek my redemption. It took a long time. It's ironic that we met again two years later at Pony Penning Days – the days of captivity and of setting free. Even so, fantasy has a way of inducing reality. Fantasies can be self-fulfilling. Gussy approached me from behind. I felt her breaths part the hairs on the back of my neck. My skin flushed and goose bumps rose down my back and the hairs on my neck stood on end. She pressed into me and I could feel her hips dip into the back of my thighs.

"Take off your shirt," she ordered in her commanding voice. "I want to see how you pruned your titties."

A jolt of warm liquid electricity flowed from my cunt upward to my heart. I could feel both my pussy and my heart opening, like a still pond stirring when a petal falls on it. The ripples wove in and out of my skin from my cunt to the curve of my cheek. It was a slow rippling of lust, a slow sipping of the skin's heady amphora.

She reached around and unsnapped the button of my jeans. I unzipped them myself and she drew her hands down the front of my panties. Her breath became more heated and more urgent. I leaned my head back against the hollow of her throat. I felt lightheaded as she reached around and parted the folds of my pussy lips. I spread my legs so she could ease her fingers into me more easily.

Gussy reached into me with more urgency. Her fingers seemed to reach deeply into my cunt. I could feel myself expanding to accommodate her. I loved the sense of fullness, even completeness, that her fingers initiated and that the firmness of her body confirmed. Her fingers became aggressive inside me. The more rough she got, the more wet I became.

She pushed me face-down on the bed. She pulled my jeans off by the cuffs in one slow, melodious movement.

"My favorite panties," she said. "I love how your red ones compliment your even, olive skin."

Suddenly, the room filled with apricot and almond. Gussy had stripped and pulled down her panties. I had memorized her smell and it was arousing as ever.

I pushed my rear end up. I knew what was coming – it was going to be both of us.

Gussy reared back and slammed her hand down on my thigh. I jumped at the surprise of it and wriggled my ass up high again, waiting for another. She didn't disappoint. She brought her hand back down on the same place. I moaned and stretched out further on the bed. The tighter my skin, the more her slaps seemed to resonate evenly around my body. My pussy was filling up with juice and I could almost hear it swash around as I moved.

She slapped her hand down again, this time on my other ass cheek. Searing heat burst through me like an explosion of lava. I grit my teeth and tears came to my eyes and I ground my hips deep into the bed. My clit and my whole body begged for a climax.

I looked back to see Gussy. Her face was framed in rapture. Her eyes half closed, I could only see their whites. Her eyes had rolled back as she fell further and further into an erotic ecstasy. She saw me only with her fingers. She was disciplining me by feel alone. I was so aroused, I almost lost consciousness. Pain was an elaboration of the skin's ecstasy. It woke up my body into a deeper and deeper rawhide intimacy.

Gussy dropped to her knees and I felt her skin on the very places she slapped me. She was pressing her cheek to the red and raised welts. Then she lifted her head, stuck out her tongue, and started licking them. Even her soft tongue stung at first, but then she blew on the red, raised signatures of her affection and the burning cooled.

Intuition struck at that moment. A thought hiding just below consciousness, like the skin's own burning, rose to the surface.

"Gussy is killing me," my skin said. "She is killing the sad, timid woman I always thought I was."

The discipline of my skin revealed the truth. The truth was that I had lived more like a whisper than a woman and that I had acted more like a shadow than an authentic submissive.

Gussy had stopped slapping my ass for a moment. She was getting her breath.

"Again," I urged her on. "Again!" *I love my adorable killer,* I said to myself. *I love her hands and the feel of her palms.*

I turned around and grabbed her right hand, the hand of my delicious discipline, and kissed it over and over again.

"Not yet, girl, get down again," she ordered. "We're not done with the lesson yet."

Gussy's hand rang down again and again on my backside. My body jumped each time. Each time, I rotated my hips toward her.

It was time, long since time, to act like an equal partner in pleasure. Sometimes being an equal partner means being on the bottom. Submission is, itself, a form of assertion.

She turned me over and gripped both of my ample breasts with her whole hand. The flesh of my titties spilled out over her hands and between her fingers. She made a tiny lasso with her thumb and forefinger and pinched my nipples. My own eyes rolled back as the delicious sting enveloped my whole body. My nipples became hard immediately and stood straight out from me hard as stirrups. The taut points pulled the rest of my breasts tight as a drum. Gussy then twisted my nipples. At first I felt pain. Then I felt pleasure. Then she pinched them hard and I didn't know the difference between pleasure and pain.

I splayed my body across the bed. After years of hiding, my body wanted to be exposed, juxtaposed, and deposed. I had ruled my body with strict timidity. Gussy's loving instruction deposed years of self-exile. My body was coming home to itself.

It can happen in a second. Just after the slap, there is an instant just before the bloom of heat that the skin is most awake and makes no decision between pleasure and pain. The mind and memories decide that. In that moment, the skin is an eager accomplice of consciousness.

The sweet sense of fullness gave way to jagged sparks all over my body. The sparks sang an incoherent chorus of stings, bristles, whip songs, and erotic relics. My body surged from a placid pool to a class five rapids. Time seemed to take on a body all its own. The skin makes its own rules of time, space and distance. The flesh makes its own equations about love and pain and the tenure of death. In that elegant, instinctive moment, heaven and earth, lust and love, touch and its exquisite absence are one.

She left me raw and ragged. It took me twenty years to accept that's what I really wanted.

* * *

Gussy and I hung out through what we used to call "The Hindenburg Years" – you know, where we crashed and burned. I felt like those trapped inside. Then there were times when we felt like the reporter screaming, "The humanity! Oh, the humanity!" as the ball of fire and steel crashed to earth.

Sometimes you really don't get out alive. Sometimes you get another chance. It was those years of ambiguity and over-certainty that bonded us. The security we found – such security in our bodies and in our beliefs about each other – steeled us against the wider world. Our bodies were bite-sized parts of the world that we could know intimately and cherish absolutely. Those were the days of absolutes and ambiguities and we were suspended between them.

I didn't see her much after high school. It was strange, we being so close and all. At least, I thought we were close. We wrote some after graduation, but each of us moved around so much in the last few years that we eventually just lost touch, meeting only again briefly that one hot July for a few glorious timeless nights.

Twenty years later, I didn't recognize Gussy at first, but noticed the woman on horseback right away. She was riding ahead of me – just the way I like it. Her hair flew behind her in a rage and her thighs sent my skin into a gallop. I could watch her all day – her lithe ass on the wide muscular haunches of her chestnut brown she called Frenzy. Her hips danced on the saddle as agile and ululating as any Malibu surfer.

She rode rough and she liked it that way. Her ass bounced so hard on the saddle, I could see her hips pound. Her inner thighs were so strong she could guide the horse with her haunches. She liked to ride no hands, reigns in her mouth, guns blazing, like John Wayne in *True Grit*.

I wanted her to ride me that same way, to steer me with the inside of her thighs. I wondered what it would be like for her to ride me no hands, the reigns of my nipples in her mouth… ah… to put me into a trot, then a gallop, bush to bush, fur to fur, our lower lips kissing each other, the wind of our breath setting fire to the brush... bruising our hair with wet bites... Now *that's* true grit.

Sometimes you just lose touch. I went away to Colorado State on an English scholarship. I majored in licking pussy, finally shedding some of my shyness. Then graduate school in post-modern Eastern European literature. Then more pussy. Gussy went to... well, no one really knew. Some say she lived on a survivalist commune in Washington. Some say she went to Tibet to missionize the Buddhists.

Wherever Gussy had gone, it agreed with her. The slender, linear algebra of her angular body had changed into the voluptuous calculus of higher mathematics.

But here we were in Chincoteague again, rounding up horses. Twenty years later, it was Gussy's hair that gave her away. Always thick and shiny, she still wore it long, in one thick braid down the middle of her back. It *had* to be her. I was delighted to see she had considerably more wind resistance in the saddle, and in all the right places. Her hips, once so narrow, had blossomed out into wide blue petals. She still wore blue jeans, and I followed her all through the ride and the corralling of the horses. We penned the horses, and threw fat bags of oats into the corral. She still hadn't seen me. The auction was the next day, so we all went into town to drink and shoot pool – two other traditions of the Pony Penning days.

I watched her dismount. She threw her hips over the saddle, her jeans tightening against her thighs and hips. She had that unmistakable, volcanic, vulva mound. The skin knows only attention or isolation. Pleasure or pain is an afterthought of the skin. To have hands on you means someone wants you – you're the Desired One. The imagining and the doing produced the same palpitations. Touch, even rough touch, quenches the skin's inevitable thirst.

There is only one great horror. This is to have no hands on you at all. Gussy's hands – and anything she held in her hands – could never cause me pain. The sweet stinging of her attention... the scalding bonds of a whip... a riding crop with its accumulation of intimacy with her rough hands, her smooth breasts...

Later, when I saw her in the bar, my panties took warm sips from inside me. I leaked anticipation. To catch my breath, I stopped to watch some pool.

"Hey, bull rider!" I heard someone call.

I turned around and Gussy looked at me from the bar. Her red hair, now flecked with grey, spilled out from her familiar straw sweat-stained cowboy hat. Her red mouth and dark eyes smiled at me.

"I'm no bull rider, "I said. "I'm a bitch rider now."

She laughed so hard she almost fell off the bar stool. She spread her legs apart as I went and stood beside her. She kept them open even after I squeezed past her. We hugged each other and I could feel how big her breasts had gotten. I wondered if she thought the same about me.

"My, my, how you've grown, little girl," she said. "Into a mare!"

"Into a stallion," I told her. We laughed.

"Do tell, do tell," she cajoled.

"Do show!" I parried.

We were picking up right where we left off.

"Well, well, you have, indeed, gone to grad school," she observed.

"Fully accredited and fully matriculated," I assured her as we paid the bill and walked out. A motel was right around the corner.

* * *

We started slow. Our bodies had all night to get reacquainted. It was good to know the embers had not gone out. I started to unsnap her cowgirl shirt with the slanted pockets. Her push-up bra barely contained her and she spilled out into my hands. The round, wide eyes of her nipples stared directly at my mouth. I cupped one of her breasts with my hands and leaned forward to take the hard, dark nipple between my teeth. She fit perfectly into my mouth. She let her head fall back. She moaned and ground her hips into mine. We were repeating out last lovemaking, but in other ways we were breaking new ground.

I wanted to break new ground without breaking her. I should not have feared.

Gussy was pleased I was taking charge. "You have had quite an education, must've been Ivy League," she remarked before I dropped my jeans to the ground. I reached into my bag.

"I've got presents," I said. "Something old and something new."

I dangled rope and a pair of small spurs between my fingers. This moment was mine.

She urged me to my knees and her zipper stared at me straight in the eyes. As I unzipped her, her smells wafted out. Pulling off her jeans and her panties in one fell swoop, she stepped out of them and I nuzzled up to her pussy. Even her smells were the same, a sage that has ripened into a deeper smell, a used and experienced scent. She smelled...*rich*, I thought.

She was shaved in a peculiar design. It look me a moment, as I ran my tongue around her pussy and over this design, but it finally came to me. She had shaved her pussy in the design of the Tarot card of The Knight. He rode a horse. It was the symbol of consistency and patience. The Prince and Princess wait for their turns to come. I took this as synchronicity – as a sign that I could buy back my hesitancies of twenty years before.

How many lovers had she had in twenty years? How much leaking, how many fingers there, how many ebbs and flows of blood, of tongues or smooth, domestic objects of uncommon delight? I wanted to taste them all – to suck into me everything that gave her pleasure.

I drew her down onto the bed and knelt over her. I lifted off my lace V-neck straight over my head and drew a map over the geography of her nakedness. My hands were wild ponies wandering across the long shore of her body. They wandered with precise peregrinations across her breasts and down to graze in the pond of her navel. I ate and I chewed her salty, sunlit grasses.

I knelt and sucked at her pussy. It was so wet I had to swallow hard not to have her juices leak all the way down my chin. Her cunt was well used. Her lips were still as wide as ever, but more languid now, more relaxed. They hung down like hollyhocks heavy with rain.

"Make me run faster," I said, handing her the rope.

She kissed me square on the mouth and bit my tongue. "Hey, this ain't no rodeo, damn it!" she shouted, smiling.

"Yes it is!" I insisted, and handed it to her. "And this is the first event!"

Gussy wrapped her wrists around the leather straps and touched the spur to my hips, pressing it all the way to my knees.

"Just my size," I said, taking her hand and pressing the spur up and down the length of my thigh. The points in my skin got deeper. It left sign languages all over, but still not deep enough. "What's the matter, you forgot how to ride? I chided. "You take the reigns in the mouth… and lead with the thighs…"

She pressed harder and the spur made tiny points in my thighs. Then she traced it around the inside of my legs like cuneiform letters pressed into fleshy tablets.[2] It felt like the rush I got from writing a poem for the first time. My body was not an agent of creation, it *was* the creation.

"Write something on me," I begged. A heat blew across my heart and plunged down into my cunt. My cunt, in fact, pumped like a heart.

I wanted Gussy to write the names of the Great Bull and her lusts all over me – every syllable and every sentence. I stretched out and arched my back to give her more space. She played me with the spurs like my whole body was a clitoris, unsheathed and exposed, the regret drained away, like the first sigh in Eden, like the last gasp of orgasm.

In that moment, I had a thought. *Eden was not a location, it was an orgasm.* It came as a flash as we lay there, Gussy licking the red lines the spur had made.

* * *

"And this..." I said later, holding up the end of a rope.

Gussy said, "The rope can bind you or set you free. So, which is it?" she asked, exploring me with her big eyes.

I took the rope, placed it in her hand, and slid the arc of the coil up and down my pussy. It was still so wet it made slushy sounds. With flicks of her wrist, she corralled my clit, stroking the rope-slick skin against it again and again. My whole vulva grew red and engorged. I was ready. The coil of the rope glistened with my readiness.

She caressed my ass with the rope at first, letting my flesh get the feel of the hemp and her rhythm. It stirred embers that had burned alone way too long. The fire licked a path from my anus to my throat.

"Make my flesh sing," I commanded her.

She slapped harder and harder. I urged her on, lost – or should I say "found" – in an ecstasy of discovery. We rode each other bareback that night through dark forests and light meadows. We splashed through streams and sliced through morning winds. We needed no saddle – no veil between us. We rode skin to skin, our bodies tight with the stinging feel of hand and lips and rope. Anything that came from her was welcome into me. My pussy felt enormous – like it could take anything inside it. But this time it didn't scare me. It enlarged me. It educated and articulated me. My cunt would speak and I would listen.

I felt like an ecstatic accommodation of skin – her roan horse. We screamed and cried and whinnied. The night was the ride on a dark horse. Sometimes we rode it. Sometimes it rode us.

Gussy's brow became beaded with sweat. My throat was raw from the sweetest extravagances of pain. She varied the intensity of the strokes like a writer varies the length of sentences. She signed the signature of her soul on mine, in the red welts and the flat of her hand. My cries cleansed memory and regret. My welts and my raised red skin were my lovely stigmata. The confession of my flesh closed the circle of our rough lovemaking twenty years earlier. The memory of lust is never wasted. Lust can always be reclaimed. It never dies.

Near dawn, we turned face to face. She opened her eyes slightly, her pupils still engorged with arousal. She leaned next to me. Her lips brushed my eyebrows. She magnified my cunt with her thumb and forefinger. I was still dilated with desire and anticipation. Shifting to my side, she slipped into me like a letter into a mailbox.

The apricot and almond smell of her was a magic carpet I rode over time. I stopped and stayed at times and places I had not visited for years and years. I floated in and out of time. Time was an elastic cunt. It can accommodate anything the heart desires. As I felt her fingers widen me and fill me up, she whispered, "All pussy, no hat."

1 I didn't know what I was saying or where that expression came from. It was only in graduate school that I learned it was one of the names that the Mesopotamian sex goddess Inanna called her lover, Tammuz. I consider this an illustration of the erotic collective unconscious.

2 The Akkadians and the Sumerians wrote their poems to the Bull Rider and his consort Inanna by pressing their stylus in soft clay.

Janice and Kyle

by
Reena Anne Hovermale

Janice walked into the interview anxiously. She wanted this job. Having just finished her degree, this was the sort of position she dreamed of. Taking a deep breath, and then having it cut off sharply, she smiled. The corset she wore under her lavender silk blouse was her encouragement from her husband, Kyle. He had told her to wear it today to remember that, ultimately, she was his and that nothing else mattered. Nothing.

Getting a boost of confidence thinking about him and the way he had laced her up this morning, a pleasant shiver ran up her spine…

Walking up behind her at the breakfast table, he wrapped a blindfold over her eyes. He pulled the chair out for her, assisted her in getting up, and led her forward a few paces. "Step over this," he instructed.

She stuck her leg out in an exaggerated fashion to avoid the unseen obstacle.

"That's my good girl." A few more paces, and he stopped her gently. "Stand up straight, Janice."

She straightened her spine and held still. The house was a little cold from the air-conditioning because he liked to see her nipples stand out. She could hear him rustling around with something and goose bumps ran up and down her skin anticipating what he might do next. Not knowing what was coming kept her senses keen; kept her wanting more. She loved being owned. Loved being his slave.

It was the secret of their marriage no one knew about. *No one.* No one would understand how she could call herself a feminist yet allow a man to completely possess her.

His body was suddenly closer. Reaching around her, he wrapped her in silky softness. Then he roughly grabbed one of her breasts and squeezed her nipple before adjusting her bosom into what felt like lace. His breath was on her neck and she leaned towards him ever so slightly.

"Stop."

"Yes, Master."

She felt the cloth wrap around her, and then tickly straps beginning to bind her tighter and tighter.

"Suck in your breath."

"A corset?" She wriggled her whole body in delight. "Oh Kyle!" Remembering herself, she dutifully obeyed.

"Almost done…" He finished lacing her up, then came around in front of her. "Now for the icing on my beautiful slave."

She felt him suck in her nipples harshly, one after the other, and then give them small little nips. "Oh!" She leaned into him. "Yes, Master. Oh my God, yes!"

He quit abruptly and she stood there quivering. With a small moan, she moved her head from side-to-side trying to 'see' where he was. Hearing more rustling, she sensed he was behind her and to her left. Suddenly he pulled on one of her nipples and shoved it into a clamp. "Yes!" She sighed. "My nipple torture. How thoughtful, dear." She could feel him screwing the clamp tighter and tighter.

He kissed her mouth. "Does that please my slave?"

"Yes, Master. Immensely."

"Good." He secured a clamp on her other nipple.

She could feel the chain that swung between them, and sighed again. The cool metal soothed the burning heat of her nipples and this duality of sensation felt wonderful.

***

Kyle looked down at his ringing cell phone and saw it was Janice. He held a hand up to his coworker to indicate he had to take the call.

"Hey. How'd the interview go?"

"Great! I think I did really well."

"Good job. I'm proud of you."

"Tell me what a good slave I am, Master."

He chuckled. "You are. You know it."

"What, can't talk right now?"

"That's right."

She giggled. "Oh really? Well then, let me tell you what I'd like to do to you. I'd like to get on my knees and beg for that big, tasty cock. Mm, that's what I'd like to do."

He felt his dick getting hard. "Hey honey, I've got to go, I'm sorry. Good job. I'll take you out to dinner tonight to celebrate."

She laughed wickedly. "Tell me you want it."

"You know I do, hon. Love you, too." He hung up.

His coworker was looking at him with a crooked grin. "The wife wanting you to make kissy face? You could have, you know, I wouldn't have minded."

"Shut up. Anyway, about this merger…"

* * *

Janice clicked her cell phone closed. Damn it but the man made her wet. She had done really well in the interview. Now she just had to wait and see if the next boss up the line approved of her. The second interview was scheduled for tomorrow.

Getting out of the car, she walked into the supermarket. If they were going to celebrate her success, then she was going to make sure they were stocked up.

***

"Say it."

She moaned.

"Say it."

Lying on her back clinging to the bed frame, her arms stretched out behind her, she mouthed breathlessly, "Master!"

"Louder."

He was fucking her so good, the strokes coming harder and faster, brutalizing her just the way she liked it. "Master!" she cried.

Clasping her hips roughly, with the chain hanging between her nipples caught in his teeth, he pulled on it and came inside her in wave after wave of violent spurts.

Wrapping her legs around him, she drew him into her even deeper and kissed the top of his bowed head between her breasts. "Mm! Baby!"

He groaned and let go of her chain as he lay down beside her, breathing hard.

"Hey!"

He smiled.

"You going to finish what you started, big boy?"

"That's not very slave-like."

She giggled. "Maybe not, but you make me so hot!"

He rolled in between her legs and licked her inner lips.

"Yes, Master, just like that..." She couldn't move her arms because they were bound to the bed frame by a smoothly knotted rope. She strained against it, relishing the restraining pressure.

His tongue quit its teasing and concentrated on her clit.

She sucked in her breath and ground her pussy into his face.

Slipping one finger inside her, and then another, he pumped them rhythmically in and out of her.

Arching into him, meeting him stroke for stroke, she moaned loudly, twisting her body within its constraints.

Not letting up on her clitoris, he thrust two more fingers into her pussy, then he slipped his other hand beneath her and slowly slid a thumb into her ass.

"Oh my God!" she gasped, and came hard, her vaginal muscles clamping down on his fingers.

He held still, letting her ride the orgasm. "Better, my little slave?" He kissed the inside of one of her thighs, and she shivered. Removing his fingers from her soaking sex, he brought them up to her mouth. "Lick them clean," he commanded.

She opened her mouth and sucked his strong, thick digits in obediently.

He kissed her brow, and then both her eyelids one by one. "I love you, honey." He began untying her.

"I love you too, Kyle." Rubbing her wrists, she smiled up at him. "Have you ever wondered if we're... I don't know..."

"Fucked up? No, hon. We know what we like and that's all that matters."

She sat up, hugging him close. "I'm just so very glad I have you. I couldn't imagine being in a relationship with someone who didn't understand."

He patted her back and copped a feel around her side, squeezing her breast. "You're a deviant, Janice." He kissed her neck. "Admit it."

"Me? What about you?"

"No, I'm just a pervert, *you're* a deviant."

She gave him a soft punch in the ribs. "Whatever. Do you think I'll get it?"

"Huh?"

"The job, silly."

"Of course you'll get it. Who wouldn't want you around, you luscious slut."

"Kyle!" Laughing, she hopped out of bed. "I have to pee, leave off!" she cried as he chased her into the bathroom, threatening to tickle her. She sat down on the toilet and waved him away. "Stop! *You're* the deviant."

He put on his best scary face and roared, "Come to me, my precious!"

"I can't pee when you're doing that!" She laughed again helplessly.

He walked out of the room, then stuck his head back in abruptly. "I hear a well-fucked slave-slut making water."

Finishing quickly, she flushed and tried to slip past him. "Kyle, stop."

He knelt on the floor and grabbed her by the knees.

"Kyle!"

"Open your legs, slave."

She obeyed.

Licking her black pubic hair, he cleaned her up completely.

It was thrilling, letting him do such a forbidden, dirty thing.

Standing, he turned her around, pushed her back into the bathroom, and shoved her up against the counter.

She was facing the mirror, and she watched him penetrate her fast and hard. Grabbing the edge of the sink, she leaned over as he pounded into her body. "Yes, Master, oh my God, yes!"

He came quickly, his face contorted by pleasure reflected above hers. He was so beautiful. She loved this man with everything she had. Being fucked so soon after her orgasm felt wonderful, and she stood there for a moment looking into the mirror at his tousled blonde hair, perspiration glistening on his body as he rested his weight gently against her back. Then the sink suddenly felt cold against her skin, so she contracted and relaxed the muscles of her sex in a way that pushed his soft cock out of her.

He groaned and smacked her ass.

She walked out of the bathroom talking over her shoulder. "That's what you get for being such a perv." She sat down on the edge of the bed.

He sat down beside her. "I'm sorry, Janice, I just... well, I just always wondered. I didn't know it would be so good."

She didn't say anything. She knew they were pushing envelopes in their relationship, but this was really strange. After the initial thrill, she wasn't sure now she felt comfortable with it. She turned her back to him. "Unlace me, please. It's starting to get a little uncomfortable. I'm not used to it yet."

He turned her back around to face him. "It might help if I take these off first." He carefully removed one of her nipple clamps.

The blood rushed back to the offended area and stung her mightily. His sucking mouth was warm, gentle and soothing. She sighed into him.

He repeated the process with her other nipple.

"Mm, that feels so good." She sighed again.

"It does to me too, Janice. You taste so sweet. There's not a sweeter woman anywhere."

She leaned forward and nuzzled his neck. "You're a sweetheart. Now get me out of this damned thing." She bit his neck playfully. "I haven't taken a deep breath all day."

He turned her around and began unlacing the complicated series of ribbons and clasps. "Good thing I practiced with this fool thing."

"You practiced?"

"Yeah. I saw all these bells and whistles and I knew I'd have to have a dry-run."

"Oh my God that's funny. And sweet. How'd you do it?"

"I just put it on a chair and laced it up a couple of times."

She turned around and gave him a deep, lingering kiss. "I love you more and more every day. Do you know that?"

He turned her around again; she was still only about a quarter of the way unlaced.

"That feels so good…" Taking another deep breath, she relished the inhale, feeling heady. "Ah!" He popped the corset from around her and even more blood rushed to her nipples. She hadn't realized how constricting the holes in front had been. "Kiss them, Kyle. They need your talented tongue."

He licked his fingers and gently rubbed one nipple, then the other.

"Thank you, but now we'd better get some sleep." She grabbed him and lay back on the bed, pulling him with her.

Sucking her nipple the whole way down, he gave it one last hearty lick and spread himself beside her. "You're a great fucking lay, baby."

"I know it." She turned on her side to face him. Kissing his lips softly, she pulled back and looked into his eyes. "I can't do without you, you know that? You're my everything."

"Janice, the world didn't exist until I saw you."

Kissing him again contentedly, she turned over onto her back again. "We'd really better get to sleep, pervert. I've got that second interview tomorrow."

"Don't worry, you'll knock 'em dead."

"If I don't get some sleep soon, I'm going to *feel* dead."

* * *

She woke up to the smell of coffee and cinnamon buns. Following the scent down the stairs and around the corner, she tried to sneak up on him, but he had heard her coming. He turned around abruptly and grabbed her, hugging her tight for a moment before planting a sloppy kiss on her mouth. He always knew when she was trying to surprise him, damn him.

She sat at the small table awaiting her breakfast. He always made her breakfast after one of their 'sessions'. It was a tradition for them, and she enjoyed the ritual.

He served the food and sat down across from her.

"As always, Kyle, you are the best cook in this house."

He smiled with his eyes as he chewed. Swallowing, he took a sip of coffee and said, "No, you're the best cook, Janice. I just play at it."

"Kyle…"

"Before you say it, *yes.*"

"You don't even know what I was about to say."

"Yes I do. You'll do well at your interview today. You're intelligent, witty, sexy and the best person for the position. I'd hire you based on your tits alone."

She laughed. "Shut up, you old pervert."

* * *

On her way to the interview, she stopped at a light and called him on her cell phone. "Thanks for last night, sexy man."

"My pleasure entirely. And by the way, when you get there, look under the passenger seat." With that, he hung up.

That devil! She ached to take a peak, but he had told her not to until she got there. She stopped at another light as it turned yellow. "He'll never know…" She leaned over and pulled out a paddle with a note attached.

I know you, and I knew you wouldn't be able to resist.
Looking forward to tonight to punish you for looking before you got there.
Love, Kyle

That bastard! The light turned green and she quickly slipped the paddle back under the seat. Smiling the rest of the way, she decided that, no matter what happened at the interview, today was going to be a really, really good day.

✱ ✱ ✱

The interrogation was exquisite. He tied her from shoulders to toes in smooth, silky rope, leaving her buttocks, pussy, and breasts completely exposed. He made her stand motionless in their bedroom as he wrapped the rope around her ankles and then up her leg, encasing her. When he was finished, he picked her up and laid her down on the bed face-up and began asking her questions.

"When did you find the paddle?"

"When I got there, just like you said," she lied.

"Why don't I believe you?" He stood up and leaned over her face, prodding her mouth with his dick. "Suck me and see if you can convince me that what you're saying is true."

Obediently sucking him, she twisted and turned to meet his thrusts.

He squeezed her breasts roughly, fucking her mouth thoroughly, not pausing for a moment. It wasn't long before his cum was shooting down her throat.

She sucked him down and sucked some more, until he pushed

back on her forehead gently, slipping his pulsing dick out from between her lips.

"I don't know," he said a little breathlessly. "Most Masters would be convinced, but I know my slave. I know how professional a performance she can give." He twisted one of her nipples. "Tell me. When did you find the paddle?"

She moaned. "When I got there!"

He lifted her up and draped her over his knee where she lay quietly, waiting.

Grabbing her ass cheeks with both hands, he squeezed them until it hurt. "What am I to do with my little liar?"

She whimpered.

"Tell me, slave. What should I do with you?"

She whispered beneath her breath, "Punish me…"

"What was that?"

She was silent.

"I said, what was that?" He thrust a finger as far into her pussy as it would go and began caressing her G-spot, rubbing firmly. "Answer me, slave."

Still very softly, but a little louder, she repeated, "Punish me."

"That's what I thought you said." Picking up the paddle that rested on the bed beside him, he stroked her ass with it gently.

Groaning with anticipation, she held absolutely still.

He swatted her cheeks three times, scarcely pausing between blows. Then he rubbed the sting away expertly with his other hand, transforming the pain into a hot pleasure.

"Oh yes, Master. More, please, Master."

He whacked her ass more forcefully, then tapped it several times in a quick succession. Rubbing her with his hand again, he inserted two fingers into her juicing pussy and finger-fucked her until, inevitably, she climaxed.

He helped her stand up and began untying her. Kissing her face, he started at the top and moved towards her legs.

She was trembling beneath his touch, and when her arms came free she grabbed him to steady herself. "Oh Kyle, that was wonderful. You're the best."

"Well, it helps to have such a prime little submissive. So, when do they call and let you know one way or another?"

"This coming Monday. I wish they wouldn't keep me hanging like that."

"Welcome to the wonderful world of corporate bureaucracy."

"Honey? Remember last night when you, um…"

"When I cleaned you up?"

"Yes." She furrowed her brow. "That… well, it wasn't all that comfortable for me. I mean, if it turns you on, then maybe I can try again, but seriously, it kind of, well…"

"Hey, I just wanted to try it, that's all. If it's something you don't like, then *I* don't like it."

She looked at him dubiously.

"No really, Janice. My job is to make everything enjoyable for you, and if it's going too far, then it's too far for me, too, believe me."

She reached up and kissed him. "I'm sorry."

"No need to be sorry. It's just something I wanted to try. Now I know how you feel."

"Thanks for understanding."

"Thanks for letting me try." He pressed her tightly against him.

She nuzzled her face into the side of his neck. "I *am* sorry. Considering everything you do for me, if you really want it, then maybe I can work past this."

"Nope. Not necessary. I just read an article about it, and I was curious." He let go of her and spread himself facedown across the bed.

"Kyle, I can tell you want it."

"Janice, I really don't. Honestly." He turned his head and smiled up at her. "I was just hoping you'd feel guilty enough to rub my back." He wiggled his tight ass up at her invitingly.

Laughing, she sat down on the edge of the bed to massage him, and soon his even breathing told her he had fallen asleep.

* * *

In her dreams someone was speaking to her about where to find something she really wanted when their voice suddenly turned into a loud, steady sound… a phone ringing. She fumbled for the receiver. "Hello?"

"Hi Janice, it's your mom."

"Mom? What time is it?'

"Oh, did I wake you, dear? I'm sorry."

Squinting at the alarm clock, she read 5:00 and winced. "What's wrong, mom?"

"Nothing, dear, I just wanted to see how you were doing."

Putting her hand on Kyle's chest as he sat up sleepily, she pushed him gently back down onto the pillows mouthing, "It's my mom."

He turned over onto his side.

"Mom, it's five o'clock in the morning here."

"Is it? I didn't realize. I've been up for a while now and just wanted to talk to you for a bit."

Grinding her teeth in silent frustration, Janice got out of bed so as not to disturb Kyle. She walked into the living room and sat down on a recliner. "Okay, I'm awake now. Tell me what's wrong."

Her mother told her how one of her friends had hurt her feelings and now she didn't know if she'd ever be able to talk to her again.

Janice's father had died five years ago, and after mourning him for about a year, her mother had suddenly turned into a social butterfly. Janice was relieved to see her emerging from her shell and venturing into the world more and more but, unfortunately, that meant she had to listen to all the slights her mother suffered. She felt like a counselor more than a daughter. She shrugged off her impatience. Her mother needed her, and she made sure she was there for her.

"Mom, this is the third time Myra has done this to you. I say drop her like a hot potato and don't look back."

"No, I just needed to vent a little, that's all."

"Well it's your decision, but if I were you, that's what I'd do. No one needs that kind of crap in their life."

Finally getting off the phone, she looked at the antique clock Kyle had bought her at an auction several years ago. It was 6:00. She might as well stay up now. She went to the kitchen and started making pancakes. She loved cooking; it was one of her passions. Stirring and pouring the batter into the hot skillet, she watched as bubbles began appearing in the middle of the circle.

She more felt than heard Kyle sit down at the table and flipped the pancake over. He was as silent as a cat.

"How's your mom?" he asked.

"Fine." It always depressed her to talk to her mother.

"Same old shit?"

"Yeah." In between the chatter about her friends, her mother had inserted carefully placed barbs directed at her daughter.

"What did the passive-aggressive old hag say this time?"

"Nothing." She flipped the pancake out onto a plate and brought it to him.

He got up and walked to the refrigerator for some syrup.

"Oh, I'll warm that up for you." She had completely forgotten about the syrup.

"No, I like it cold sometimes." He sat down again and slathered his pancake with it while she poured more batter into the skillet.

"Damn but you make good pancakes." Getting up again, he went and got some milk from the refrigerator.

"Oh, honey, I'm sorry." The milk too? She *was* tired.

He poured himself a glass, and then another one for her. Getting up yet again to hand it to her, he leaned up against the counter and stared at her.

"What?" she asked.

"Out with it, Janice."

She sighed. "She said that by the time she was my age she had three kids already. She asked me if I'd seen a fertility doctor."

"That's none of her business."

She shrugged, put down the glass untouched, and concentrated on not burning the pancakes. They had decided a long time ago not to have children. They liked their life the way it was and didn't feel the need to procreate. It still bothered her, however, that her mother could get to her like that.

He went back to the table, but waited for her to join him before he kept eating.

She sat down and they enjoyed their breakfast in silence.

When she was finished, he took their plates and put them in the dishwasher.

She was thinking about how her mother always managed to catch her off her guard and slip her a good verbal punch. When she got her degree, her mother had responded by saying, "It's about time, dear, your sister had one years ago. Now, if you had children, I wouldn't have said a word." For one sweet evil moment she thought about changing her phone number. She loved her mother, she just didn't know if she could ever *like* her.

"Still thinking about your mom? I have just the ticket." He pulled her chair out with her still in it, grabbed her hand, and led her into the bathroom. "Stay here." He made her sit on the lid of the toilet as he turned on the shower. "Nothing better than to wash that sort of shit right off you. I'm going to give you a shower you'll not soon forget."

She smiled up at him.

"There it is, my smile. Come on, hop in here." He got into the tub and held the curtain open for her.

Her smile deepened as she joined him.

Grabbing the soap, he lathered it up into big bubbles, making a dramatic to-do about it.

Standing in the flow of water she watched him, loving how the droplets played over his hairy chest. She loved his hair. Bending over slightly, she sucked in a little mouthful of it and licked his skin.

"Now, now, none of that,' he scolded. "If I let you get started, I'll never get the filth off of you." Rubbing her tits with his hands full of bubbles, he washed her thoroughly.

"Kyle, I think my breasts are clean now. I do have other body parts you know."

"I know, I'm getting there, you impudent little bitch." He turned her around and kissed the back of her neck, making her feel wet from more than just the shower.

Pushing her ass into his crotch, she wiggled it against his hard cock. She reached a hand down between her legs, grabbed his erection, and guided it up into her pussy. He slipped inside her, and she braced herself on the slick tiles in front of her.

"You're a dirty little whore, Janice," he said, fucked her with vicious energy for so early in the morning, bracing himself by cruelly clutching her breasts. "I'm going to wash that pussy inside out!"

"Yeah, baby." She loved it when he talked dirty to her.

"Tell me, slave."

She knew what he wanted to hear and purposefully didn't say it, enjoying how wet and hot and hard everything was around her and inside her.

"Tell me, *slave*."

In the sweetest tone she could muster, she asked, "Tell you what?"

He let go of one of her tits and smacked her ass. "Tell me *now*."

"Fuck me, Master!" She relented breathlessly. "Fuck me just… like… that…"

He pulled out of her.

"Hey!" She turned around. "I thought I was supposed to be getting a good cleaning."

"You did, you nasty little whore."

She bent over and found the soap. She lathered it up and gripped his cock, making him suck in his breath.

He pushed her away from him, turned her around again, and spanked her. "Little slave, I think you're pushing it. Maybe I need to go get that paddle again."

"Better watch it, Kyle. I just may take you up on that."

"Devil cat."

Smiling, she reached for the shampoo and began washing her mother's negative vibes right out of her hair.

* * *

After kissing Kyle and seeing him off to work, she did the dishes and tidied up the house a little.

Seated on their big comfy couch, she finished the last chapter of a book by an author she was beginning to love. When she turned the page and realized there was no more, she felt deflated; it had been such a lovely book. The characters had come alive in her mind and she had been taken away on a verbal journey full of conquest and suspense.

"Damn it." She closed the novel and looked around her.

She was going to miss being home all the time. These past few weeks had been wonderful just sitting around and cleaning and reading and cooking. No classes, no term papers, no deadlines.

She scowled realizing that getting a job meant she was going to have all those headaches again, just in a different form.

She got up, put the book away, and looked for something to do. Oh yeah, that's why she wanted to go to work. Well, that and the paycheck.

Walking into the bedroom, she made the bed. Eyeing her little bag of toys beneath it, she thought, why *not*?

Releasing the slipknot on the cloth bag, she upended it, dumping all of its contents onto the bed. "Okay, so it looks like you, Jean-Paul." She had nicknamed the eight-inch-long red dildo after a favorite musician she'd had a crush on in her youth. In her naiveté, she had imagined all men had red dicks because she'd heard her friends call a dick a "red rocket". It had made sense to her then, because she knew the blood rushed down 'there'. When she saw the dildo in an adult book store one night with Kyle, she immediately grabbed it.

No longer fantasizing about Jean-Paul, she imagined Kyle at home with her now. Taking off her clothes, she sat on the bed and leaned back against the headboard. Spreading her legs, she took the dildo and wrapped her warm vaginal lips around the cool head. She shoved it partway inside her with small, quick strokes.

The phone rang.

Slipping the dildo out of her, she reached for the receiver feeling guilty. "Hello?"

"Hi babe, it's me. I'm at lunch."

"Hi. I'm so glad you called. I was just thinking about you."

"What are you doing, Janice?"

"Um, nothing. Why do you ask?"

"Because I can hear that horny blood flowing."

"Well, actually, I was just getting ready to fuck myself with Jean-Paul." She knew she was teasing him and relished her power.

"That's nice. I'm glad you're making good use of your time."

"Did somebody walk up?"

"Yes. Listen, I'll call you back in a few minutes."

"Okay. Get somewhere where you can stroke that thick cock while I fuck myself."

"Absolutely. Give me about five minutes and I'll get back to you on that."

She laughed and hung up. He was so corporate.

Leaning back against the headboard, she penetrated herself with Jean-Paul, this time managing to push it all the way up inside her. She was excited that Kyle had called her just when he had. Then she waited, tormenting herself with the lifeless dildo's thick, motionless presence. Thankfully, it wasn't long before the phone rang again.

Squeezing her thighs together, she answered, "I'm here, Master, fucking myself thinking about you."

"Mm. Tell me all about it."

"Okay." She balanced the phone on her shoulder and grabbed the plastic cock with both hands. "Do you have your dick out, Master?"

"Let's just say the pump is primed and ready."

"Good. Are you in the car?"

"Yes. In the parking garage. Now, tell me, where are you?"

"I'm on our bed, completely naked, laying on top of the covers."

"Mm. Wish I were there with you."

"Me, too. I wish your mouth was on my pussy right now while I fucked myself with this big dick. I could use your mouth on my clit." She penetrated herself for a few slow strokes. "Oh… that felt good… this dick is really getting me off. You know what I'd like to do?" She began fucking herself more quickly. "I'd like to have you in my pussy and then shove this big fat dick inside me, too."

"Really? Wow. Tell me about it."

"Yeah. I want to try that. I want to have two dicks in my cunt all at once."

"God damn it, you're driving me crazy, Janice."

"Oh, Master…" She gripped the base of the dildo with both hands, shoving its full length deep inside her over and over again, rubbing it against her clit on the way in and out. She went silent as she started coming.

"Janice? You still there?"

"I'm here, babe. I'm… oh yeah…" She moaned into the phone, completely forgetting herself for a few moments.

"That's it babe, come for me."

"I did." She quickly pulled the dildo out of her and lay comfortably back against the pillows. "Oh Kyle, you have the sexiest voice."

"You're not finished yet, slave. I want you to go get your nipple clamps and put them on. Now."

"They're here in front of me."

"Good, now put them on, and no cheating, slave. Make them good and tight."

Still balancing the phone between her head and shoulder, she did precisely what he said.

"Are they on?"

"Yes, Master."

"Good girl. Now I want you to get that little vibrator that can fit inside your pussy and be turned on by a little remote control."

"Yes, Master." She fished it out of the pile, checked the batteries, and slipped it inside her. "It's in, Master."

"Turn it on. Mm… I can hear it."

Her pussy was still pulsing with aftershocks of pleasure from her orgasm, and now it clenched expectantly around the new pacifying plastic penis. The feeling was one of pure torturous satisfaction. "Oh yes…"

"I want you to talk dirty to me, slave. Talk dirty and get me off. I've got my cock out in my hand and I'm stroking it thinking about you."

"Close your eyes, Master. I'm there on the seat next to you, watching your big dick getting stroked by your strong hand. You're making me so hot, Master. I'm fingering myself thinking of that big cock inside me. Oh, I want it so bad! My clit's getting all hard and demanding so I touch her. I'm rubbing her with my fingertips hard and fast, in little up and down motions while I stare at the head of your dick playing peek-a-boo with your palm. It's getting me all hot thinking about that head inside my mouth and inside my pussy. I want to put your big hard-on in my mouth and wrap my tongue around it. I want to shove it into my mouth over and over letting you feel the deep warmth and the sucking moisture."

He groaned into the phone.

"That's right, Master. I'm sucking you so good, making you feel my lips catch under your head as I pull away before I shove you deep down into my throat again, sucking and fucking your big beautiful dick." The little vibrator was making her cunt tighten with the onset of another climax. "You've got me all wet, Master. My pussy aches for your cock but my mouth is too greedy, it has to taste you, it has to feed off your cum."

He gave a low growl.

"That's right, Master, come all down my throat."

"Fuck me... you're a pro, Janice..."

Her pussy hadn't let up and she hissed softly as she sensed him ejaculating on the other end of the line.

"Good, it's beginning to work," he said a little breathlessly. "I want you to leave that in all day, slave. If the battery runs out, replace it, then put it back in immediately."

"But I have to go to the store, Master..."

"Then you'll wear it there as well."

"But everybody will know!"

"Slave, are you questioning me?"

"No, Master..."

"Then do as I say. In fact, I want you to go to the store right after we get off the phone. I'll be calling you in about twenty minutes, and I'd better hear people in the background."

"Yes, Master."

"Good. Now I've gotta go for the moment, but I'll be calling you back shortly."

"Is there anything I can pick up for you?"

"Yes, get some lubricant. I plan on using a lot of it tonight and I don't want to run out."

"Yes, Master."

"Good girl. Now get going."

***

Walking into the store, the little vibrator churning away sounded so loud in her ears she was sure everyone could hear it. She walked quickly, passing people in an embarrassed rush.

Her phone rang when she was in the Produce department.

"Hello, my little slave."

"Hi…" She couldn't call him Master in public.

"Good girl. I can hear people in the background. Where are you in the store?"

"Produce."

"I want you to go get me some chili."

"But that's at the other end of the store," she protested.

"Exactly. Now go get it. I'm going to listen to you while I work."

She quickly headed towards isle with the chili.

"Slave?"

"Yes?"

"Slow down. I can tell you're walking fast."

She cringed inwardly, but slowed her pace.

"No one can hear it, slave. There's too much background noise. Relax."

She heard someone walk into Kyle's office and begin talking to him. He answered them, and then she heard the door close again.

"Slave, do you have the chili?"

"Yes."

"Okay, now go get some crackers."

The crackers were in the next aisle over from the Produce. She made her way back through the store. "Okay, I'm… oh!" She suddenly started coming. Grabbing the shopping cart, she looked wildly around her to see if anyone was watching her. She moaned softly, completely helpless as her body took over.

"I can hear my sexy little slave juicing up for me."

"Oh my God, Kyle," she whispered breathlessly into the phone. "Oh my God…"

"That's right, pet. Come for me."

Someone walked into the aisle and she stood up straight, pretending to be intensely interested in the cans in front of her even as she climaxed silently and intensely. Oblivious, the person turned the corner.

"Don't forget the lubricant I require, slave."

"Okay..." Recovering herself, she heard him typing in the background. "Kyle?"

"Yes, slave?"

"I don't know how much more I can take of this."

"Good. We're testing your limits today. Do you have my lubricant yet?"

"Not yet."

"Go get it then check out. And I want your bag carried out by the bagboy, slave."

"You're evil!"

"No, I'm your Master. Now do as I say or suffer the consequences."

"Fine!"

"Are you prepared for tonight, slave?"

"Tonight?"

"Yes. We're going to explore exactly what your limits are."

"We are?"

"Yes, we most definitely are. Are you in checkout yet?"

"Almost."

"Good. I can torture you a little longer."

"Kyle, I know that... *you* know."

"You're fine Janice. Listen. Do you hear the sounds of people talking? The sound of the scanner reading barcodes?"

"Yes."

"Those are much louder than your little vibrator, so relax."

She took a deep breath. He was right.

"When are you going to learn to trust me, slave?"

"I do trust you."

"No, I mean completely. I'd never put you in a situation where you could be exposed or humiliated. Never."

She knew he wouldn't, she was just nervous. This was Kyle, her love and her husband for the last fifteen years. He would never harm her, not without her consent. "I know that, Master."

"But since you've been such a good girl for me, Janice, you can take the vibrator out when you get home."

"Yes, Master. Thank you, Master."

* * *

When she got home, the first thing she did was slip the vibrator out of her deliciously tortured sex, then she took off her shirt and very gingerly removed the nipple clamps. It hurt like hell; she had left them on way too long. She touched her nipples tentatively. They were intensely sore.

As she put away the groceries, then washed the vibrator, she tried to imagine what her Master had planned for her tonight. If it had anything to do with her breasts, he was out of luck. She got a small washcloth and ran it under some cold water. Squeezing the water out, she used it as a small compress to sooth her aching nipples. "Poor babies," she murmured.

Heading upstairs, she decided to take a nap. The strain of going out in public so completely exposed had worn her out.

"Shit." All their toys were still lying on the bed. Taking off the rest of her clothes, she pushed them to one side and settled down for a nice catnap.

She woke to the unmistakable sensation of her lover penetrating her.

"There you are," he breathed in her ear. "You were looking so beautiful lying here, I just couldn't resist."

She slapped his hand away when he made to caress her breast. "No, baby, way too painful."

"Are you okay?"

"I will be." She arched into him.

He smiled. "Always able to scrape up a good fuck for me, huh? That's my perfect slave."

Making love to her gently, but never letting up, he brought her to a gentle climax and then changed his angle and began beating himself quickly against her. "You're such a wet… slutty… slave…" he accused her in rhythm with his thrusts. "I'm so proud of you for going to the store like that today. I had a hard-on all day thinking about it. Fuck you're gorgeous!"

Afterwards, they held each other tenderly.

"Master, do you think your plans can wait until tomorrow? My nipples are really sore."

He lifted her chin with his finger and gave her a soft kiss. "Absolutely. Is there anything I can get you to feel better?"

"Some ice would be nice."

He got up to get her some while she went into the bathroom and turned the faucet on in the tub. Making the water a little cooler than she normally liked it, she slowly sat down in the growing pool.

"My poor baby." He brought her ice wrapped in a dishcloth, and she placed it gratefully over her nipples. "Listen, Janice, I'm sorry. I completely forgot to tell you to take off the nipple clamps."

"It's not your fault, Kyle. I forgot, too. Everything was just feeling so good."

"Well, we'll not use those for a while. We need to get you a pair that are little more gentle."

"Yeah." She smiled up at him. "I'm fine. Really."

"I'll go get you a drink. I'll also make dinner tonight."

"Thank you, Master." She relaxed into the tub and closed her eyes, smiling.

* * *

Eventually, the smells wafting up from the kitchen roused her from her daydreams and made her realize she was starving. She toweled herself dry, slipped into her robe, and padded barefoot down the steps into the kitchen, where she stood in the doorway watching Kyle at work. He looked incredibly handsome to her walking here and there, spicing this pot and stirring another. "What are you making?" she asked eagerly.

"Want a taste?"

She went over and savored a mouthful from the spoon he offered her. "Oh, that's *good*. What is it?"

"It's a chili-dip with vegetables. Get the chips, it's time to eat."

They sat facing each other enjoying the meal and the company in silence.

"This is nice Kyle," she spoke finally.

"It's just a little recipe I saw in a men's magazine that was supposed to be quick, and it was."

"I wasn't speaking of the meal, although it's nice, too. I was talking about how nice it is to be around you."

He put his spoon down and grasped her hand. "I think so, too. I love you so much, Janice."

"I love you more."

"Not possible. Are you feeling better?"

"I am. I'm still a little tender, but I'm almost like brand new."

"So you still want to hold off on my plans?"

She laughed. "You are the horniest man on the planet, Kyle. As long as it doesn't involve nipple torture, I'm game."

"I'm glad to hear that." He stood.

"Where are you going?"

"You'll see." He returned carrying a bag from which he extracted a black metal bar with cuffs on either end. He placed it on the table. "It's a leg spreader bar," he explained.

"*A what?*"

"A leg spreader bar. Here, I'll show you." He picked it up, grabbed her hand, and led her to the couch in the living room. He made her sit down, then snapped the cuffs around both her ankles, adjusting the bar so that she was slowly cranked more and more open.

"You think you can keep me open for business even when it should be closed, huh?" she teased.

"You're always open for business, whore."

"Oh yeah? Tell me what a naughty girl I am."

He shook the bar, testing its strength. "You're in my clutches, slave." Grabbing her arms, he lifted her up and set her down about a foot away from the couch.

She had to seriously use her leg muscles to maintain her balance, and the strain felt good.

"Who are you?" he demanded harshly, reaching into the bag again.

"I'm your slave, Master."

"That's right. And who do you belong to?"

"To you, Master."

"That's right, slave. You were such a good girl today going to that supermarket with your pussy all juicy." He tapped the riding crop against his palm. "Problem is, slave, you questioned my judgment. You didn't trust me." He walked behind her and swatted her ass with the crop.

"No, Master. I mean-"

"I don't care what you mean, slave. I told you to do something and you tried to bend the rules by running through the store."

"I didn't *run*."

He smacked the back of her thighs with the hard leather, stinging her. "Don't interrupt me. You know you tried to bend every command I gave you. Then you had the audacity to question whether or not I had your best interest in mind." He whacked her ass cheeks a few times as her legs quivered to absorb the shock and maintain her balance. Then with his mouth right up against her ear, he said very softly, "I would never expose you, Janice. Never." He smacked her ass with his open palm this time, and it burned wonderfully.

"I'm sorry, Master. Please forgive me."

"Forgive you, when over and over again you question my commands?" He walked in front of her and looked sternly into her eyes. "Why should I forgive you? You'll only disappoint me again."

"I'll do anything, Master, anything! Just *please* forgive me. I know you wouldn't do something that cruel. What can I do to make it up to you?"

He cocked his head to one side, considering. "Hmm. Well, let me see. There is *one* thing that you could do to make it up to me, but no, you'll just bitch and moan. Never mind."

"No, tell me, please, Master. I'll do it."

"You're sure?"

"Anything!"

"Don't move and don't speak." He walked out of the room and left her there to balance on her own.

She stood there for what seemed like hours, perspiring from the strain. He had cranked her into a position that was a little too wide for standing comfortably and her muscles were already aching. "Kyle?"

The minute she called out he stepped into the room. "I'm here. I knew you'd bitch and moan. Look at you. You said you'd do anything, and now you're having trouble following a simple command." He strode up to her and smacked the side of her leg, making her knee buckle. He grabbed her arm and helped her stay upright.

"I'm sorry, Master."

Kneeling, he unlocked the mechanism and helped her sit down. The cuffs still on her, the bar bent, he pointed to the lock.

"If you're ever truly worried, this catch here will release you. I expect you never to use it except under extraordinary circumstances. Understand?"

She rubbed her legs. "Yes, Master."

"Good." He cranked the bar back into position. She was sitting on the couch with her legs forced wide open in front of him. He walked away, and returned a moment later with some things. Bending over her, he put a blindfold on her, tying it firmly. "Can you see?"

"No, Master."

"Good."

She heard his footsteps padding on the carpet, then some sounds she couldn't quite identify. What was he doing? What was he going to do? The mystery thrilled her.

He gripped the bar between her ankles and pulled on it until her ass was hanging off the couch. Lifting the bar, and her ankles with it, he positioned her with her legs in the air.

She felt cold lubricant on her labia and jumped from the shock of it.

"Hold still, slave. Remember, you said you'd do anything."

"Yes, Master."

He lubricated her pussy with two fingers, then she felt an impossibly thick pressure at her opening. Whatever he was forcing inside her was part warm and part cold and so huge his fingers kept slathering more and more lubricant around her lips to help accommodate it.

"Oh... oh yes, Master...." Whatever it was, it was in her at last, and it felt so incredibly good she almost couldn't bear it. It must be him, or at least attached to him, because she could feel him between her legs, his balls slapping her asshole as he fucked her. The sensation was unbelievably intense. It was almost painful, but so good, too, her clit rubbing right up against his pubic bone she was stretched so wide open. She could feel him lifting the bar between her legs until it hit the couch behind her, contorting her body with it.

"Oh my God, Master!" He was pounding himself to the very bottom of her cunt and rubbing her clitoris in the process in a way that made her suffer tiny little climaxes beneath his driving strokes. She felt inundated by him, completely filled and fulfilled by his powerful strokes. When he started coming, pulsing and swelling inside her, his erection forcing her straining hole even more wide open around his thrusts, the pleasure was so intolerable she nearly screamed as an orgasm ripped through her.

He slipped out of her hot cunt and it suddenly felt devastatingly empty. He gently pulled her legs back down, and she heard the mechanism unlock. He uncuffed her ankles so she was free of the spreader bar, and leaning over her brushed her body with his. When he removed the blindfold, she had to blink wildly as her eyes adjusted to the light. She saw him standing before her holding the blindfold, smiling down at her. Moving her gaze down to his crotch, she saw what he had been using on her.

"Oh Kyle, you used a strap-on, and with Jean-Paul!" She grabbed both his cock and the dildo. "You sneaky bastard! Thank you!"

He unbuckled the harness and dropped the dildo down on the couch. "You deserved a reward, Janice." He sat down beside her and put an arm around her. "You've been such an obedient slave." He kissed her long and deep. "But most of all, you're the best wife a man could ever dream of."

"Thank you, Kyle. I love you so much." She hugged him hard against her, not caring that her nipples still hurt like hell.

A Night Without A Moon

by
N.T. Morley

She's got nothing on under the tiny, almost see-through dress – nothing at all.

She knows that fact is obvious to anyone who sees her – but she thinks, or hopes, no one can see her. And if it wasn't for the light-sensitive camera, she'd be right – because she's walking down an alley without storefronts, without streetlights, six hours after dark, on a night without a moon.

But I can see her. I can see the way the skintight material exposes her nipples, hard with the cold and doubtless with fright. I can see the way she tugs down the hem of the dress, trying to keep it from creeping higher up her thighs and exposing her shaved sex.

I can see the way she quivers in the darkness as she sways her way down the alley, tottering on heels so much higher than she's ever worn before. Her eyes are wide, her breath comes short. She makes her way down the alley toward a dead end strewn with garbage.

"Go," I tell them. Two men leave their chairs and head for the alley.

* * *

Autumn has to know what's coming – *has to*. It's haunted her dreams, her nightmares, for years. It's a fear and a longing that troubles the thoughts of all women like her. Women with her desires, with her fears, spend their lives with this event in the backs of their heads, in a mélange of raw hunger mixed with dread mixed with knowledge.

The thought that she is somehow wrong, somehow guilty for *wanting* this – those thoughts are furthest from her mind, because Autumn knows, now, that this is the night, a night without mercy, and her fears and anxieties are focused not on the tainted nature of her soul but on the imminent corruption of her body.

Perhaps she knew this was the night as much as thirteen hours ago, when she first unwrapped the black ribbon around the black gift box and took out the absurdly skimpy dress – the kind of dress a girl wears when she's "asking for it."

Maybe as she enacted the lengthy ritual to prepare herself for this moment, to conjure up her darkest hungers, she began to understood that it was to occur tonight, without possibility of escape, and that she would walk into it with her eyes open and her pussy wet.

Maybe she understood what was to happen to her – not sometime, in the distant future or in a secretly-scrawled journal tucked between mattress and box spring, but *tonight* – when she read the directions pinned to the driver's side window of her sports car, directions that guided her from her uptown apartment to the warehouse district.

Perhaps she figured it out as she drove past streets choked with drug dealers and streetwalkers, into a deserted region between the slums and the long-dead ports. Or maybe it dawned on her when she arrived at the dark alley, parked her Lexus in the appointed spot, locked it, and dropped her only set of car keys down the sewer grate.

Then again, maybe even now, as she walks down the alley, she doesn't know what is going to happen to her.

But when the door bursts open between her and the street, when she sees the two big men coming for her out of the dark, when she feels them grab her arms and drag her toward the door – then she knows, in a rush, that her ravishment is moments, not hours or months or years, in the future.

And that's when she opens her mouth to scream.

Even then, there may be doubt in her mind. She might think, *This is all a game, right? He could never really do this to me. He loves me, I know it.*

But then she knows the answer to that question when the woman in question is a woman like her.

Even if there was anyone to hear her in that garbage-strewn alley, they wouldn't, for the heavy steel door slams shut behind her, and she is drawn into darkness.

By then, there is no doubt: she knows. Autumn knows she is about to be taken, and no power she possesses can prevent her absolute and ultimate submission.

It's all a test, you see. One last, critical test, held in the darkness of a night without a moon.

* * *

It's no small matter, this sort of thing; it takes months of planning. It takes a certain kind of naiveté, like the creation of any work of art – a belief in the supernatural, the magic of happenstance. The ecstasy of surrender, even – or especially – when that surrender is reluctant.

Autumn has been carefully prepared. She was given the dress just this afternoon, moments before I undressed her and put her to bed, lulling her off her regular schedule with a sleeping pill. *What is it?* she asked, and I just looked at her, not even smiling.

She swallowed.

Lulled by the pill, Autumn slept from three-o'clock until midnight: I wanted her both well rested and disoriented, her circadian rhythms all but obliterated for the night.

I woke her with a phone call, her sleepy "Hello?" eliciting only a hang up. She found the first note on the bathroom counter when she went in to brush her teeth. I know (or surmise) that she followed the instructions to the letter; she showered, shaved herself – legs, armpits and pussy.

She then went downstairs to find a DVD in the player and a box marked with a big red "1." She did not open the box yet. She also did not eject the DVD, did not look at the title; I'd hidden the box so she would not know what to expect until she saw the action on the screen.

I know (or suspect) that her first sight of the images on the screen made her pussy wet, her clit hard, her nipples firm and aching.

As instructed in the note, she brought herself to the edge of orgasm, never taking her eyes off the screen, never turning away from the sight of the bound and nude woman being tormented, teased, pleasured, punished, and invaded – with paddles, whips, canes, clamps, vibrators, and dildos. These are a few of Autumn's favorite things, and the mere mention of them during sex will often to bring her to orgasm. Watching them on a video screen was assuredly more than enough to get her off.

She did not allow herself to come, though – that is, if she followed the instructions.

If she did not, I'll know the instant my cock slides into her. There is no mistaking a pussy that's been swelling and aching on the very brink of orgasm for a matter of hours.

When her orgasm had faded away, she was allowed to return to masturbating, starting the DVD player and witnessing, once again, an unnamed woman's torment. I had selected this video for two reasons: first, because the activities visited upon this woman match almost exactly what Autumn likes to fantasize about. Second, and more importantly, the woman in question eerily resembles Autumn, not so much in facial characteristics but in body shape and behavior: slender, blonde, with tits the size of small apples and a tendency to spread her legs very, very wide when being fucked – even when shackled to a table.

While watching, Autumn used each of the toys in turn, in their prescribed order: nipple clamps, vibrator, dildo. When she approached orgasm, she stopped both the DVD player and her own play. Without removing the nipple clamps, she ate the meal I'd prepared – something bland, because I knew at the height of her arousal the last thing she'd want to do was eat.

Thirty minutes later, she started the DVD player again, removed the nipple clamps, massaged her nipples until the pain stopped. Then she opened the second box. When she reached the edge of orgasm again – this time with the anal plug inserted and an appreciably larger dildo, not to mention a much more powerful vibrator – she returned to the shower without climaxing.

Following the instructions – if she did, and I'm quite sure she did – she used the shower massager on herself, always a sure-fire method of making her come. She coaxed her body once more to the edge of climax but backed off at the final moment. By then she was frustrated, painfully frustrated. She wanted very badly to come. She would have done anything to come – anything, I hoped, except disobey me.

It's no small matter to plan something this elaborate – even to the point where Autumn left the shower, toweled off, climbed into her dress, buckled on her impossibly high heels, and left the apartment.

To say nothing of what it takes to plan what comes after – Autumn's abduction into a warehouse filled with pain and humiliation, the ravishment she's dreamed of since she was too young to know how unthinkable it was.

It took an elaborate plan, and lots of money. It was quite a big deal for me to arrange Autumn's ultimate fantasy.

But now, as the cogs of my perfect machine begin turning, I know it will prove a much larger matter to my victim than it ever has to me.

***

They force her down a long corridor while she writhes and struggles against their arms – and screams at the top of her lungs. There is no one to hear her screams, here in the abandoned port district at three in the morning. Her struggles increase in urgency as she is frog-marched down the hall and into a large, open area draped with chains, racks, and tables. You would think the strength would go out of her as she realizes how helpless she is – that there is nothing, absolutely nothing, that can stop what is going to happen to her.

The two men who have abducted her are not the only ones. There are more in the makeshift dungeon – the crew totals half a dozen, she thinks, never knowing whether more wait in the shadows of the warehouse, their cocks hard with anticipation of the fun they'll have with her.

Just the sight of the other men is enough to make her shiver and slump into the arms of the two holding her. They appear to be dressed in a kind of uniform. Big boots, tight leather pants and tight black T-shirts. They're big, to a man – or at least they look that way from her perspective. While each of the six would bring a slight linger to her glance if they passed on the street, calling them "handsome" might be pushing it a little. More importantly, it would be an unhelpful generalization, especially given the variety of men involved – two are black, three are white, and the other is of mixed heritage, which she might notice, if she had time to think about it. Nonetheless, they are all of a type to which Autumn is inexorably drawn – masculine, well built but not bulky, tall, broad-shouldered, and a distinct personality carved into their features. Most of them are cleanly shaved, but two of them sport black goatees I know she thinks are sexy. She might have thought twice before giving me unfettered access to her photo albums, with all the pictures of her ex-boyfriends to guide me even better than the rather frank comments she makes, often at my urging, about men she meets. With such guidance, I'm quite confident I've found men Autumn is, even now, reacting to sexually.

In another context she would find them attractive. She would flirt with them. She'd like that they were looking at her tits.

In this context, she's not sure what she feels, or perhaps she doesn't want to admit it – except to admit, since she can do nothing else, that she feels weak, suddenly, as they surround her, as they look at her, as she succumbs to them. The strength goes out of her muscles, and her struggles cease, because only now does she understand how inevitable her ravishment is. There is nothing she can do to stop it. She is going to be taken. She is going to be possessed, by all these strong, leather-clad men. She's about to be – she knows with an intensity that sends a surge of exquisite anticipation through her cunt – seriously fucked.

She is limp now, her eyes wide with fright and some other unfathomable emotion. The strength has gone out of her; she has to be supported by the two men holding her.

Her arms are forced behind her back; her forearms are placed in a heavy leather sleeve attached to chains depending from the ceiling. The sleeve laces tight and padlocks. There are restraints for her feet, too – manacles, circling her ankles, as each man takes a leg and holds it still so she can be immobilized.

Her feet are forced wide apart so her legs are spread. The dress has begun to pull up her thighs, and if she struggles much more her shaved sex will be exposed – if they let her wait that long.

The ankle restraints lock into place over the straps of her

high-heeled shoes. Soon those will be all she's wearing, and she knows it.

"Please!" she wails, her red-painted lips quivering. Tears have begun flowing down her cheeks, running in black rivulets as her mascara disintegrates beneath her distress. The strength comes back into her muscles and she fights against her restraints – but by now it is too late, much, much too late for her to mount any resistance.

One of the men reaches around and pinches her cheeks firmly, forcing open her perfect mouth. The other man shoves in a metal ring gag sheathed in rubber, preparing those luscious lips to do what they were born to do – suck cock.

She prides herself on what her lips were made to do, loves to hear the word "cocksucker" aimed her direction. She loves to slide those lips down a hard shaft and show a man just how brilliant she is at that filthy art, her tongue eliciting moans as she puts her natural proficiency to good use.

But that pride is the enemy of her surrender – when a woman sucks cock, really *sucks* it the way she was born to do, ravening, devouring a hard prick with years of hard-learned technique and admirable enthusiasm, she is very much in control. Even though she may be down on her knees, as she usually is, even though her wrists may be handcuffed, as hers often are, even though there may be a hand tangled forcefully in her hair, as it generally is, even though she may be called a cock-sucking whore, as she always is – even then, when she sucks cock, a woman like Autumn is firmly in control. It is the cock that is at her mercy, and such a cruel kind of mercy it is.

Tonight, Autumn will not be in control, not even when she sucks cock. The ring gag ensures she'll do it without skill, without technique – her mouth is now nothing more than a hole to be violated, to be used.

The ring is secured behind her teeth, holding her mouth wide open. A strap holds it in place, unseen hands lifting up her long hair so the buckle can be secured at the back of her head.

The fear mounts in her eyes now that her mouth, like her cunt and her ass, has been rendered indefensible.

I don't know for sure what she's thinking, but I can speculate – a very educated kind of speculation – and it makes me so fucking hard I want to ravish her right then and there rather than make her wait. She's thinking that when she leaves here – after the experience she longed for, begged for, dreamed of – she will be wrecked, destroyed, savaged, never again the woman she was when she parked her car and walked down the alley. She will be nothing like she ever was. She will be something that, right now, in this final moment before the event, she can't even conceive of.

Her hair is lifted again by those unseen hands. A leather collar is placed around her neck, just snug enough to make her worry. It closes with a padlock.

She utters a desperate plea from behind the gag, a wordless wail; the ring is so wide it keeps her from forming coherent words.

I don't know if this particular thought has occurred to her, but it would frighten her to know it: the ring *has* to be large, because the men who will take her were selected first and foremost for their endowments. An average-sized ring never would have accommodated them, would never have permitted the ravaging of her mouth and throat the way they will be ravaged this dark night.

The two men who brought her in are the first to get a crack at her. This is their payment for doing the work of grabbing her – because men like this don't do it for money.

***

Autumn feels their hands on her; their touch brings a shudder. First the one behind her pulls her hard against him, hands on her breasts, and pinches her nipples. They are erect, whether with fear, cold or arousal no one but her – maybe not *even* her – can know. She gasps as he pinches them, squeezing and fondling her tits. Men look at them all the time; she often sees in their eyes the desire to *take*. Now those breasts are being taken, against her will, while she struggles and whimpers and sobs.

He releases her nipples, grasps her dress at the neckline, and pulls.

The flimsy material rips down the front, disintegrating like tissue under the onslaught. The man in front of her yanks the bottom hem up to her waist, exposing her sex. He thrusts both his hands between her legs. He feels immediately that she is shorn, shaved smooth like a stripper, but she doesn't even have time to feel embarrassed at his discovery before he spreads her lips wide and thrusts the fingers of his other hand into her – three of them, all at once, no warm-up, enough to make her gasp and then wail as she is violated. Her pussy, tight and swollen with intense arousal and repeatedly denied orgasm, is stretched painfully. The man thrusts his fingers as deep as they will go, and she feels the cruel stroke to her core.

His fingers come out wet shining with her juices. He smiles.

The man behind her squeezes and pinches her now-naked breasts as the one in front of her shoves his three cunt-glistening fingers through the ring gag. He does not thrust them deep enough to test her gag reflex, but still her throat contracts. She can taste herself. He is reminding her that she wants this – that she all but asked for it. That she *did* ask for it, by putting on such a dress and walking down that dark alley. She begged for it, and her pussy tells the tale, gushing the juice of her arousal even as her immobilized mouth struggles to form the word "No." The humiliation is tangible, burning in her eyes.

The "no" comes out as a gulp, a choking sound of distress as her mouth wrestles with the ring gag.

The man in front of her presses himself close so she can smell him, as if he's going to kiss her, but her wide-open mouth can no longer be kissed. He shoves two fingers inside her this time, finger-fucking her as he smiles into her eyes. The man behind her is still having his way with her tits, squeezing them, slapping them, pinching her nipples. When the man before her tires of her pussy, he slides his fingers out and puts one arm around her, grasping her ass and pulling her body firmly against his.

He does this for two reasons, and both have the desired effect. First, she can feel his cock straining through his leather pants hard against her belly.

Second, she can feel his hand on her ass – not grasping her cheek, but firmly in the center, where she can feel his finger touching her cleft.

She must have seen this coming, but perhaps she hadn't fully faced it with so many other things to think about. Well, she sees it now, and the knowledge savages her. She is going to be taken there as well. In her ass, where she doesn't even let her lover take her, except on very, *very* special occasions.

She is a perceptive woman. She sees men looking. Men look at her ass almost as often as they look at her tits, and she knows it is not innocent admiration; she knows what they want to do with it. She knows what every man wants to do with every woman's ass. She knows, in particular, that uncounted men have fantasized about violating that back door of hers, cradled as it is by those perfect, firm cheeks. Many of them – almost all of her numerous lovers – have even asked for it. Some have begged. Only a small number have been allowed to use her there. Even fewer have done it without extensive romantic persuasion. None have done it without hours of foreplay.

Only very special men are allowed into Autumn's ass – but these men are very special, in their own way.

Tonight, they'll be allowed in – she's helpless to stop them from taking her there, in a way that humiliates her. That knowledge sends a pulse of heat into her pussy as the man behind her works his fingertip into her anus, lubricated only by the juices of her unwilling arousal. She cries out, but from her forced-open mouth it is a pathetic sound; a bleat. I can see the fear and hunger in her eyes. If anything, her cunt is wetter than it was when she was brought in. Even her fear can't stop the uncontrolled lubrication of her sex. On the contrary, it's increasing it.

Not a word has been spoken. The men assaulting her don't care to brag about what they'll do to her. They prefer to let her figure it out, because they know the knowledge of this frightening yet exciting potential lurks in the mind of every woman, and the fact that it's real is the only thing she might now have trouble accepting.

The man in front of her snaps his fingers. Someone behind him retrieves an implement from one of the tables and hands it to him. She sees it is a scalpel. He snaps off the guard and brings the scalpel to her belly.

The man handling her tits pulls down the bottom of her dress, then seizes the remains of its top and holds the shredded fabric up for his accomplice's attentions.

The tattered dress comes open almost without a sound, slit from the terminus of the jagged tear to the hem – barely decent at the best of times, and now of no consequence at all. The cap sleeves go quickly, too, and the ravished garment falls like a pool of white moonlight between her spread feet.

The two men withdraw, one of them kicking the dress away. They leave her hanging spread and naked, open to my gaze from where I watch her onscreen. The very color of her eyes reveals she understands that someone is watching. She knows it's me.

I look her over, giving her a long, languid caress with my eyes – shackled ankles to shaved sex to reddened breasts and pink nipples. Then I look at her lovely face, its pretty innocence ruined by the ring gag opening it, the soiled tears streaming down her cheeks, the fear in her eyes.

She can see the shadowy figures closing in on her.

Another wail escapes her forcibly-opened mouth as half a dozen men move in to feel her. She recoils from each touch – but there is nowhere she can recoil to. She is surrounded.

* * *

I lose her in the press of male flesh. My eyes cannot fully capture this chapter of her debasement, with so many men on her at once. Hands explore her – six, eight, ten, twelve at a time, depending on how tight the men close in. Fingers violate her shaved pussy, marveling at its smoothness, two and three hands at a time, jockeying for position.

Then one hand fingers her cunt while another rubs her clit – different men, each time, sometimes more than one at each place. Thumbs part her cheeks, opening her wide, middle fingers testing the tightness of her rear entrance. Mouths suckle her breasts, tongues and teeth massage her firm nipples. More tongues taste her everywhere – her face, her throat, her belly, her thighs, the small of her back. One tongue, nudging a violating finger out of the way, traces its way down her crack furrow and wriggles its way into her asshole. Two different men hold her cheeks wide open for the man rimming her. Cruel hands grip her hair and pull. They test the tightness of her collar, circle her throat beneath and above it just to tell her they're there.

I can see her eyes widening as her anus is violated by a tongue. The man buries his face between her forced-open cheeks and devours her. Two more men feast on her breasts, mouths open and tongues working hungrily.

Hard cocks rub against her from time to time – against her hips, her thighs – and the smells must be overwhelming her, too; the smell of so many men, all over her. She knows the scent of every man she's been with – can recall it vividly, without struggling, can catch a whiff of it in her nostrils when she thinks of him. She's written about them in her journal. She'll think of these men's smells for the rest of her life.

A new man takes his turn between her spread cheeks, tonguing her, and yet another man kneels before her and plants his mouth on her shaved sex, three fingers invading her slit. That brings a savage convulsion to her body as she fights against the onslaught of sensation – her clit and ass being licked at the same time as the two men in front of her suckle, tongue, and bite her nipples. She can climax, sometimes, just from having her tits nursed on, if an hour goes by. With her cunt, clit, and ass being worked on as well, that time is telescoped immeasurably.

She knows it will happen, and the men know it, too, because I've told them. I know it will happen soon. That instant of release will initiate her absolute submission as no mechanical violation ever could. I can see it in her face, the pressure that builds as she squirms on the edge, her eyes glaze incoherently in their sockets, roving, rolling back.

It's not going to happen yet, though. There's more that she must endure, in her memories, forever. It's not enough for me to know she will vividly remember her first orgasm of the long ordeal. It's not enough to know she was conquered by her pleasure, that she was brought off by strangers, mouths on her nipples, tongues in her pussy and ass. Her place is not to merely be pleasured, serviced against her will. Her place is to be taken. She exists to be used.

She's not going to come without a cock in her mouth.

I step out of the shadows.

* * *

The men withdraw at my command, leaving her naked body glistening with her perspiration, her thighs and breasts moist with their spit. Her pleasure-dulled eyes look at me, glazed, unbelieving. My cock is hard, stretching my jeans.

I don't say a word, at first, although I can tell she wants me to.

I snap my fingers and gesture to one of the unseen men. The chain that connects to her wrist restraints goes slack, rattling through the pulley overhead.

She tries to remain standing, but her legs are too weak. One of the men behind her props her hips up while I grasp her hair and pull her down toward my crotch. The chain slackens until she is bent over fully.

She tries to pull her head away as I guide my cock toward her mouth. I slap her cheek, gently at first, then again harder as she continues to struggle. She tries to stand up. I slap her a third time. When she doesn't settle down, I nod at the man behind her.

Someone else retrieves a cane from the dress rack and hands it to him while a second man disappears behind me to retrieve the nipple clamps.

I let her stand upright then, regarding her glazed eyes with pleasure. She brings her wrists down in front of her, covering her breasts as if that can protect her. She's been so lost in her struggles she doesn't even know the cane is ready.

She wails beneath the first stroke – a good smart blow across her ass. She lunges forward and totters, then manages to straighten herself – no small task with her legs spread like that, her feet forced into a tiptoe posture by the high heels. The cane whizzes through the air again. Her whole naked body explodes in a spasm of pain, but she doesn't bend forward. I nod at him, and the man behind her gives her six rapid strokes, enough to make her scream behind the ring gag.

It takes two more strokes. I catch her as she drops, her wrists twisting up over her head. I make sure the posture is correct, her wrists behind her, the chain tight above her, her face level with my crotch. One of the men seizes her shoulders and holds her down. Another man kneels beside her, nipple clamps shimmering in the indirect photofloods.

She gasps as the clamps go on. Her nipples are so sensitive. I know she must be hurting.

The nipple clamps are clovers connected by a Y-shaped chain, its terminus bearing a clamp that would usually go on her clit. Instead it attaches to the manacles that secure her ankles. The clover clamps tighten with pressure. For her to straighten up now would be impossible, even if I wasn't gripping her hair tightly.

With a signal, I have the cane man give her six strokes on the back of each thigh. She spasms and shudders beneath each of the twelve blows, trying to straighten and shrieking as the agony in her nipples holds her in place.

He hits her just hard enough to leave angry welts down the backs of her thighs. I'll trace those marks with my hand or my tongue in the coming weeks – any time I need to remind her of the price of passion.

Her face is cradled against me now, immobile, unresisting, ready to be taken. But I don't take her yet, because she's angered me by resisting.

I slide my hand over her, taking a long time caressing the small of her back – she is very ticklish there. Her shivers and shudders make her chains pull taut, and I hear the whimpers as her nipples are tormented.

I ease my hand down her crack, parting her cheeks so she knows I can have her ass taken in whatever manner pleases me. Then I curve my fingers in to violate her cunt. It's dripping, tight, swollen. She obeyed me, I know now – she's been on the verge of orgasm for hours, never crossing that line, never bringing herself to a climax.

The pain has distracted her, and her sex tells me exactly how much. She's still on the edge, yes, but not as close as she was. Not nearly close enough to satisfy me.

I remove my hand and wipe her juices on her face, close to her nose so she can smell them when I violate her mouth, just in case she could ever forget how fucking wet she is.

I jerk my head toward two of the men. One of them kneels underneath her, between her spread legs, and molds his mouth to her sex. The other bends low behind her, parts her cheeks wide with his hands, and plants his mouth between them. She utters a helpless moan as she feels tongues invading her sex and her ass.

She's on the edge again in less than a minute. I couldn't miss it if I tried. I grasp her hair and force her head up so I can look into her eyes as they go vacant with the approach of her climax. She tries to close her eyes as she gets ready to come. When I slap her face, she opens them again, the first hint of obedience I've seen all night.

Her nipples can make her come, but they can also keep her from coming, and my arm hooked under her shoulders can make her nipples keep her from coming. I do that now, because I've determined she will not come without a cock in her mouth.

I lift her body slightly, and she cries out as the chains pull taut and the clamps compress her nipples. She utters a wretched groan, and I pull her body up more firmly. The men continue to work on her pussy and ass, and I hold her face upturned with my hand firmly buried in her hair. I'm cutting it close, I know – sometimes pain in her nipples can drive her over the edge, rather than preventing her orgasm.

I see the flare in her eyes that tells me she's almost there, and I bark a wordless command to the men working on her. They withdraw into the darkness.

It's much like a sob, the sound that erupts from her mouth. She wants very badly to come. Almost anything would do it. She *wants* those strangers on her clit and in her cunt and their tongues up her ass. I steady her face with one hand and with the other I point my cock at her mouth.

She makes a gagging, choking sound as I slide my cock to the back of her throat. Her tongue works feverishly – whether trying to get me off or push me out, I'll never know. Her throat, however, is doing nothing if not trying to prevent its own forcible violation. Its muscles tighten as I push in, and the violent surge they give makes me pull out just enough so she can gasp in a lungful of air. She takes it. Her throat accepts me. Muscles still straining, she is forced to open up and feel my cock jutting down her neck.

Autumn absolutely loves deep-throating. She loves it because men so prize it, because once she's deep-throated a man, swallowed his cock to its foundation, she knows (or hopes) she's done something few, if any, of his other lovers did without being asked. That, she thinks, makes her a prize to be cherished. This is a way in which sucking cock puts her firmly in control.

Once I've violated her, the muscles of her throat go slack, as if her throat, like the rest of her, is slowly accepting its fate – to be an object of pleasure, not fit for breathing or eating only fit to be fucked by hard cock. Her throat is well trained, having pleasured numerous cocks in its time in moments when she was in control. But now, being fucked like this, she is *not* in control, and that is what I know will make her come harder than ever before.

I don't watch her eyes as that moment of surrender overtakes her, because it's more important that something else happen before she can use those finely-toned muscles to give herself something she must learn is no longer hers to give.

I nod to the man one who caned her, for two important reasons. First, he is the most skilled with a cane, and he performed a critical service to me by helping destroy her will to resist.

Second, and much more importantly, he has the biggest cock in the room.

She doesn't expect it. I don't even think she feels him up against her or recognizes the weight of his body against the backs of her thighs or knows what's coming when he parts the lips of her shaved sex with his fingers.

Perhaps she's so lost in the strokes of my cock down her throat, trying so hard to time the rhythm of her breathing to the invasion of her neck, that she's unaware of the rest of her body.

But when his cock-head stretches her pussy, her attention is suddenly focused there, and only there.

I slide down her throat as I see his hips surge forward. She can feel his cock-head opening up her cunt – not entering her yet, but preparing her for the thrust that will violate her.

The muscles of her throat tighten around me as a cry attempts to escape her filled throat. Her naked body wrenches against both of us – far, far beyond trying to get away, beyond even trying to fuck herself onto his cock, beyond everything except orgasm.

I slide my erection all the way down Autumn's throat, my hand tangled in her hair.

I nod at him, and he shoves his cock inside her.

She comes the moment he penetrates her.

Even though she can't scream – she would scream if her throat wasn't filled with my cock – I know the tension of that naked body, the way that back wants to arch. She tries to, but this only heightens her suffering by pulling the clamps on her nipples. Yet the sensation of pain in her breasts can't stop the orgasm that thunders through her. When she gets to this point, pain only makes her come harder. And she comes hard, hard enough to sob as the man thrusts his thumb into her anus, perhaps the last thing she expected, and perhaps the one thing that could make her come even harder than she's already coming.

He fucks her violently as she climaxes, and her hips begin to buck wildly, impaling herself on his cock, meeting each of his thrusts with her own. It takes her a long, long time to finish. Half a minute, perhaps more, the whole time her hips bucking violently and her back straining against the pull of the clamps on her nipples.

When I slip my cock out of her mouth, a moan erupts from her like the wail of an insane woman, a woman driven so far over the edge she is now in free-fall.

The man pauses in his thrusts, and his nod tells me he can still feel her cunt clenching around him. I cradle her face against my cock, the rigid shaft laid against her cheek. We let her finish, his cock no longer pumping into her but his thumb visibly wriggling in her ass.

He and I make eye contact as he waits to find out what he'll do to her.

I've been struggling with this moment since the start of it. At one point is her surrender absolute? Do I let another man fuck her, is that enough? Do I allow her to be fucked in the ass? Will orally servicing every man in this room, kneeling with her wrists bound behind her, push her over the edge and dissolve her resistance forever? Or does it take the most intimate and thorough of violations – another man's seed exploding deep inside her?

I nod to him, and he begins to pound her viciously, driving his cock deep inside her in the rhythm that every man follows when he's fucking to come.

She knows it, she knows he's going to come inside her. As her eyes turn up to me, I see what I want to see in her eyes – I see fear, the flicker of resistance. And then – as he fucks her cunt harder and faster, seeking his satisfaction without any thought for her – I see what I really want, what I've always wanted, what she's always wanted to give me.

There's no way she could fail to recognize this moment. She's felt it enough times before. She's felt a man pounding himself into her, striving after his own orgasm, without regard for hers. And that moment devours her every time. Late at night, when she's being fucked, when *I'm* fucking her, in whatever position – missionary, doggy style, bent over the vanity, pushed up against the railing of the balcony overlooking the pool – however it's being done, there's one thing that drives her over the edge. It's not my careful thrusts, calculated to hit her G-spot just right. It's not my hand working her clit. She can come that way, sure – the first few times, mild orgasms, rapturous pleasure – but if she's tired, or distracted, or not sufficiently turned on, it's the pounding that'll make her come harder than ever.

"Jacking off inside me," she once explained it to me, and just saying that gave her naked body a shiver. When she masturbates, her fantasy is often about just that moment – being fucked when the man is about to come and he doesn't care if she does or doesn't.

Now this nameless man is jacking off inside her, using her cunt as carelessly as he would his closed fist. He's not wearing a condom. He's not going to pull out, and she knows it. She's on the pill. She and I have never used condoms, we've fucked flesh-on-flesh since our first date, but that does not lessen the extremity of this invasion. On the contrary, it vastly increases it. Her body is about to be flooded with this stranger's cum, her womb drenched by his essence. It would be bad enough if she was just being fucked, but she's also being filled with his sperm, and this is the fact on which this whole experience hinges – she trusts me. She knows if he's coming inside her that it's safe.

The feel of a stranger's cum inside her is, I know, more precious and terrifying than almost any other gift I can give her.

This is her breaking point, then, the moment at which she either trusts me or despairs that she doesn't trust me.

Her face upturned, her eyes fixed on mine, I'll see which path she's taken, trust or despair. I have to admit, I'm not sure it'll be trust that this moment elicits from her. That's why this is a test, for both of us.

Her words are clear in my memory: *Anything, darling. Anything and everything. No boundaries. None.* I even said it, *Fucked by a stranger without a condom?* She shivered when I said that and answered, *Yes, I need to know you'll do anything to me – anything, absolutely anything.*

So that's what I've given her – the hot spurt of a stranger's cum. I can tell by the sudden arrhythmic bucking of his hips that he's shooting deep inside her. Autumn knows it, too. She's an experienced woman and knows what a man feels like when he's coming, when his hot jets of sperm erupting inside her.

I could tell you that the violent, screaming orgasm she has on the man's unprotected cock as he ejaculates inside her is what tells me she's turned to trust rather than despair, but the truth is that an orgasm is frequently followed by despair. But she definitely comes again so soon after her first climax. She wails, bucking against him, her back straining as she pounds back onto him. The clovers are built so that they can't pull off. They do anyway, and she shrieks as her nipples come free. She shudders all over.

He finishes inside her, sighs, and pulls his softening cock out of her cum-drenched pussy.

I release my grip on her hair, step back, and leave her hanging, bent over, her cunt utterly violated, her mouth forced wide open, her face coated with perspiration and mascara-blackened tears.

She looks up at me then, eyes dazed.

"Take her down," I say in a tone of voice I'm shocked to hear myself using. Perhaps it's me who's gone beyond into the badlands where Autumn is just a tool to elicit pleasure in men. It certainly seems that way, because as my henchmen take her down from the chains, the things I know I'm about to do to her would have terrified me only an hour ago. Now they just make my cock harder than it's ever been.

* * *

There's a low table in the middle of the room. At each corner it bears sturdy rings. At its center it tilts up down so she can be bent over it with her ass in the air and her face at crotch level.

The men unfasten the sleeve that holds her arms behind her. I'm surprised to see her struggle as they force her wrists into restraints. The struggling is fruitless, of course. The restraints circle her wrists and cinch tight. The padlocks attach to the rings as two more men work on her ankles. It's a broad table, so there's plenty of room for them to spread her legs *wide*.

I take off all of my clothes as they get her ready for me.

A thick leather belt goes over her back, holding her to the table so she can't even try to get her exposed pussy and ass out of the way of what they have coming to them. The table is built for no earthly purpose except fucking a restrained submissive. Autumn knows this, and this knowledge makes her wriggle and squirm against the restraints, whimpering.

Her pussy is spread now, open for me. Shaved as it is, it's lovely in the indirect light. Her clit stands pink and erect, no doubt sore from all the suckling. Her entrance pulses between her shorn lips, glistening with another man's semen.

Her asshole, too, is opened, forced wide by tongues and fingers.

Her legs form a luscious V, the manacled ankles and high-heeled shoes offering a dissonant pairing of violence and femininity. Down the back of each thigh is a line of angry stripes, but her white buttocks are maddeningly unmarked. I snap my fingers, and someone hands me the cane.

I don't bother to have her kiss it. I don't tease her with it before I give her the first blow. She yelps, and her body jerks against the tight restraints. I draw three lines across each of her buttocks, and each blow brings a cry and then a low moan from her.

I draw the tip of the cane up her inner thigh, watching her shiver as I near her sex. I tease her swollen lips with the tip of the cane, then draw slow circles around her erect clit. I slide the cane inside her, deep into her cum-soaked channel.

Now I'm going to have her kiss it. I listen to her moaning as I work the tip of the cane around inside her. Then I draw it out, step over to her face, and look into her eyes.

The cane slides as easily into her forcibly opened mouth as my cock did. I stroke the tip of the cane against her tongue, just in case she had any doubts there really is another man's cum inside her pussy.

I come around behind her again and give her six more strokes, making her naked body jerk and twist. Then I discard the cane and mount the table between her spread legs.

I bring my cock to her entrance and feel its tightness, her muscles cinching to resist me as I work my way into her. I drive into her hard, feeling my blood rise as savagery overtakes me.

I can tell her pussy is sore, but not from being violated, since it has barely been violated at all. It's sore because she's come so hard. Her muscles are not just tight because she's still resisting, they're tight because my cock sliding into her causes her the pain of too much fulfillment. Just a few thrusts open her up, though, and she's soon moaning, straining hopelessly to push her cunt onto me. She can't, of course, for the belt holds her down. She can only lie there and get fucked, and I give it to her in short, violent thrusts ameliorated by slower ones as I catch my breath, followed by even more swift and violet penetrations. Now she's open wide, moaning in pleasure as I do my best to violate a cunt so hungry nothing can satisfy it.

But violence is on my mind, and I can't bear to let Autumn rest in the glory of her ravishment.

A gesture from me brings another man to her face. His cock is hard and slides easily down into her throat as mine did – more easily because now she's been fucked wide open. I hear her gagging only a little as she takes the new stranger's cock. He begins fucking her, holding her hair, savaging her face as I penetrate her pussy. I wave another man over, and he brings a tube of lubricant. He stands beside

Autumn, and she gasps as two of his fingers, cold with the jelly, slide into her anus.

I can feel the pressure of his fingers inside her through the membrane that separates one hole from the other. I listen to the gagging sounds as her throat is violated and feel the clench of her muscles as her ass is opened for me. The sight, the smell, the sensation of it all is starting to make me come, and I know nothing can hide this knowledge from her. I start fucking her even faster, banging her brutally, and I feel her muscles tense with anticipation. *He's going to come inside me*, she might be thinking. *My lover is going to come inside me.*

I wave the fingers away and they slide out of her ass. I lean forward onto her, lifting my hips, sliding my cock out of her cunt. I perform the switch quickly, not giving her time to adjust to the knowledge that she's about to be violated anally, in that private place where only the loved ones have gone.

I drive firmly into her slick anus, planting my cock deep inside her. The man fucking her face is watching closely. He anticipates my action and draws his cock out so I can hear her gasp of shock. Then he fills her mouth again as I begin reaming her with the savagery that comes from my imminent orgasm.

It's never easy for me to come in Autumn's asshole. Something about the shape, the texture, the tightness, the curve of her buttocks, the gentleness I always apply when I'm inside her back passage distracts me and makes me go slower. This time, however, there's nothing to stop me. I pound her ass harder than I've ever pounded her cunt, listening to her wails of dismay each time the other man's cock slides out of her mouth.

I'm jacking off inside her the way she so guiltily loves, only this time not in her cunt. Yet it has the same effect, and the muscles of her anus, for some reason, are infinitely more powerful. I can feel them quivering, tightening in spasms as rapturous moans emanate from her throat around my thrusting erection.

She comes before I do, and the man fucking her face lets her moan and wail as she climaxes, cupping her face and positioning his cock right at the entrance in the ring gag between her open lips. Then her wailing turns to low, sobbing moans as I keep fucking her ass with all my strength.

I'm shocked to hear it when I come – a savage, bestial roar. I ejaculate deep inside her, filling her bowels with my seed, growling and clawing at her back. She shudders and wrenches against the restraints, pushing up against the belt holding her down. My cock-head, thrust as deep inside her as it will go, fills her with cum, and she milks it from me, moaning softly until the moment when the other man's hard-on once more violates her throat. And then he's giving her that moment in her mouth – the moment of jacking off heedless of her pleasure – and the openness of her throat makes it easy for him. When he looks at me, I toss my head carelessly, and he pulls out just enough to fill her mouth with his sperm.

Four more men are waiting their turns, standing naked and erect in the reflected glare of the clamp lights.

I step around to face her, reach under her long hair, and unbuckle the ring gag. She gasps as it comes out of her mouth, and then swallows convulsively.

There's one more piece of dedicated furniture in the warehouse – an old divan covered in red velvet with a texture that reveals its age. Narrower than most sofas, it's the perfect width for a woman's legs to spread elegantly around it, toes touching the floor, with just enough space between her sex and the surface for a man to lie beneath her. The divan abuts a sturdy table, the perfect height for a man to sit and be sucked down by the same woman crouching over another cock. But that fact probably hasn't occurred to her. She only knows, I suspect, that she's about to be fucked in all three holes at once. She knows that because she wants it so bad.

Three of the men are behind her in seconds, unfastening her restraints. She's weak enough that she has to be lifted off the table, but once she's propped up on her feet, she moves with a ballerina's grace despite the two strong hands circling her wrists and frog-marching her across the warehouse until she's standing over the divan. She looks down at the man lying on his back across it, his leather pants long since gone, his cock standing straight and rigid as he holds it up for her to sit on.

She doesn't look at me. Instead she looks at the cock before her as she's guided – almost lifted – over it. She struggles a little, half-heartedly, as if to keep up the charade that she doesn't desperately want to be forced onto that cock when, in fact, at that moment, she lives for nothing else. And that cock is hard, hefty, held in the exact right position for her to sit on it. She stops struggling, and the man behind her frees her wrists. She is now crouched over the hard dick being held up for her. Five other men circle around her, and she probably does the math in her head.

Now, for the first time tonight – since the moment she crossed the border of that darkened alley – Autumn is allowed control.

Which is probably why it happens the way it does. When she lowers herself, it almost looks like she's falling, and it probably feels that way, except that she settles with exactitude on the up-thrust cock, guiding it inside her with her hand and moaning, her face contorted in ecstasy as it penetrates her. She descends on it eagerly, pushing it as deep as it will go inside her, and when she slumps forward onto the man's chest, others are already moving into position. One man mounts the table, presenting his erection for her mouth, his hand tangling in her hair as if forcing her, but she's ravenous when she swallows it. One easy thrust past her lips and deep into her throat it goes. While she sucks him down, first one of her wrists and then the other is seized and her hands are guided to the hard-ons of the men who crowd on either side of her. Only one final place remains open for the fifth man, and though she must expect it, she puts on a good show. She makes them hold her tight as he lodges the head of his lubricated cock in her sphincter and plunges through her tight ring.

It is no simple matter to be fucked by five men at once, and that fact is evident from the initial awkwardness she exhibits. If these men were less experienced, she would find it much more difficult, but their motions are coordinated perfectly, and within moments she's relaxed completely into their collective grasp, supported by their straining muscles. She holds on to two cocks, gets fucked by one, sodomized by another, and never, for more than an instant, loses that ravenous hunger for the cock in her mouth. I can tell when she climaxes, about ten minutes into it, which is the five men's cue to swap. One is close to coming – the one in her ass – and he gives me a glance. I shake my head. He pulls out, and with her lying on her back this time, her body spread on top of another man, a new erection is guided into her ass. She goes crazy, shuddering all over as she's penetrated afresh at an even more excruciating angle. The one who was fucking her ass crouches over her and quickly finishes himself off on her breasts. He steps aside and another man mounts her while two other men put their erections into her hands as yet another man tips her head back over the edge of the divan and easily plunges all the way down into her neck.

She is sandwiched between two rutting men, grasping a throbbing cock in each hand, her face fucked like a cunt, and I know she's happier than she's ever been. She finishes off one of the men, displaying her expertise at the hand-job. Then the man in her ass groans and shudders beneath her while the man fucking her pussy pulls out and ejaculates on her belly. There's one cock in her mouth and one in her hand now, and they take this opportunity to switch. She's lifted to her feet, where she slumps into the arms of one of the bigger men. The man she was sucking lays down on the divan, and she's guided onto his cock while the last man penetrates her ass from behind, driving his dick in deep, and together they fuck her harder than she's ever been fucked before.

With her mouth no longer filled with cock she can cry out as much as she wants to, and she does. The man driving into her ass finishes long before the one sliding in and out of her pussy.

Only one more thing remains to be done. I don't even have to order her. As the other men move away, I take my place on the divan, and she crawls onto me.

She spreads herself wide and comes down on me with a gasp that sounds almost like a sob. Then she makes love to me, rising and falling on my cock, and when I climax she moans softly against me and nuzzles her face into my neck.

"Thank you-" she begins, but I silence her with a savage kiss, and her naked body shivers in my arms.

* * *

"I think I'm still going to be walking funny when I walk down the aisle," she says, her voice slightly hoarse from the number of cocks that have savaged her throat.

I smile. "Isn't that the idea?"

She takes my hand as I turn the car onto the onramp. She's curled up in the passenger's seat wearing sweats and a T-shirt and the seatbelt, at my insistence.

"Yes," she whispers. "I know I can do it now. You passed the test, baby. I know you're the one. You can give me everything I want. Everything, and more."

"Good," I say, "because the caterers have already been paid."

She doesn't respond to my sarcasm; doesn't seem fazed by it in the least. She's accustomed to the dry wit of a man who can have her taken by half a dozen strangers and subject her to things other women can only dream about.

I probably won't tell her about the week I waited while the recruits got their test results, or the month before that while I checked their references, sneaking cell phone calls all over the country in between meetings at work. She doesn't need to know the details of how her husband recruited a small army to gangbang her, or how he made sure it was safe.

Because she doesn't need to know it *was* safe. For that she has trust, unshakable and absolute. It's important for Autumn to accept that she doesn't make any decisions about how safe or unsafe her ravishment was. She has to know that her mind, like her body, has been *possessed*. That moment of trust I saw in her eyes – that was the test. Not for her, but for me, because a woman like Autumn doesn't give that trust unless it's been earned with chains and cum.

There are many nights in our future, nights without a moon, and I would never cheat her of any of them.

Something has been awakened inside me. That bestial growl when I came was not an act for her benefit, nor was it a simple expression of male savagery. I can still feel it burning inside me – the hunger to take absolute possession of her – and when each of us says "I do" it will only be the icing on the wedding cake. We were married the moment she surrendered her body and mind to my care, however brutal that care should prove to be.

"Hungry?" she asks.

"Famished," I reply.

"There's some roast chicken left."

"I ate it this afternoon."

"I could heat up a frozen pizza."

I chuckle as I turn down our street. "I think you should rest."

She smiles. "Why, because I just got gang-banged?" She laughs.

"And most of them fucked you twice."

"*You* certainly did! God, I thought you were never going to come. I didn't want you to. I wanted you to fuck me so *fucking* hard. I wanted you to fuck me forever!"

I pull into the driveway of our house. "That's what I'll do," I tell her. "Forever."

When I look over at her, she's breathing hard, her face pink and her breasts heaving. She giggles nervously, as if to cover up the intimacy of that terrifying moment, though she was the first to use the word "forever". When I echoed it, it was enough to take her breath away.

I seize her and kiss her hard, tasting cum and not caring. "I'm going to fuck you forever!" I whisper fiercely.

There are tears in her eyes, so I kiss her again, my tongue ravishing her mouth. Her nipples harden against my chest. She's not quite spent. I feel the ache of my cock getting hard. Even after a night like tonight, she can still arouse me.

"I know," she says, and sniffles a little. "I know."

"Let's get upstairs. I don't need dinner."

I get out of the car, but she lingers, staring out the window. I come around to her side and open the door for her.

She looks up at me. "It's dark out tonight," she muses, the fact as self-evident as it is magical.

"Yes," I say, "but it's almost sunrise."

"Mm!" She reaches up for my hand without looking at me. "I hope the sun never comes up."

Natural Bondage

by
Maria Isabel Pita

I walked out the kitchen door to light the gas grill on the back porch, but then I just stood there, entranced by the impossible sight of a black moth hovering in mid-air without moving even though its wings were beating wildly. Wow, I thought, I didn't know moths could do that! An insect with the gravity-defying soul of a hummingbird? Something didn't feel right... I realized then that I was witnessing not an enchantment but an entrapment. The black moth was helplessly caught in the web of two red-and-yellow spiders swiftly converging on it from opposite directions. Amazed the invisible filaments were strong enough to hold a winged creature twice the size of its captors, I grabbed a grill fork, and with devilish pleasure destroyed the vital work of one species to temporarily become the guardian angel of another. The spiders had no right to use the leg of my grill as a post for their cruel dining room; I was delighted to have arrived just in time to free their unwilling feast. The transformed caterpillar flew away as I lit the grill, smiling. It would live another few minutes, at least, while the spiders hungrily re-constructed their delicate white dungeon to put another creature in sticky bondage.

I was living in a big city at the time I met my Master online. Our virtual paths did not cross on *alt.com*. I was looking for mental stimulation, respect and profound, lifelong affection, and my one experience with this alternative dating service had disgusted me enough to convince me I would be better off searching for my soul-mate somewhere more "normal". It was a matter of priorities – I wanted love, which would hopefully involve kinky sex. I wanted the milk you stir the chocolate into, but on *alt* all I seemed to find was the emotional broken glass of promiscuous perversions secretly shattering marriage vows – an inordinate amount of the men who contacted me were married and looking for a slave or slaves on the side, not a loving wife. In my opinion, a life worth living is by necessity subtle and complex. *Alt.com* is tuned into the loudest – the most obvious – facts and ideas about BDSM, a thrilling playground for some, a frightening wasteland for others, myself included. I wasn't looking for a sadistic man who played by the perversely conventional rules of traditional SM (as I was more or less able to make sense of them) because there were simply too many clauses in that particular lifestyle contract that made me sick to my stomach. The more profiles I read, the more turned off I would get. So I put my submissive desires on the back burner to search for the light of true love on a different site. I had tried my luck on this particular service a few times before and had been pleasantly disappointed every time by men who were attractive and intelligent but who all lacked something vital – the first promising but as yet unfinished sketches of my true Master, who I knew had to be out there somewhere. I never lost faith that my life would someday intersect with the man who would fill all the empty places inside me in every sense. I could almost feel the web of time and space vibrating as from different directions we both converged on the sensual feast of our destiny together. It was only a matter of time before we met, I simply had to believe that, so I put up a new profile, and only a few days later received the e-mail that changed my life.

I won't go into the details of our courtship, which happened with the rationally blinding swiftness of lightening striking and dividing my life in half like the birth of Christ did the historical timeline. It's perfectly natural for me to think of my life as "before Master" and "after Master" existing as I do in a different world now with a richer, more fulfilling atmosphere where everything feels easier and more enjoyable and where vibrant colors don't affront the black-and-white melancholy I so often suffered from before.

Before I met my Master "discipline" was only an abstract concept to me. I now understand what it means to be disciplined much as a plant appreciates being pruned, watered, protected from predators and in every way cared for. My Master is merciless with those aspects of my personality that struggle against my higher, submissively peaceful instincts. He never lets me get away with a helplessly negative perception of any situation or event. His relentless understanding grasps my thoughts and emotions, twists them around just so, and forces me to face this new difficult conceptual position with the invisible restraints of his willpower and concern, which I initially resist before submitting to gratefully. The man I have been living with for over five years is the Master of my ever-sharpening perceptions and deepening self-esteem. He is the warmth and energy, the focused perceptive intensity, stimulating and cherishing the growth of my being. This may sound over-the-top, but I assure you it most definitely is not. I am not the same woman I was five years ago. I am older, and much more beautiful.

I never use Master's given name when we're alone. I call him "Master" dozens of times a day as casually and yet as respectfully as Jeannie addressed Major Nelson. My vivid sensual imagination is contained in the bottles of my books, and Master's scientific cool might sometimes seem to clash with my passionate perceptions but, in truth, if it wasn't for him, I wouldn't have explored enough to become who I am now. I've shared erotic experiences with him that, before we met, seemed as impossible to fulfill as breathing on the moon. During our first two years together, I was very often bound hand and foot, but it was never just for fun. Master wanted me to reflect on what I had done wrong, to isolate the thoughts and emotions that had twisted themselves up into a defensive bird's nest inside me that caused me to lash out at him. My wrists crossed and bound against the small of my back, my bare ass thrust up into the air, my ankles attached to my wrists so

I couldn't move an inch, my cheek pressed against the muffling mattress, a blindfold covering my eyes, I was the helpless yet deeply loved embryo of the beautiful slave I longed to be as beneath my Master's patient silence and unwavering affection my soul felt perfectly safe and at peace. Unable to do anything else, I was forced to analyze my reactions, to go over the whole chain of events again and again being as honest with myself as I was physically powerless. By the time I felt my Master kneeling behind me, and his hard cock sinking into my wet pussy, I had been possessed by a revelation that made his penetrations feel even more pleasurable, like a glorious reward for my profound sensitivities as his erection helped me get to the bottom of my rebelliousness.

I looked up from the notebook I was writing in. Master was setting another log on the dead stump, balancing it with his fingertips before lifting the axe straight up over his head with both hands. He paused for a split second to hone in on the grain in the wood even as his whole body rose up into the air and he brought the weapon down with deadly force. There was a sharp crack followed by a dull thud as two perfect pieces of firewood fell off the stump onto the grass. He was replenishing our supply for next winter. When he informed me that this particular tree was dead, it reinforced the unnerving knowledge of how much I need a man like him around to manage fives acres of land, not to mention a house that will inevitably need repairs now and then. This doesn't even include all the wonderful additions he has already made to our home – a fireplace in the living room and a hot tub outside the bedroom, both of which he designed and built himself – or similar future projects, including a pool where we can swim like pharaohs surrounded by trees and sky and the animated hieroglyphs of cows and birds decorating the southern horizon.

The dead oak tree was growing perilously close to the house, and hurricane season will be here again soon; it can be dangerous living out in the woods if you don't know what you're doing. I have a lot to learn, and even then I'll never possess the physical strength necessary to chainsaw massive trunks and split them up into manageable logs. I don't like to wonder what I would do without my Master. The thought of a world in which he still didn't exist is so terrible that, whenever I dare to picture it, my stomach aches with anxiety as I imagine myself all alone out here just trying to survive instead of relishing every second of my life.

I tore my eyes away from the sight of his strong arms and looked back down at my notebook for a moment before setting it down beside me on the wooden swing hanging between two trees. I stretched my legs and rocked it gently back and forth, contentedly watching him work as my mind wandered through one of my favorite subjects...

Erotic pain is its own dimension, a vivid, powerful dream that's hard to remember afterwards when I "wake" from it. At first it was merely a nightmare, a sensation that made everything go dark beneath its hot flash. When my Master first punished me for lying to him, I swallowed every inconceivable burst of agony silently, like an unholy communion. Amazingly, it wasn't long before I actually found myself craving the unbearable, not as punishment but as mysterious stimulation. Nevertheless, I'm still glad it's a rare event. Master is wise enough to understand that such an intense experience can only happen once in a blue moon.

"Don't you need a break?" I called to him, feeling a little guilty about how hard he was working for us.

"No, thanks."

I picked up my pen and notebook, but then just sat staring at the flexing muscles in his arms as I struggled to understand, by somehow putting into words, why I love being used so roughly during sex by a man who otherwise treats me with such tender respect. I was never this happy in any of my other relationships, and perhaps it's the fact that I can't control my Master that makes me love him more every day. Sometimes I catch myself trying to subtly manipulate him the way I sometimes did my previous boyfriends, but it never works, and how ashamed I am of myself for trying can't compare to how thrilled I am by the excitingly firm, inviolable core of his personality my attempts fully expose. He sees right through my thoughts and actions when they aren't completely sincere, and then it feels right that he should punish me for being selfish and weak; for continuing to indulge those parts of myself I'm strivng to rise above.

I gave up on writing for the day and got up, heading for the house to get my hardworking lover a glass of ice water. It's nearly impossible to capture in words what it feels like to be caned and then fucked so violently from behind that I'm literally suspended on his stabbing erection, my wet-hot pussy a witch's cauldron in which every sensation –the constricting strain on my wrists and arms suspended above me, the burning marks crisscrossing my skin, his fingers digging cruelly into my breasts as he braces himself with them – is alchemized by the driving strength of his thrusts into a haunting negative of pleasures that is very hard to remember clearly and almost impossible to explain reasonably.

Today – every time I touch my left shoulder blade – I suffer an inexplicably sweet discomfort in the tender flesh that flows up into my neck. Master took me from behind last night, the full weight of his body pinning me down against the bed. He bit me as he drove into me, the sharp pressure of his teeth intensifying with his penetrations. The harder he fucked me the more viciously he sucked on me, and his guttural grown – in which I heard intense satisfaction combined with a dangerously growing need for even more of me – was an aphrodisiac of the most irresistible kind to my absolutely yielding pussy. The burning pain in my neck flowed straight down into my sex like supernatural blood lubricating his hard-on and making it easier and easier for him to thrust into me, as if I were bottomless. The more completely I yielded to him the more I stoked his lust, and I experienced a little of what prey suffers in the jaws of a powerful predator – a mysteriously submissive peace at being so desirable. A certain amount of pain turns me on, and it isn't mental; it's purely and intensely physical. When Master spanks me really hard my pussy gets as hot as my ass. The tyranny of my clit was overthrown the moment I realized that totally relaxing and absorbing my Master's controlled force in whatever form it takes – a whip's cruel licks, his punishing hand, his rampant cock – makes my sex wet like nothing else.

I love being properly fucked by my Master, but the truth is that I obsessed about sex when I lived in cities more than I do out here "in the middle of nowhere". The borders of my sensuality have blurred to include the world around me in a way that's simply not possible where the earth is buried in concrete and the moon and stars are often invisible behind skyscrapers and light pollution – nature in environmentally cruel bondage. Inevitably, I've begun to wonder about the relationship between BDSM and civilization. How much did the sensual frustration of the box-like apartments I was once condemned to – not to mention the sense of powerlessness that comes from being just one stubbornly creative little statistic in an increasingly violent and pain-filled world – have to do with the seductively sinister allure of sado-masochism in my mind and libido? I expressed these thoughts to Master one evening when we were sitting out on the front porch (which he had just finished screening in) having a drink before dinner. He agreed they probably had something do with it, but only to a certain extent because, as he often reminds me, everything is more complex than it might at first seem. I had to agree. Almost everywhere I look now I see natural examples of SM and bondage, yet I don't believe people are merely playing at the food chain in kinky nightclubs.

I fell silent and sipped my Chardonnay savoring the golden light pouring between the trees to our west as the sun slowly set. On the occasions when our distant neighbor's tractor competes with the lovely conversation of birds, the intense molten light imbues him with the aura of a knight in modern armor morphed with the roaring dragon he's forever fighting. It's really impossible to describe the enchanted quality of that light, which brings to my western mind the sword of Excalibur and the magic of Merlin still living in our forest. I love it when the last rays of the sun gild my Master's face, which is more intensely handsome in my eyes than any of the ancient pharaohs whose golden funeral masks have been discovered. His features are a blend of cultures and centuries that almost make it possible for me to remember, as we look silently into each others eyes, experiences I had when the naked energy of my spirit was bound in different forms altogether…

"Shall we go lock the girls in?" he asked.

I smiled. "Yes, Master."

A wind almost always wafts in from the southwest, refreshing the air in summer and making it even cozier to go inside and light a fire in winter. Our fine wine glasses, ordered from *crateandbarrel.com*, looked incongruous sitting on top of an old railroad tie turned fencepost when we set them down to enter the area in which our three Rhode Island Reds roam free. Wine glasses are not a classic element of this rustic scene, which becomes even more intriguingly rich with their slender and fragile forms outlined against the sky, the vanished sun seeming to have left behind in them some of its luminous blood. I never could have imagined how much I enjoy watching our chickens feasting on untold varieties of bugs while occasionally clucking excitedly. The adorable cooing sounds they make delight me, and it always relaxes me to watch them as they scratch and peck, scratch and peck, scraping their splayed toes over the grass to reveal the dirt beneath, then staring straight ahead for a split second of intense anticipation before launching their beaks at the ground, where there always seems to be something delectable for them to eat. It reminds me of the way I sometimes get when I'm surfing the Web, clucking on my keyboard and scratching my mouse across the wooden desk searching for interesting things. Master built our girls an adorable little coop then put chicken wire up around it, extending the fence all the way to one border of our property so they have plenty of space in which to forage. They don't seem to mind their generous confinement one bit, and after the sun sets they willingly walk up a ramp into their wire-mesh cage. I close it and lock it behind them, and they sleep safely at night protected from even the most tenacious predators. Master and I don't make our living farming, so there's no pressure, we simply enjoy indulging in its pleasures, which are quite different from the ones we were obliged to cultivate in the city. We can drive into town for the weekend and see pretty human females at fetish parties posing in cages because they *want* to be eaten alive, but it would be impossible to merely dabble in the very personal relationship we're nurturing out here with the soul of the land and with each others.

Lately when Master punishes me it's not because I've been bad in the sense of disobeying him, as I often did in the beginning when I was still learning to trust him and to accept my submissive devotion to him, Over five years spent in the company of my Master has smoothed the ruffled feathers of my mistrust and now, on the rare occasions when he disciplines me, it is because he knows physical pain has the power to soothe, and (at least temporarily exorcise) the emotional and spiritual turmoil I often wrestle with. Moving out to the country, for example, made me fully aware of what I had been missing most of my life as far as a truly intimate connection with nature. How many more pleasurable possibilities I suddenly had at my fingertips reinforced and intensified my environmental concerns and stirred up all sorts of conflicts inside me because (unlike many of the people I met when I was more socially active) I am definitely not an anti-civilizationist. Our generator is always filled with gas so we can run the two refrigerators and keep our computers hooked up to the satellite Internet whenever we lose power for more than a few hours. Ideally, we would love to free ourselves from the electrical grid with solar energy, but unfortunately we don't have money to burn. Central air conditioning congests me – for three months out of the year it's difficult for me to breathe – yet I would be much more miserable without it. My addiction to physical comforts has made me a slave to progress – a totally willing slave – the satellites hovering in the atmosphere above us metal shackles connecting me to the excitement of countless people simulating me with the caress of their thoughts and feelings and their seductive perceptions of reality. There is something magical about the lovely blue lights flashing on the black tower linking our computers with the orbiting dish that serves up so much mental nourishment. Science and technology have tapped into a whole other dimension were matter ceases to be imprisoning in its inflexible solidity and reveals itself as units of energy in mysterious bondage to each other, electrons dancing submissively around a dominant nucleus. It fascinates me, for example, that the sky would not be blue if it wasn't for the way our visual cortex works – for the way the unique palette of our physical senses interprets the pure forces of creation, tying them down with the dark mortal "toys" of our veins and organs and muscles and skeleton which we use to experience the world even while retaining the haunting freedom to conceive the possibility of infinite other realities.

Master and I could not relish our sensual isolation without all the technology that keeps us in touch with the world that finances my philosophical and metaphysical contemplations. Our bank accounts are bound by the desires – at once inspired and selfishly destructive – of the powerful society into which we were born naked and helpless. As I struggle with these and other issues full of the knots of seemingly irreconcilable paradoxes, Master watches me with an appreciative smile that turns into a displeased frown only when I take my fears and frustrations out on him by raising my voice and losing my temper as though it's all his fault. A few months, ago when this kept happening, Master commanded me to take off all my clothes, to put on my six-inch black heels along with my black-leather training collar, and to wait for him upstairs in the guest room that also serves as our playroom. Naturally, I obeyed him at once, and sat waiting for him on the couch I had covered with a red velvet spread, my hands crossed on my naked thighs, my back straight and my mind pleasantly blank for a change. It had been a long time since Master disciplined me, and I was conscious of how desperately I needed it. The room was lit softly by a small lamp, and when he entered, I was thrilled to see he had changed into clothing he hadn't worn for a while – tight black leather pants, heavy black boots, and a short-sleeved, dark-gray shirt that molded to his strong chest and broad shoulders.

"Very good, my slave." He sat down beside me and began caressing me, gently kneading my breasts and sucking on my nipples. The subtle sensation raised goose bumps across my flesh and made me sigh with pleasure. His large hands stroked my thighs, spreading them open so he could finger my labia teasingly, for we both knew he wasn't going to fuck me anytime soon. First he was going to punish me. I was wet and languid by the time he stood up, opened our black toy box, and pulled out several coils of smooth white rope it is my task to put away again neatly after every session.

"Kneel on the floor and rest your head on the sofa," he commanded quietly.

I obeyed him silently, and held myself as still as possible while he tied me up, leaving my bottom cheeks fully exposed. I remember everything clearly up until he began spanking me, then the relativity of time was easily proved without the need for multibillion-dollar particle accelerators or any other equipment besides his hard hand and my soft ass.

"Do you understand why I'm punishing you?" he asked.

"Yes, Master." *Please don't make me talk!* I thought, and thank God, he did not.

He spanked me with excruciating, concentrated vigor, and the first blows hurts so much I was sure I couldn't take anymore. I whimpered and moaned and started crying, but he never once let up, and I loved him passionately for it. The burning misery in my buttocks incinerated all my thoughts, granting me a blessed release from myself as I became conscious only of the body sustaining this awareness. At some timeless point it happened – I felt a part of me that I choose to call my soul begin riding the pain's darkly cresting waves. My skin stopped cringing in resistance and instead began absorbing the searing sensation, letting it deeper and deeper inside me as my soul surfed its unrelenting, inarguable and inescapable power. When the punishment finally ended, I thought only fifteen or twenty minutes had passed. I was intensely relieved even though I was also a little disappointed the excruciating ordeal had been so brief, until his hard-on surged into my unbelievably wet pussy, then I let out a purring moan because there was nothing in the universe I wanted more than the feel of a big hard cock pounding into my cunt. The more violently he fucked me the more strangely transcendent was the contentment that possessed me. I imagined kneeling in that helplessly bound position for hours while one attractive masterful man after the other got himself off inside me like this, swiftly and selfishly, using my body like a sacred ritual vessel...

Afterwards, Master gently untied me and helped me sit back up on the sofa since I was stiff from kneeling. "How do you feel?" he asked, draping an arm over my shoulders to hold me tenderly against him.

"Wonderful!" I sighed.

"You went into one of your trances again."

"I did?" I couldn't remember going into a trance, in fact, I was quite sure I hadn't.

"Do you have any idea how long I punished you?"

"It felt like about fifteen, twenty minutes?"

"I spanked you for almost an hour, dear."

"Get out of here!" I pulled away from him and stared incredulously up into his eyes.

He smiled. "It's true. You were somewhere else. It was very interesting. I could tell when you started riding the pain instead of fighting it. Every few minutes you stopped struggling and I waited for you to come down before I started up again."

I was fascinated, but worried. I didn't remember those intervals of perversely orgasmic respite; the beating had seemed constant and inescapable. I count on being mentally in control of myself even when I'm physically helpless, and this lapse in my awareness – when time and space distorted to the point where they essentially ceased to exist – at once exhilarated and frightened me. I grew up with the famous maxim, *I think therefore I am*, but even though I stopped thinking during my discipline I still very much *was*. It seemed a thrilling clue to an identity inside me independent of my brain that mysteriously resides in the organ of my flesh which enables me to catch firsthand glimpses of a timeless energy pain and ecstasy are only faint reflections of.

Then there was the day I was beaten by the tulip tree we sacrificed limbs from for the sake of satellite TV. We noticed we were losing channels, but couldn't really bring ourselves to care until we suddenly got no reception at all. I helped Master carry his twenty-six-foot ladder out of the shop, and watched anxiously as he positioned it against the tulip tree that had leafed out and blocked the three satellite receptors jutting eternally erect towards the heavens. He climbed up slowly and carefully while I pretended to brace the ladder at the bottom; there really wasn't anything I could do to hold it up if it fell with all his weight on it. I had eyes only for him and the dangerous operation he was performing from the uppermost rungs. He had ingeniously extended a pole pruner using some of the same smooth white rope he tied me up with so he could reach all the culprit branches. Without looking down, he commanded me to get as far away from the house as possible. He didn't have to tell me twice, and I continued watching from a safe distance while one branch after the other crashed into the bushes growing outside our bedroom window. When he finished, I would pull them out and drag them into a pile of future kindling. I wasn't really nervous; I have full confidence in my Master's abilities because he never does anything without thinking it through carefully first, and he never overestimates his own strength and skills. I was confident he wouldn't damage the roof and that we would soon have full satellite reception again.

He trimmed all the smaller branches first, then he looked down to make sure I was well out of range before he began working on the biggest, heaviest limb. It took him some time, and considerable effort, to saw through it. Finally, he wrapped a long rope around it, descended, and slowly pulled on it so it just barely grazed the roof as it landed ponderously behind the house. There was a loud cracking sound followed by the rustling of living green branches cascading to the ground, then I heard myself scream as something painfully hard whacked me fiercely across the back just above my right shoulder blade. I looked wildly around, suffering the impression that some invisible force had stepped up right behind me and used the wooden rod lying at my feet to beat me with. It had hurt like hell.

"Are you all right?" Master hurried over to me. "What happened?"

"What *happened*? That thing flew right at me! I'm lucky it didn't hit me in the head!"

"That's not possible," he said quietly, picking up the thick two-foot long segment of tree limb and studying it.

"It may not be possible, but it definitely happened!" I insisted impatiently; shock and pain don't take kindly to scientific detachment.

"Wow… that's really strange."

I had never seen my Master so perturbed – almost in awe – of something before. "I just don't see how this piece could have split off the main branch and propelled itself all the way over here like that. It's not physically possible," he concluded.

"I know why it happened." I sniffed. I was crying mainly because I enjoy drama, and because I *was* rather stunned by the seemingly deliberate force that had defied gravity to deliver a blow with brutal precision where it would seriously hurt me without doing any real damage. "While I was watching you cutting so many of its branches off, I didn't once think about how the tree felt. I didn't wonder if it was in pain, or ask its forgiveness, or anything. I was just worried about you, and selfishly looking forward to having television again. I don't blame it for being angry and hitting me. I deserved it."

Master looked deep into my eyes, but he wasn't smiling as he dropped the branch and took me gently in his arms. "I made absolutely sure you were standing far away enough that you couldn't possibly be hurt even if it didn't fall exactly where I wanted it to, which it did. I really have no idea how that piece got detached and flew all the way out here."

I was both chastened and excited. I felt guilty and yet also blessed by the attention I felt the tree had paid me. The following day, I planted both my palms against its smooth bark and apologized to it for my callous selfishness. I also warned it that we would probably have to trim more of its limbs in the future. I thanked it for sacrificing parts of itself for the sake of our pleasure, and for gracing our home with its majestic presence. I urged it to look forward to growing in different directions, because we would never really hurt it. I gazed up at its branches, growing towards the atmosphere, then down at its roots penetrating the earth as I caressed its firm, slightly rough skin with assuaging respect.

Out in the country, it's not uncommon to see a falling star streak across the sky and vanish behind a tree where it transforms into a firefly gliding over the grass that never flashes again where you expect it the way a wish never comes true exactly how you imagined but instead takes you on a journey of highs and lows and dark times where you almost lose hope until it suddenly comes alive right beside you. Whenever I dreamed of true love as a little girl it never involved a white wedding dress or a flower-filled ceremony with elegantly dressed guests. My Master first told me he loved me in a swing club where we were surrounded by other naked bodies and it felt completely, beautifully, right.

Sunflowers are slaves to the sun and grow even taller than my Master, who is forced to brace them with ropes so their slender bodies don't droop and break as they turn to follow their lord's passage across the sky.

By mid-summer our little forest becomes a shadowy dungeon of spider webs in which creatures are bound like naked slaves covered in sticky, glistening cum waiting passively in their corners to be used with absolute selfishness by their owners.

A grape vine twines itself around a phallic trunk, thriving on its strength, and in the end it refuses to let go, stubbornly holding the tree up even after it's dead in its hunger for light. My life – who I am – would not be the same if I had not met my Master. The intimate relationship between all things in nature makes its individual wonders possible. When one species vanishes others inevitably follow. Naturally, I would survive if my Master died, but I would never be the same again inside. The way I feel everyday affects the way I think which influences what I do, and this process would be very different without our love. I wouldn't be as happy. The "Lord God bird" would have flown forever from the forest of my feelings, leaving me only with the memory of how enchanted the world is when you intimately share everything with someone you truly love. To steel myself against such drastic loss with thoughts of moving on and maybe meeting someone else in the future is disrespectful to the unique wonder of what my Master and I have together. Every loving union between two persons is an irreplaceable way of experiencing the world. Untold numbers of marvelously unique forms of life become extinct every day as couples break up and sign divorce papers. Absolutely everything is related in a way that is extremely disturbing because so few people believe it. Civilization has become the earth's relentless master, and it hasn't given her a "safe word". Still, she has her ways of rebelling, of

NATURAL BONDAGE

struggling to break free when man goes too far and begins seriously hurting her. Shiny slick impenetrable rubber concealing living skin beneath plastic ball-gags and trendy gas masks speaks of oil-spills, landfills and pollution. It's hardly surprising that more and more beautiful Dominatrixes are getting rich off tormented businessmen.

I love watching threesomes of fantastically large yellow-and-black butterflies ascend into the sky over baby purple banana leaves that haven't yet learned to dance in the slightest breeze like their older green siblings. Sluggish caterpillars transformed into swift winged beings... a submissive crawls even while exercising the confidence of thoughts and desires working in unquestioning obedience to love's elevating nature, because the uniquely human metamorphosis of striving to make our fantasies come true rises above merely being stepped on by someone else's will.

Magic Carpet Books Catalog

MAGIC CARPET BOOKS

Order Form

Name: _____

Address: _____

City: _____

State: _____ **Zip:** _____

Title	ISBN	Quantity

Send check or money order to:

Magic Carpet Books
PO Box 473
New Milford, CT 06776

Postage free in the United States add $2.50 for packages outside the United States

magiccarpetbooks@earthlink.net

Visit our website at:
www.magic-carpet-books.com

Maria Isabel Pita

Maria Isabel Pita is the author of three BDSM Erotic Romances – *Thorsday Night, Eternal Bondage* and *To Her Master Born*, re-printed as an exclusive hard-cover edition by the Doubleday Venus Book Club. She is the author of three Paranormal Erotic Romances, *Dreams of Anubis, Rituals of Surrender, The Fire in Starlight* and of three Contemporary Erotic Romances *A Brush With Love, Recipe For Romance,* and *The Fabric of Love*. Three of her erotic romances (Dreams of Anubis, Rituals of Surrender, The Fabric of Love) were re-printed under one cover as *Cat's Collar – Three Erotic Romances*. Maria is also the author of the critically acclaimed *Guilty Pleasures* – a book of romantic erotic stories set all through history – and of two non-fiction memoirs – *The Story of M – A Memoir* and *Beauty & Submission*, both of which were featured selections of the Doubleday Venus Book Club. *The Fabric of Love* and *The Story of M – A Memoir* have been translated into German and published in Germany by Heyne/VG Random House GMBH. Maria won second place in the New England Association For Science Fiction & Fantasy for her story *Star Crossed*. She was also a finalist in The Science Fiction Writer's of the Earth Award and the L. Ron Hubbard Award for Science Fiction Fantasy. You can visit her at www.mariaisabelpita.com

SEPTEMBER 2006

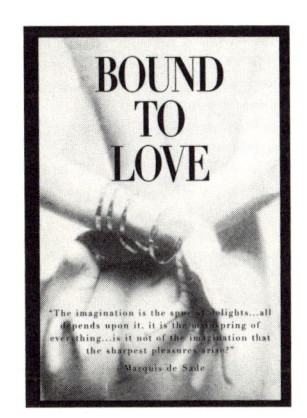

Bound to Love:
A Collection of Romantic BDSM Erotic Stories
Edited by Maria Isabel Pita

Fiction/Erotica • ISBN 0-9766510-4-1
Trade Paperback • 5 3/16 x 8 · 304 Pages
$17.95 ($24.95 Canada)

In *Bound to Love*, Maria Isabel Pita has gathered together nine erotic love stories written by some of today's hottest writers of erotica. In each story the darker side of sexuality is explored through realistic, well-developed characters deeply in love with each other and otherwise leading normal lives together. The men and women in *Bound To Love* are involved in serious, long-term relationships in which their deeper feelings for each other are inseparable from their erotic interaction. The stories in *Bound to Love* are some of the best in their genre precisely because they transcend it.

NOVEMBER 2006

THE COLLECTOR'S EDITION OF VICTORIAN EROTIC DISCIPLINE
Edited by Brooke Stern

Fiction/Erotica • ISBN 0-9766510-9-2
Trade Paperback • 5 3/16 x 8 • 608 Pages • $17.95 ($24.95 Canada)

Lest there be any doubt, this collection is submitted as exhibit A in the case for the legitimacy of theVictorian era's dominion over all discipline erotica. In this collection, all manner of discipline is represented. Men and women are both dominant and submissive. There are school punishments, judicial punishments, punishments between lovers, well-deserved punishments, punishments for a fee, and cross-cultural punishments. These stories are set around the world and at all levels of society. The authority figures in these stories include schoolmasters, gamekeepers, colonial administrators, captains of ships, third-world potentates, tutors, governesses, priests, nuns, judges and policemen.

Victorian erotica is replete with all manner of discipline. Indeed, it would be hard to find an erotic act as connected with a historical era as discipline is with the reign of Queen Victoria. The language of erotic discipline, with its sir's and madam's, its stilted syntax and its ritualized roles, sounds Victorian even when it's used in contemporary pop culture. The essence of Victorian discipline is the shock of the naughty, the righteous indignation of the punisher and the shame of the punished. Today's literature of erotic discipline can only play at Victorian dynamics, and all subsequent writings will only be pretenders to a crown of the era whose reign will never end.

Victoria A. Brownworth

Victoria A. Brownworth is the author of nine books, including the award-winning *Too Queer: Essays from a Radical Life* and editor of 14, including the award-winning *Night Bites: Vampire Tales of Blood and Lust.* A syndicated columnist, her work has appeared in numerous mainstream, queer and feminist publications, including the *Baltimore Sun*, the *Philadelphia Inquirer*, the *Village Voice*, the *Advocate, OUT* and *Curve*. Her erotic writing has appeared regularly in anthologies and magazines, and she is a former contributing writer to the lesbian sex magazines, *On Our Backs* and *Bad Attitude*. She has published several erotica collections, including most recently, *Bed: New Lesbian Erotica*. She also publishes gay male porn under a psuedonym. She teaches writing and film at the University of the Arts in Philadelphia where she added two new courses to the literary curriculum: Writing Below the Belt and Smut. She has also taught safe-sex education classes as well as classes on S/M and B/D for various lesbian and bisexual venues. She lives in Philadelphia.

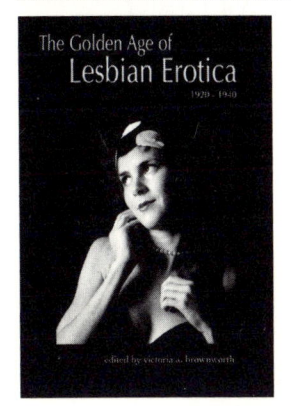

JANUARY 2007

THE GOLDEN AGE OF LESBIAN EROTICA
Edited by Victoria A. Brownworth

Fiction/Erotica • ISBN 0-9774311-4-2 • Trade Paperback
5 3/16 x 8 • 320 Pages • $17.95 ($24.95 Canada)

Lesbian erotica of the 1920s through the 1940s had a bold new cast to it. Unlike the tender and affectionate eroticism of the Victorian era with its naughty schoolgirls, convent antics and ladies-in-waiting, these 20th Century tales brought verisimilitude and fantasy together. While Radclyffe Hall was being prosecuted for obscenity for her depiction of "sapphics" and "inverts" in the classic lesbian novel *The Well of Loneliness,* her friend Natalie Barney was riding naked through the streets of Paris on horseback with her lover, the poet Renee Vivienne and Anais Nin were penning lurid and lustful tales of very bad girls while yearning for Henry Miller's sensual wife, June.

MARCH 2007

THE COLLECTOR'S EDITION OF THE IRONWOOD TRILOGY
by Don Winslow

Fiction/Erotica • ISBN 0-9766510-2-5
Trade Paperback • 5 3/16 x 8 • 480 Pages • $17.95 ($24.95Canada)

The three Ironwood classics revised exclusively for this Magic Carpet Edition

IRONWOOD, IRONWOOD REVISITED, IMAGES OF IRONWOOD

In IRONWOOD, James Carrington's bleak prospects are transformed overnight when the young man finds himself offered a choice position at Ironwood, a unique finishing school where young women are trained to become remiere Ladies of Pleasure. James faces many challenges in taming the spirited beauties in his charge, but no test will prove as great as that of mastering Mrs. Cora Blasingdale, the proud Mistress of Ironwood. In IRONWOOD REVISITED we follow James' rise to power in that garden of erotic delights, that singular institution, where young ladies were rigorously trained in the many arts of love. We come to understand how Ironwood, with its strict standards and iron discipline, has acquired its enviable reputation among the world's most discriminating connoisseurs. In IMAGES OF IRONWOOD, the third volume of the infamous Ironwood chronicles, the reader is once again invited to share in the Ironwood experience, and is presented with select scenes of unrelenting sensuality, of erotic longing, and of those bizarre proclivities which touch the outer fringe of human sexuality.

MAY 2007

MASTERPIECES OF VICTORIAN EROTICA
Edited by Major LaCaritilie

Fiction/Erotica • ISBN 0-9774311-6-9
Trade Paperback • 5 3/16 x 8 • 320 Pages • $17.95 ($24.95 Canada)

There is no shortage of great works to compete for the title "masterpiece of Victorian erotica." Indeed, as readers familiar with Dickens or Trollope can attest, the Victorians were nothing if not prolific. Yet to be a masterpiece, a work has to distinguish itself in many ways. It can be without equal in its subgenre or the apotheosis of its tradition. It can offer a deeper insight, a more vivid image, or a more surprising turn. Or it can be unique, truly peerless in its style, plot or execution. Having distinguished themselves in these ways, the works in this volume represent the very best of the Victorian erotic imagination. There's poetry and prose, narrative and instructional guide; there's fetish, queer, s-m, and vanilla; and there's bawdy, tender and daring. For the newcomer to the Victorian erotic universe, these stories are the place to start. For the connoisseur, this collection offers undiscovered delicacies. For everyone, these stories cannot fail to arouse, stimulate and amaze with their delightful sexiness and bold originality.

JULY 2007

HOWEVER YOU WANT ME
by Les Bexley

Fiction/Erotica • ISBN 0-9774311-5-0
Trade Paperback • 5 3/16 x 8 • 320 Pages
$17.95 ($24.95 Canada)

Pity poor Heritage College. It's hard to be a holier-than-thou Christian girls' school without a dirty little secret or two. And that was before April Cartier even set foot on campus. The banned activities listed in the college's morality code are April's to-do list; the college's dirty little secrets, her major. But it's not just the college that has secrets. Professors Jessica Rowley, Klaus Binder and Alex Gould have made secrets a way of life, and April isn't the type to leave anyone's skeletons in their closets. When this cast of characters finds itself in the perfect storm of desires and taboos, naked appetites and raw emotions, they become more exposed and more intertwined than any of them could have possibly imagined. Sexy and daring, unflinching and humane, *However You Want Me* tells the story of people whose deepest secrets are kept not from others but from themselves.

BACK IN STOCK

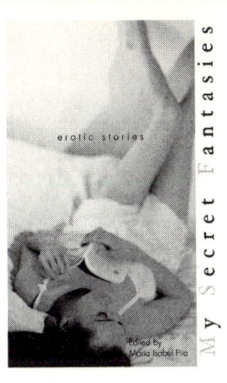

MY SECRET FANTASIES
Fiction/Erotica • ISBN 0-9755331-2-6
Trade Paperback • 5 3/16 x 8 • 256 Pages • $11.95

Secret fantasies… we all have them, those hot, vivid daydreams that take us away from it all as we wonder, *what if...* In My Secret Fantasies, sixty different women share the secret of how they made their wildest erotic desires come true. Next time you feel like getting your heart rate up and your blood really flowing, curl up with a cup of tea and *My Secret Fantasies*… Beneath the covers of *My Secret Fantasies* you will find 60 tantalizing erotic love stories.

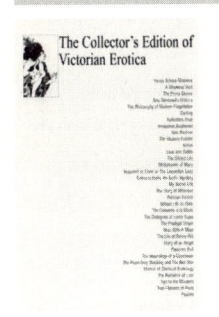

THE COLLECTOR'S EDITION OF VICTORIAN EROTICA
Edited by Major LaCaritilie
Fiction/Erotica • ISBN 0-9755331-0-X
Trade Paperback • 5-3/16"x 8" • 608 Pages • $19.95 ($18.95 Canada)

No lone soul can possibly read the thousands of erotic books, pamphlets and broadsides the English reading public were offered in the 19th century. It can only be hoped that this Anthology may stimulate the reader into further adventures in erotica and its manifest reading pleasure. In this anthology, 'erotica' is a comprehensive term for bawdy, obscene, salacious, pornographic and ribald works including, indeed featuring, humour and satire that employ sexual elements. Flagellation and sadomasochism are recurring themes. They are activities whose effect can be shocking, but whose occurrence pervades our selections, most often in the context of love and affection.

THE COLLECTOR'S EDITION OF VICTORIAN LESBIAN EROTICA

Edited By Major LaCaritilie

Fiction/Erotica • ISBN 0-9755331-9-3

Trade Paperback • 5 3/16 x 8 • 608 Pages • $17.95 ($24.95Canada)

The Victorian era offers an untapped wellspring of lesbian erotica. Indeed, Victorian erotica writers treated lesbians and bisexual women with voracious curiosity and tender affection. As far as written treasuries of vice and perversion go, the Victorian era has no equal. These stories delve into the world of the aristocrat and the streetwalker, the seasoned seductress and the innocent naïf. Represented in this anthology are a variety of genres, from romantic fiction to faux journalism and travelogue, as well as styles and tones resembling everything from steamy page-turners to scholarly exposition. What all these works share, however, is the sense of fun, mischief and sexiness that characterized Victorian lesbian erotica. The lesbian erotica of the Victorian era defies stereotype and offers rich portraits of a sexuality driven underground by repressive mores. As Oscar Wilde claimed, the only way to get rid of temptation is to yield to it.

THE COLLECTOR'S EDITION OF THE LOST EROTIC NOVELS

Edited by Major LaCaritilie

Fiction/Erotica • ISBN 0-97553317-7

Trade Paperback • 5-3/16"x 8" • 608 Pages • $16.95 ($20.95 Canada)

MISFORTUNES OF MARY – Anonymous, 1860's: An innocent young woman who still believes in the kindness of strangers unwittingly signs her life away to a gentleman who makes demands upon her she never would have dreamed possible.

WHITE STAINS – Anaïs Nin & Friends, 1940's: Sensual stories penned by Anaïs and some of her friends that were commissioned by a wealthy buyer for $1.00 a page. These classics of pornography are not included in her two famous collections, *Delta of Venus* and *Little Birds*.

INNOCENCE – Harriet Daimler, 1950's: A lovely young bed-ridden woman would appear to be helpless and at the mercy of all around her, and indeed, they all take advantage of her in shocking ways, but who's to say she isn't the one secretly dominating them?

THE INSTRUMENTS OF THE PASSION – Anonymous, 1960's: A beautiful young woman discovers that there is much more to life in a monastery than anyone imagines as she endures increasingly intense rituals of flagellation devotedly visited upon her by the sadistic brothers

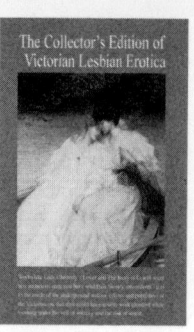

CAT'S COLLAR – THREE EROTIC ROMANCES
by Maria Isabel Pita
Fiction/Erotica • ISBN 0-9766510-0-9

Trade Paperback • 5 3/16 x 8 • 608 Pages • $16.95 ($ 20.95 Canada)

DREAMS OF ANUBIS: A legal secretary from Boston visiting Egypt explores much more than just tombs and temples in the stimulating arms of Egyptologist Simon Taylor. But at the same time a powerfully erotic priest of Anubis enters her dreams, and then her life one night in the dark heart of Cairo's timeless bazaar. Sir Richard Ashley believes he has lived before and that for centuries he and Mary have longed to find each other again. Mary is torn between two men who both desire to discover the legendary tomb of Imhotep and win the treasure of her heart.

RITUALS OF SURRENDER: All her life Maia Wilson has lived near a group of standing stones in the English countryside, but it isn't until an old oak tree hit by lightning collapses across her car one night that she suddenly finds herself the heart of an erotic web spun by three sexy, enigmatic men - modern Druids intent on using Maia for a dark and ancient rite...

CAT'S COLLAR: Interior designer Mira Rosemond finds herself in one attractive successful man's bedroom after the other, but then one beautiful morning a stranger dressed in black leather takes a short cut through her garden and changes the course of her life forever. Mira has never met anyone quite like Phillip, and the more she learns about his mysterious profession - secretly linked to some of Washington's most powerful women - the more frightened and yet excited she becomes as she finds herself falling helplessly, submissively in love.

GUILTY PLEASURES
by Maria Isabel Pita
Fiction/Erotica • ISBN 0-9755331-5-0

Trade Paperback • 5 3/16 x 8 • 304 Pages • $16.95 ($20.95 Canada)

Guilty Pleasures explores the passionate willingness of women throughout the ages to offer themselves up to the forces of love. Historical facts are seamlessly woven into intensely graphic sexual encounters. Beneath the covers of *Guilty Pleasures* you will find eighteen erotic love stories with a profound feel for the times and places where they occur. An ancient Egyptian princess… a courtesan rising to fame in Athen's Golden Age… a widow in 15th century Florence initiated into a Secret Society… a Transylvanian Count's wicked bride… an innocent nun tempted to sin in 17th century Lisbon… a lovely young woman finding love in the Sultan's harem… and many more are all one eternal woman in *Guilty Pleasures*.

THE STORY OF M – A MEMOIR

by Maria Isabel Pita

Non-Fiction/Erotica • ISBN 0-9726339-5-2

Trade Paperback • 5 3/16 x 8 • 239 Pages • $14.95 ($18.95 Canada)

The true, vividly detailed and profoundly erotic account of a beautiful, intelligent woman's first year of training as a slave to the man of her dreams.

Maria Isabel Pita refuses to fall into any politically correct category. She is not a feminist, and yet she is fiercely independent. She is everything but a mindless sex object, yet she is willingly, and happily, a masterful man's love slave. *M* is erotically submissive and yet also profoundly secure in herself, and she wrote this account of her ascent into submission for all the women out there who might be confused and frightened by their own contradictory desires just as she was.

M is the true highly erotic account of the author's first profoundly instructive year with the man of her dreams. Her vividly detailed story makes it clear we should never feel guilty about daring to make our deepest, darkest longings come true, and serves as living proof that they do.

BEAUTY & SUBMISSION

by Maria Isabel Pita

Non-Fiction/Erotica · ISBN 0-9755331-1-8

Trade Paperback · 5-3/16" x 8" · 256 Pages · $14.95 ($18.95 Canada)

In a desire to tell the truth and dispel negative stereotypes about the life of a sex slave, Maria Isabel Pita wrote *The Story of M... A Memoir*. Her intensely erotic life with the man of her dreams continues now in *Beauty & Submission*, a vividly detailed sexual and philosophical account of her second year of training as a slave to her Master and soul mate.

THE TIES THAT BIND

by Vanessa Duriés

Non-Fiction/Erotica • ISBN 0-9766510-1-7

Trade Paperback • 5 3/16 x 8 • 160 Pages • $14.95 ($18.95 Canada)

RE-PRINT OF THE FRENCH BEST-SELLER

The incredible confessions of a thrillingly unconventional woman. From the first page, this chronicle of dominance and submission will keep you gasping with its vivid depicitons of sensual abandon. At the hand of Masters Georges, Patrick, Pierre and others, this submissive seductress experiences pleasures she never knew existed...